I0600982

THE ARROGANT BILLIONAIRE

THE BALTIMORE BOYS
BOOK 2

SAMANTHA SKYE

ISBN 978-0-6457144-3-2 (ebook)

ISBN 978-0-6457144-4-9 (Paperback)

ISBN 978-0-6459897-6-2 (Alternative Paperback)

Cover Design: Angela Haddon

Editor: Nice Girl Naughty Edits

Proofreading: Kimberly Dawn

❀ Created with Vellum

CONTENT INFORMATION

This book contains spicy scenes, swearing and descriptions of violence. It also contains information and dialogue on domestic/partner violence.

It is a single mom, fake engagement, opposites attract, billionaire romance that will have you hot under the collar and keep you on the edge of your seat.

Enjoy.

1

EMILY CARR

We push our way through the already full crowd, making our way to the back of the bar. Friday night drinks on Leslie Street is always a bad idea, but every year on this date, this is where we come.

"I'll get the champagne!" Sarah hollers as she detours across the room to the busy bartender as Allie and I grab the last table before anyone else can.

"I hate this place," I say to her as I slump into the chair, looking around at all the arrogant suits in the room. They've no doubt just come off a hectic week of working day and night to try to make their next million.

My skin prickles with a mixture of anxiety and fear, but I push through it, knowing my beautiful daughter, Rosie, is tucked in at home, nice and safe. I should be with her; the mom guilt of leaving her never goes away, but I know she thrives in her independence when we are apart, regardless if I like it or not.

"Come on, it isn't all bad. There's some eye candy in

this place, don't you think?" I roll my eyes. That's what I thought when I first met Jeremy. What a terrible mistake that was. Allie is younger than me by about four years, and even though at twenty-nine, I am not old, I feel like I have lived three lifetimes already. We've only just arrived, and I already can't wait to get home and sit on the sofa with a good book.

I see the door of the bar open again and another five men walk in, all looking distinguished, dapper, and totally full of themselves. I huff out my frustration. We come here every year just for this purpose. It's a reminder of everything I have been through and never want to go through again.

"They only had the expensive stuff, so I thought we would treat ourselves tonight!" Sarah says as she puts an ice bucket with a bottle of French champagne on the table, followed by three champagne glasses. "It is raining men here tonight." Taking a seat, she surveys the room.

"It is a meat market and hasn't changed a bit in the twelve months since we were here last," I sass as I spot a few men hanging by the door, but just one look at their suits is enough to make my stomach curve into itself.

"Give me that bottle." Grabbing it from the table, I rip open the foil. I no longer drink very much, but like a professional, I grip the bottle at the bottom, hold the cork still, and twist the bottle in my hand exactly six times. The cork pops quietly as I lift it gently with my hand, the small fizz only reaching my ears, and I pour three glasses while still holding the base. I am nothing if not well trained in the art of how to open and pour champagne.

"Happy anniversary!" Sarah and Allie sing in unison, holding up their glasses.

"Thank you, girls. I wouldn't have survived without you," I say, smiling, thankful they have both been in my corner these past few years.

We sip our drinks, and I take a moment to gather my thoughts. I always feel on edge in the city. *What if I see him? What if he spots me?* I'm constantly looking over my shoulder. The need to be both smart and safe while maintaining a normal life is such a balancing act. But this reminder of my former life is necessary, no matter how much my anxiety skyrockets from it. It gives me the courage to continue. As I sip on my champagne, I think of all that has happened and feel the small bubbles dance in my mouth. The sensation fills me with glee. I've come so far. I made it out unscathed.

Well, almost.

"So tell me about your week," I quiz Sarah, wanting to hear all about her latest interaction with our new school gardener. There is a no fraternizing policy at William Heights Elementary School, so staff members are off-limits to each other. So far, Sarah has been adhering to that policy, but their flirtation is off the charts. It really is only a matter of time.

"He picked me a bunch of roses from the gardens and left them in my classroom this morning," Sarah says wistfully, and I notice a blush creeping up her neck.

"Oh, how sweet!" Allie exclaims. She is the romantic one of us. Always dreaming that a charming prince will come in and sweep her off her feet. If only she knew that wasn't how the real world works.

I wish I was still as naive.

"So what are you going to do?" I press, wondering what their next move will be. The gardener is extremely good-looking in a rugged sort of way and appears to be a total gentleman, but I'm not sure she will give it a chance to blossom.

"I mean, he is nice..." She ponders her words for a moment, her small smile giving her real intentions away.

"Nice! He is delicious, that's what he is!" Allie exclaims while fanning herself with her hand, causing us all to laugh.

"Speaking of delicious..." Sarah's attention wanders to a gathering of men by the bar. One, in particular, stands out, purely because he is so tall, broad, and looks like a wall of muscle. His white shirt is rolled up at the sleeves, his tanned skin peeking out. I divert my eyes before I find him any more attractive, not wanting to ever entertain a man in a bar such as this. I gave up men in suits a long time ago and have remained single since. Thank God for my battery friends.

My eyes roam the rest of the room, relieved that I haven't seen anyone I know. Not that I expected to; my past life is now long behind me and there wouldn't be anyone here who would have the first idea of who I was. Most of the men in this bar are too self-absorbed to care about anything else other than their whiskey and the nearest set of tits.

"I've gotta go to the little girls' room. You two can survey the man meat without me." It takes an hour to drive into the city from where we all live in the suburbs, and given I don't drink much anymore, my bladder doesn't always agree with the alcohol. While Sarah pours another round–our last for the night, because all three of us are keen to get back home and away from the city before it gets too dark and rowdy–I step away.

As I maneuver past a group of more corporate men and women filling the space, I get a push from behind and fly forward, slamming into a hard wall of chest.

"Sorry," I mumble as I try to take a step back, but the crowd is closing in, and I don't get far before I am pushed again, and large hands grab my waist to steady me. His hands are big enough that they nearly encase my entire waist, and I am staring right at his chest. Looking up, it feels like it takes forever to get to his face. It is the same man we were all admiring earlier. He is well over six feet tall and so broad I can't actually see around him.

"It's okay, I am used to women falling for me," he says smoothly, his deep brown eyes looking right into mine, with a smirk I want to slap off his face.

"Oh, of course you are. It must be so hard catching us all?" My tone is saccharine, not in the mood for another cocky man like him. This place is swarming with them, and I really need to get out of here before my history becomes my undoing. His eyebrows raise in a challenge.

"Well, I have a lot of practice. Only, you might just be the most beautiful yet." *Great.* He is flirting with me. I can't believe this talk actually works on some women.

"And such big, strong hands to catch little ole me." I bat my eyelashes and give him a fake grin.

"That is not all they are good for." I refrain from rolling my eyes.

"Oh really? Please, do tell…" I purr, pretending to give in to his charm.

"Hmmm, I could always show you," he offers, his thumb rubbing where it still rests on my waist, and I still. His hands feel good. Too damn good, but I've taken the teasing too far.

"Ugh, I do *not* want to know. Get your hands off me." I groan as I step back, creating distance between us.

"You are the one that ran into my arms, sweetheart. I merely caught the cargo," he says with a shrug, then slides his hands in his pockets.

"The cargo? Oh my God, you are such a Neanderthal." I find myself shrieking a little. I need to rein it in before I start to sound like a crazy woman. I can't help it, though. These places always put me on edge. It's almost like I stepped back in time, but with the years of experience to make me stronger, if not entirely pessimistic about it all.

"A Neanderthal, huh? Well, don't stop with the compliments, Mrs. Doubtfire. Please, continue." His tone is amused as he rocks on his heels, smirk still intact.

"Mrs. Doubtfire?" My head falls back as I look up at him, and my hair flows down, reaching where his hands just seared my back with his touch. It makes me shiver.

"Well, if the shoe fits." His piercing eyes look up and down my body, and understanding washes over me that he is insulting my wardrobe. I came straight from school, not bothering to change, so I am very G-rated compared to all the other women here.

I shake my head in annoyance. These suits are all the same.

I get another push from behind and land against his hard chest again with a huff, and I do not miss the warmth. My breasts are firmly squished to his solid form, and I take a deep inhale of his cologne. It's a dangerous woodsy aroma mixed with deep desire, distracting me enough that I don't notice I'm still flush against him until his grip around my waist gets tighter. My skin tingles where his hands touch my body, and I need to shake my head to get the thought of wanting to stay in his protective embrace from my mind.

I go to step away again, but then I am whisked up, my feet no longer touching the ground. I exhale a small shriek as I grip onto his shirt, white-knuckled, as he twirls me around and swaps positions with me. My back now against the bar, and my waist cold, he moves his hands onto the bartop on either side of me, caging me in and barricading me from the pushy crowd at the same time. He is getting nudges into his back now, but he doesn't seem bothered.

"What are you doing?" I ask him, my steely gaze drilling into him as I try to remain composed.

"Protecting you." He smirks at me in a cute yet totally annoying kind of way.

"I don't need protection." The audacity of this man. I have been on my own a long time. I can look after myself.

"Benjamin," he states, his eyes piercing mine.

"What?" My eyebrows furrow, trying to understand what he is talking about.

"Benjamin. My name is Benjamin. You can call me Ben." His mouth lifts a little on one side as he introduces himself. Years ago, I would have swooned, but I am not the same woman I once was.

"That's nice; however, I really need to go, so if you will excuse me..." I duck under his arm and walk away from him toward the bathrooms, not once looking around or looking back, even though I really, really want to.

But men in suits have no place in my life. Not anymore.

2

BENJAMIN LANGFORD

I watch as the little firecracker with the pouty lips walks away. She called me a Neanderthal. Who even says that word? Her plump ass sways in her god-awful attire, not that I care about what she's wearing. I am not sure what law firm she works at, but I know it isn't mine.

Our interaction lasted five minutes, yet it was the most fun I have had in months. Her sultry lips and her quick wit has my mind racing. I've never had a woman banter with me like that before. I usually get the yes women, those who will do anything I ask, anything I want. It was new, and I liked it. Even if she toyed with me and threw insults my way.

I wasn't wrong when I called her Mrs. Doubtfire. The name was said in jest to match her ridiculous name for me. I liked pushing her buttons and I saw her eyes flame as soon as it left my mouth. But the name fits. She has every inch of her skin covered in her basic black pants and white shirt combo and looks out of place in a bar like this. The women crowding this bar are much more liberal, showing off everything they have to offer, and I mean *everything*. I have already had two offers for a quick fuck in the bathrooms, and while I said no to both, after my run-in with her, my senses are awake and firmly looking for attention. Preferably from a short, sassy, dowdy-dressed woman.

I learned from a young age that appearances are everything. My mom always used to say *Dress to impress, Benjamin.* I can still hear her shrill voice in my head, and I shake it to remove it entirely.

"Want another?" Tennyson asks me, making my eyes leave the woman's ass to land on him. He is younger than me by two years, and I eye him suspiciously. He loves nothing more than a night of drinking and ladies, so I need to make sure he doesn't stay out too late tonight. I don't need to work all weekend to take down paparazzi photos of him doing things he shouldn't be.

"Sure," I say with a nod. He grabs my glass and drops it on the bar behind us, and I take another look in the direction of the bathroom but see no one. The hallway is now empty.

"Who's the nun?" Eddie asks as he comes to join our circle to get away from the crowd. He himself is trying to detangle from the manicured hands that appear on his arms regularly.

The three of us stand at the bar, oblivious to all the looks we are getting. We are DC's richest most eligible bachelors, our faces recognizable to the city's female population. We even trend with our own hashtags at times.

"No idea," I reply, taking a swig of my fresh glass of whiskey that has appeared. She didn't give me her name, something she clearly wasn't keen to offer. Again, another first for me. Most women I meet friend request me the minute they leave my side, yet this one didn't fall for my charm. I spot red fingernails inching up and down Tennyson's arm, as yet another woman tries to lay claim to him for the night.

"She didn't look like your type," Eddie says, standing next to me, as Tennyson edges out of the conversation and stalks off to indulge in the red-nailed assassin.

"What is my type?" I ask him inquisitively, already thinking I may have found a new type. The kind of woman who is smart as a whip and sexy as a minx all together in a small package that would give me nothing but trouble. I am sure of it.

"Tall, Amazonian supermodel," he fires back a little too quickly.

"I have dated other women." I'm feeling defensive, but I'm not sure why.

"Literally your last three girlfriends have all been from the front covers of the top fashion magazines. They are carbon copy versions of each other. You don't stray, so you have a very clear type." Eddie smirks, and I hate that my history proves him right.

"I don't have a type." My eyes flick toward the bathrooms again, still seeing the hallway empty.

"Sure, you don't. What about Sasha?" he questions, pushing his point.

"Let's not bring up that disaster," I murmur, wanting an end to this conversation. I grit my teeth at the memory.

I feel no pain, simply embarrassment for being so fucking stupid. As I wait for him to push me, he downs his drink.

"I'm off. I need to get up early and check out the building on the east side. Good luck with that Monday morning meeting you were talking about." He shakes my hand, and we do the manly backslap before he slinks through the crowd, dodging other's handshakes and attempted flirtations.

I'm feeling unsure about that meeting and have talked at length about it tonight with my brothers. I am still waiting for the full details, but Jonathan Beasley is our biggest law client, so regardless, we'll have to be successful. He makes us millions each year as we try to protect and rescue him from business deals gone wrong, along with a few misdemeanors in between. We just settled his third divorce, and he is extremely happy with our service to date, given that we have made him more money than ever. His eye is now firmly set on an elementary school property on the outskirts of town in a lower socioeconomic suburb. He wants to use it as a new piece of land to develop into condos, such is his main business. From all the paperwork, it appears that it is a good move.

But navigating the suburbs and entering neighborhoods can be tough. There is a lot of community communication and collaboration that needs to happen, especially since the school is community managed but privately owned. Even more so now that my brother, Harrison, is governor. But as usual, Beasley just wants to throw money at it and get the land. And he will, because money always talks.

Given that we will make a few million on the deal, I can't really complain. It is just business.

I stand at the bar, swirling the whiskey in my glass, my eyes flicking to the empty hallway a few more times before surveying the room. It is the usual people here tonight, men in suits, women sipping champagne, hoping to be the next missus to many of the men here tonight, including myself.

But being wealthy makes me a magnet for gold diggers, as I learned with Sasha. We dated for twelve months before I caught her with another man. There is a myriad of emotions that run through your body when you catch your partner with someone else. Shock, anger, sadness, disbelief. She totally blindsided me, because I thought what we had was something semiserious.

Now I only do casual hookups. The shitty outcome of my parents' marriage is enough to turn any man off from the act. My mother, who was loyal and caring, changed almost overnight when my father died, leaving a string of girlfriends behind, all who were a surprise to her and us boys. It left us all on edge. None of us like the thought of commitment anymore, except Harrison. He found Beth and hasn't looked back since, the two of them governing Maryland like they were born to do it.

I tip my glass back and finish the whiskey, spotting a posse of women looking at me from across the bar. Nodding, I turn away from them, not feeling it tonight. I mentally scold myself when my eyes look toward the bathroom. Again. Before I can get too far, I feel a hand wrap around my forearm, and I look down to see painted red glossy nails. I wonder if it is the same woman who was just wrapping herself around Tennyson.

"Well, hello, handsome," a feminine flirty voice skirts over me, and I feel disappointed that it isn't the mystery woman from earlier. Looking over the sea of people, I see Tennyson locking lips with a blonde. He has her pushed up against the wall in a small alcove, but not completely out of sight. Just around the corner from him, I finally spot the woman from earlier with two other women, laughing at something that seems to be incredibly funny as they grab their bags to leave. She looks even better with a smile. I wish that she smiled like that for me. My eyes remain fixed on them, feeling jealous, because I would rather be over there with her in fits of laughter than where I stand right now.

"Come here often?" the woman who is currently attaching herself to my arm asks, not catching my silent hint. Ignoring her line I've heard a million times, my eyes remain on Doubtfire as she walks through the crowd toward the door. She must feel my gaze, because her eyes flick back to me, then to the woman who is currently cemented to my side, before rolling her eyes and walking out the door with her friends.

I think I will call it a night.

3

EMILY

This can't be happening. I feel like my heart is going to explode from my chest. I am about to have a full-blown panic attack or throw my glass of water against the wall. Either one of those is highly likely at this point.

My fingers grip the letter as my eyes run over the words. The fancy paper rests thick and heavy in my hands. I want to rip it up and pretend that we never received it. But I learned long ago never to put my head in the sand. To always stand up for what is right and fight the good fight.

"Don't look so grim. It was bound to happen," George says from across his desk, looking too calm in this situation. He is my rock, and I have no idea what I would do without him.

"How are you not upset by this?" I ask, perplexed. My blood is already boiling, my grip tightening, the paper almost to the tearing point. He is protective of me, but I am equally as protective of him.

"I have been expecting it for a while. Ever since those new condos went up on Smith Street. Progress is happening. We are not immune." George remains stoic as ever, but his shoulders are slumped and his face is resigned. I hate seeing him like this. I want to take it all away.

"Well, there won't be any future progress if we can't educate these kids. They will fall through the cracks if they can't come here. William Heights Elementary is all they've got!" I plead my case to George like he doesn't already know it. He does. As do I. As does everyone who works here and everyone in the community. Everyone except the big-city billionaires who think they can walk in and wave around their millions. Their only motivation is to demolish, build a row of condos, and resell, then making a tidy profit, no doubt.

"I just won't accept the offer," George says with a sigh, sitting back in his office chair. It was donated, just like most of the furniture and décor around the school. The black leather has a tear in the side where the seam once used to run. Our school is like this—run-down, old, in need of repair. But these walls are so full of love and joy, things I never thought I would have in my life, yet George is the one who helped me find it.

We met a few years ago when I was at rock bottom. If it wasn't for him, I am not sure I would have found my way out. He gave me a job, he gave me a home, gave me purpose to my life, and he gave me hope. Now it is time for me to return the favor.

"It's five million dollars!" I say with exasperation. It is a lot of money. George would be a fool to reject it. He could do so much with it. But with George, it is always more about giving than taking, and I already know he will indeed reject every offer, regardless of how many zeros are attached to it. I'd like to think that some of his strength has passed on to me after all these years. God knows I've needed it.

"There is more to life than money. We both know that." He is right. We do.

"So what happens now?" I ask, throwing the letter back onto his desk, observing him from where I sit opposite in the hard timber chair. He is a tall, stocky man. Protective genes run through his body. He takes care of the kids. He takes care of me. My heart starts to slow at the thought, the anger subsiding a little.

"Well, most likely, I will ignore the letter, then another one will come, along with a suggestion to meet them at their swanky office in the city. That is what happened to the fruit shop down the road." I watch him rub his brow, the stress of the unknown building. We can do this. We can save the school. We have to. There is no other choice. If I don't have George or this school, then my life takes a severe turn into the cold dark lanes of poverty. I've been there, and I don't want to go back.

I think back to the family-run shop which is no longer. I did love that fruit shop. Their strawberries were amazing. Now instead of strawberries, there are parking problems and congestion on the adjoining streets.

"Imagine what you can do with five million, though," I murmur, remembering that he and Glenda wanted to take a cruise before she got sick. They never got to make that trip.

"Not what needs to be done. What needs to be done is

educating these kids. Give them the right start in life. I want to spend the years I have left looking after you and Rosie. You're like a daughter to me, and these kids... we are all they've got." I smile then. My daughter Rosie is the apple of everybody's eye. The holder of my heart.

"But I will need your help with this," George says, bringing my attention back to the subject at hand. I admire his determination. Most people would take the money and run.

"Sure. Anything," I offer, because I would do anything for George. He helped me at my lowest, and I am in deep debt to him.

"I want your support. I want your legal expertise. You know these city folk as well as I do. They will stop at nothing to get their greedy hands on my land, and I need someone who understands all this jargon to help me navigate what they will throw at me. I am not selling, no matter what. I will die before that happens." He is steadfast in his words. They fill me with both pride and determination. We can do this. I will do this... I hope.

My pulse stalls for a beat, my past coming back to me and making me dizzy. Something that I skirt around daily. The dark cloud that constantly shrouds my life. My ex is the sole reason I didn't further my legal career, solitude being just one of his many tactics that impacted my life. I nod to George then. Pressing my lips together, I straighten my shoulders that are already heightened to my ears.

"But I've never practiced," I say, my confidence quickly dwindling. I have no idea how useful I will be, and I don't want to mess this up even more.

"You studied law at college, and that's enough for this. You're smart, Emily. I need you with me. I need you to represent me." I can't turn him down. My college textbooks disappeared from my life a long time ago, along with mostly everything else. But I will do anything I can to support George.

"Tell me what you need," I confirm I am all in. Because George is right. I do know these city types. And they stop at nothing until they get what they want.

No matter the consequences.

4

BENJAMIN

I rub my face, seeing double. My eyes are dry and tired as they fly across my cell phone, reading an urgent email from my client, Jonathan Beasley.

"Benjamin! No phones at the table!" my mother berates me like I am twelve and not thirty-one, and my eyes flick to hers, our matching scowls a reflection of our relationship. I grit my teeth so I don't say something I am sure I will regret. I am stressed with work, and dealing with my mother is the last thing I need right now.

"Fuck me," Tennyson murmurs from where he sits next to me. Mother's stink eyes move to him, but she remains silent. They haven't talked for years. I am not sure how that conversation would even go now.

"What's happening at the firm?" my older brother, Harrison, asks. I haven't seen him for a few weeks. His new position of governor has taken him from CEO of our firm to traveling around the state, shaking hands and kissing babies. Now as CEO of Langford Law in his place, my workload has exploded, and my stress levels have peaked. There is a lot to do and even more for me to prove.

"Beasley wants a meeting about the property he is considering buying on the outskirts," I tell him. And as soon as I open my mouth to give him more details as I finish reading the email, I'm predictably interrupted.

"Benjamin!" my mother almost screams again, so I pocket my cell and pick up my cutlery. The meat on my plate is dry and unappealing, just like the atmosphere around the dinner table. But the sooner I eat, the sooner I can leave and get home to my den and bury my head back into work. This deal is not going to make itself, and I need to move fast.

"He mentioned that to me at an event the other week. I told him to reach out. Put Michael on it. He will get that sorted," Harrison offers, and I nod. I appreciate his advice. He, more than anyone else, knows what time and energy it takes to run a law firm and Langford Law is not just any firm. Our client list is long and profitable and one I want to maintain. Harrison started the firm, and I want to build it now, make it my own.

"What property is he looking at?" my brother Eddie pipes up. The youngest of us four boys, he now manages our real estate portfolio, so his interest is not personal.

"Some school, William Heights," I say, looking back at my email and trying to gather the facts. My teeth grind into the meat, my mouth taking my stress out on the meal.

"For God's sake, boys! No phones!" my mother shrills. I take some deep breaths and remind myself why we all bother coming here for our regular monthly dinner with her. She is not the easiest woman to be with. In fact, she is downright despicable most of the time. But we are all she has, and her life is not yet settled after my father died.

"I'm out," Tennyson says as his cutlery clinks against his plate and his chair scrapes on the floor. Standing, he throws his napkin on the table in frustration. I rub my head, wondering if there will ever be a time when we can all have a nice dinner together, but deep down, I know that day is a long way off.

"I'll walk out with you. I need to get home to Beth, and then I have to be in DC early in the morning," Harrison says, standing slower, and I watch Tennyson throw back what is left of the whiskey he was drinking before sliding the empty glass on the table and stalking off to the door.

"Thanks, Mom." Harrison says his goodbyes, giving Eddie and me a brief nod before he follows Tennyson out the door. The room is quiet for a beat, and I see my mother purse her lips in annoyance before she takes a big breath and looks right at me. My nostrils flare as I wait for her assault.

"So... Benjamin. Tell me, how is Sasha?" she asks before putting a pea-sized amount of food in her mouth. I watch her chew it over and over like it is steak, not the soft potato mash her chef prepared. She chews exactly fifteen times before she swallows, taking a small sip of water and repeating the action again.

"Sasha and I broke up a few months ago, Mom. I told you that." She doesn't care. She only cares about appearances, not whether any of us are happy with the women we meet.

"Of course, but I thought you would be back together by now. She is fantastic for your reputation," she says proudly, and I cringe. Sasha was a gold digger, plain and simple. Like every other woman I have ever met. Only after money or status. It is so hard to find a genuine connection these days, so I prefer not to bother looking anymore.

I arrived at Sasha's apartment one night after she flew home from a fashion shoot in Paris, letting myself in with my key. Needless to say, after what I walked in on, I left the key on her kitchen bench and never answered her calls and have avoided her like the plague ever since. But to this day, she is still persistent. Often showing up to work unannounced, calling and texting me regularly, and it's becoming a problem. She doesn't appear to be taking no for an answer and there will be no other answer. I will never be going back to her. Cheating is the one line I do not cross.

"What reputation is that, Mom?" I toss back and see Eddie watching the exchange with interest from across the table. His eyes ping between the two of us like he is at a tennis match instead of family dinner.

"All you boys are workaholics. Just like your father. Sasha is a model, a socialite. You need to take her out again. Rekindle the flame. She can get you out of the office, lift your personal brand. Keep you on the front pages and ensure you are relevant." My head tilts, and I bite on my back molars, tempering the words on the tip of my tongue.

"Well, it is a bit difficult to take her out on a date when she is busy fucking every old rich man in the city."

Nothing beats walking into the apartment to surprise your girlfriend, then coming face-to-face with her jumping up and down on another man's cock. A man old enough to be her grandfather.

"Benjamin! No foul language at the dinner table!" My mother throws her napkin, not unlike Tennyson did moments ago. The two of them are more alike than he would admit.

"Suffice it to say, Sasha is a gold digger and we don't need any more of those in this family," Eddie offers, taking a sip of his water, clearly referring to our father's affairs. My mother's face blanches for a second before it hardens again. The reminder of her husband's philandering ways is something she will unlikely escape for some time.

"Yes. Well. We have the gala coming up soon. Please make sure you all have dates by then." The one in honor of my father, with money raised going straight to the Heart Research Center. Not that any of that matters. This is a party for our mother. So she can play the sad widow and garner the sympathy of society. She needs to stay relevant somehow.

I crack my neck and let go of the breath I was holding. I have no idea who I will take to this gala. It is not that I find it hard to get a date, but a woman who can hold a conversation and leave her cell in her handbag rather than in front of her face would be preferable.

"Yes, ma'am," Eddie mocks with a salute, and she sends a scowl his way.

"Who will you bring, Edward?" she asks, and I tune out now that her focus is not on me. My cell vibrates again, and I pull it out. *Speak of the devil,* I think to myself as I see Sasha's name lighting up my screen. I hit ignore and pocket it again. Her not taking the breakup very well, considering her new hobby of being on her knees for every rich man in town, comes as a surprise. But then again, everyone wants to marry a Langford. Our name opens doors, comes with status and money. Apparently not enough for Sasha, though.

"Isn't that right, Benjamin?" my mother says, smiling with glee. My eyes flick to Eddie, who is red, his teeth clenched. It looks like he is about to explode.

All in all, it is just a regular monthly family dinner in the Langford household.

5

EMILY

I spent all day yesterday preparing. I may be a special needs elementary teacher now, but I studied law in college and know my way around a contract. And George needs me for this. As the only father figure I have after losing both my parents, he deserves my efforts. So I will give it my all and that includes researching all weekend.

It isn't every day that a large property developer wants to purchase the school and is doing every underhanded tactic to get it. Our school is small, underfunded, but badly needed. I look after ten kids, all of whom have no other special needs school nearby to go to instead. If the school closes, then their only option is to attend a regular nearby elementary school, which has no funding for special classes or teachers. Their families would have to move.

George and I squeeze into the elevator, both of us taking a deep breath as soon as the doors close. I hate coming into the city, but I dressed for the part. I found an old black corporate-approved dress in my wardrobe that hugs my figure in all the right places without being too revealing. With my black patent leather pumps on my feet, my makeup perfectly done, and my hair silky and flowing down my back, I look like every man's wet dream. Little do they know, I am their worst nightmare.

George, who is well into his seventies, tugs at his tie, his nerves clear to me as I see him fiddle with his cuff links and run his hand through his hair. Usually, he is not so rattled. He is stoic, sure, dependable, so his clear uneasiness is carrying over to me. Maybe this is not going to be as easy as I thought.

As the elevator stops on the 33rd floor, I step out and the extravagance slaps me in the face. Everything is shimmering and looks brand new. Glass and stainless-steel surfaces reflect off each other, black leather armchairs placed strategically around reception, and dark woods polished beneath our feet. These city office buildings all look the same, and I am reasonably confident that the model-esque woman behind the desk will be entirely unhelpful. As if on cue, the receptionist looks at George and me, but boredom crosses her face and she glances down at her nails instead of greeting us.

"We are here to see Mr. Bennett and his client Jonathan Beasley," I say to her, and she doesn't reply, but I hear the annoying click of her long lacquered nails as they tap on the phone system.

"Hi, Sandra, Michael's ten a.m. is here," she whines through the phone before hanging up without saying another word.

George is pulling at his tie again, and I take another

deep breath to prepare myself for the meeting. They requested a face-to-face. Not totally unheard of, but a community meeting is usually how these things run in the suburbs. But as usual, men with money think they can buy themselves out of the inconvenience of going through the correct channels, which already tells us the man wanting to buy the property is not at all interested in looking after the school, the students, or the families that rely on it.

Assholes. All of them.

"It will be fine, George. Don't worry," I say with a small smile, which appears to do nothing to alleviate his fears.

An older, more refined woman appears, waving for us to follow. "Miss. Carr, Mr. Wellington, please come this way." With one more reassuring look at George, I take the first step to walk after her down a small corridor to the conference room, him walking beside me. I subtly smooth my dress and wipe my sweaty palms, trying to feign the confidence I need.

She opens the oversized opaque glass door and walks in, holding it open for us. As I step through, the first thing I notice is three men in the room, standing for our arrival. The second thing I notice is that the man now drilling me with his eyes is regrettably familiar.

While researching this firm yesterday, I discovered my run-in from this weekend was the CEO. His headshot on their website had me doing a double take, and then to read his last name... I was sufficiently caught off guard. He's a Langford. The brother of our new governor. I almost laughed to myself, thinking back on how I spoke to him. But out of all people to see in this meeting, I didn't expect it to be him. Given he owns this law firm, doesn't he have more important matters to attend to?

I watch as his handsome features morph from shock to intrigue, until they finally settle into a small smile, the kind that shouldn't make me melt, but it does a little. My knees feel weaker than they were two minutes ago, from just looking at him. His suit fits his frame just right, and I watch as his hand comes to his jaw, rubbing his cheek as his eyes travel down my body. Nice to see that after all the effort I put into my appearance this morning is worth it.

"Doubtfire?" he says suddenly, the curiosity in his tone evident, and I stop in my tracks.

"Neanderthal, I would say it is a pleasure, but it really isn't." I try to act unaffected as I attempt to get my racing heart under control. "Hi, I am Emily Carr. Nice to meet you," I say, extending my hand to the other lawyer in the room, Michael Bennett, and ignoring Benjamin Langford, who is standing mouth agape, still staring at me. Michael is the leading lawyer for the Langford Law Firm in which I am now situated.

"Jonathan Beasley," the other man says, but doesn't reach out to shake my hand, and I don't either. He obviously licks his lips as his eyes peruse my body in an entirely inappropriate manner. One that doesn't feel at all comparable to how Ben just looked at me. I mentally shake that thought away. I don't need to be giving him any bonus points for not being a total perv.

"What are you doing here?" Ben asks, slowly taking it all in.

"I am here to represent William Heights Elementary

School, and you are?" I say as professionally as I can, letting my sentence stretch, waiting for his response. We didn't introduce ourselves at the bar, so he doesn't have to know that I know exactly who he is. He might be a bigwig around this city, but his arrogance could use a check.

"Benjamin Langford. My name is on the door," he replies with a grin, his tone almost condescending, with a little nod toward the door.

"How lovely." My smile's fake, not wanting to give him an inch. I know how men like him operate. He will now think he has the upper hand in all these negotiations. Only, there will be no negotiations. George and I want this deal dead in the water. We only came here to tell them no.

George and I have spoken at length about this situation. We will continue to decline their offers, but they will play dirty. Probably tamper with the school, try to remove our funding, try to increase costs and pressures in some other underhanded way. We're mentally prepared; we know how this game works.

As we take our seats, George and I sit on one side of the table, with the three suited men opposite us. It is uneven, just like this negotiation is going to be.

"So, George, Emily, we have the paperwork all here for you to sign. As stated in our email, Mr. Beasley wishes to purchase the property and has offered quite the sum, as I am sure you can appreciate," Michael says as he pushes the paperwork over to us. George clears his throat but doesn't say a word.

My eyes flick to the paperwork. Five million dollars is a lot of money. George could do so much with it, but he has made it very clear that we are not selling the school. Not for any amount.

"Thank you for your very kind offer, Mr. Beasley, but as I am sure *you* can appreciate, the school is actually not for sale." I offer a small smile as I push the paperwork back across the table.

"It's five million dollars, Emily. Take the money," Ben interjects, appearing flabbergasted that I would decline such an offer, which is over and above market rates.

"Unfortunately, Mr. Langford, not everyone can be bought." Piercing him straight in the eyes, he meets my gaze. My fingers intertwine under the table, my body feeling hot. The way he looks at me is intense.

"What will it take?" Mr. Beasley asks, breaking the staring competition that Ben and I had started. He appears keen to get his grubby hands on our school, and his tone is demanding, but it's nothing I haven't heard before.

"As I said, we are not interested in selling the property."

"Ten million!" the balding fat man shouts at me, like he is bidding at an auction, and Ben looks at him sharply. He and Michael are obviously the ones who need to do the negotiating. Their client is now going rogue, a good sign that we have ruffled feathers. That was my main aim of being here to discuss this in person, after all.

"Once again, Mr. Beasley, we thank you for your offer, but we are not selling the property. That's final," I reinstate calmly, in a measured tone, which I know to men like him is extremely frustrating. As if on cue, a vein pops out of his neck and starts to throb.

"Emily, it's ten million dollars; you will never get that kind of money from anyone else. Take the cash," Ben says to me. He's trying to remain stoic, but I can hear a sense of urgency in his voice.

"Again, as I said, we thank you for the offer, but we are not for sale." I turn to look at George, who looks back at me proudly, and we both stand. I think I've repeated myself enough. "Pleasure to meet you all. We can see ourselves out," I say with a nod, my eyes looking quickly at the bowl of Milk Duds on the table, my tongue itching to taste one. They are my downfall, those delicious chocolatey treats.

Ben stands quickly and follows behind me as his client and colleague remain in their seats, still sitting in shock at our rejection.

"Are you really just going to walk away from ten million dollars?" he hisses at me as we walk through the door into the quiet corridor.

"Emily, I need to go," George says. This is the last place he wants to be, and I can tell he's itching to get back to school where he's needed.

"Go, George, I will meet you there later." He nods and walks briskly to the elevator, getting out of the building like it is on fire.

I turn and look at Ben, clearing my throat to make sure my last denial is firm. "We are really not interested in selling, no matter the price—" I stop mid-sentence as my eyes flick around his shoulder, my heart dropping through the floor at who catches my eye. I suddenly can't swallow, and my body begins to tremble.

Desperation kicking in, my head whips around frantically, trying to find a place to hide. Anywhere before he sees me.

"Emily?" Ben asks, his brow furrowed when my eyes land on him. "Are you okay?"

"Shit, shit, shit..." I say over and over to myself, shaking my head as I spot a vacant desk not too far away. I make a mad dash for it, past a tall potted plant, and down the hallway a bit, and then drop to the floor onto my hands and knees and crawl underneath the desk to hide.

"What the hell are you doing?" Ben follows right behind, looking down at me.

"Shhhhh," I say just as *he* approaches.

"Benjamin, good to see you, my friend," his voice booms, and I bite my tongue, forcing myself to stop breathing, hoping like hell he doesn't see me. I squint my eyes closed and clutch my hands to my chest, feeling my heart pumping hard underneath.

"Jeremy, nice to see you," Ben says as he positions his body so he is hiding me more, seemingly protecting me so Jeremy doesn't notice me. I give a silent thanks to the universe that Ben hasn't outed me, that he's actually helping.

"I would like to stay and chat, but I must keep moving. See you around. We must play golf sometime soon?" Jeremy says as he is walking toward the elevator.

"Sure, we can set something up," Ben replies dryly, and I feel like I am turning blue, with not enough oxygen getting to my lungs.

"Great, speak soon." I peek through a small crack in

the desk and see Jeremy enter the elevator, the doors closing on his frame.

Finally exhaling, I crawl out from under the desk, trying to settle my already shot nerves. Ben extends his hand to me, and I grab on to it like a life raft as I get to my feet. As I stand up, my eyes flick to the elevator one more time before I push my shoulders back.

"Thank you," I state like nothing just happened, fixing my dress and pushing my hair out of my face.

I look up at him and can't help but notice he still has hold of my hand and I am still trembling.

"You want to tell me what's going on there?"

"Nope," I say, popping the *P* in reply and taking a big gulp of air.

The last thing I want to admit is that I hide from my ex. It's been a while since I saw him last, and I would like to keep it that way.

Ben turns sharply and begins to stalk down the hall-way, further startling me from my thoughts. He hasn't let go of my hand, so he is dragging me behind him, and I have to run in my heels to keep up with his large strides.

"Hold my calls, Sandra," he tells the woman who showed me to the conference room earlier, her eyes widening as we walk into what I assume is his office, and then he's closing the doors behind us.

His office is huge, bigger than my whole apartment. A large timber oak desk sits front and center, with two black leather armchairs in front of it. A sofa and another armchair are off against one wall, the thick carpet between them creating a sitting area the size of most people's living rooms. There even appears to be a private bathroom through another door to the left, which boggles my mind. Everything about this office screams money, including the amazing view of the city through the enormous floor-to-ceiling windows. It makes me want to vomit.

"Start talking," he says as he leans against his desk, his arms crossed in front of his chest, demanding answers that I don't want to give.

I stopped answering the demands of men years ago, and I don't plan on sharing my personal life with my opposing lawyer today. My lips remain tight, and my eyes don't waver from his as I stay silent.

He stands up from this desk and walks over to me slowly, stopping right in front of me. Looking up at him, his eyes are intense, like he is trying to read me. Now my body is shaking for an entirely different reason as I feel his chest so close to mine.

"You are shaking. Are you okay?" His tone is soft as his eyes drill mine with palpable concern, and the armor around my heart cracks a little. This is new. A rich man in a suit, probably worth more than most people in the country, and from the Langford family to boot, and he is asking after my welfare.

I take another big breath and sigh. "I'm fine." Plastering on a fake smile, I step back from him before I do something stupid like fall into him and never let go. It has been a long time since I was in the arms of a man, and I have a weird feeling Benjamin Langford's arms would keep me safe from a myriad of things.

He nods, clearly not believing me, as he continues

watching me. His hands firmly in his pockets, an undercurrent of sexual tension sparks around the room.

"Ten million is a lot of money..." he says, assessing me.

I laugh then. *God, I am such an idiot.* I shake my head at my stupidity. Of course he didn't drag me in here because any part of him cares. He is just like every other suit; he wanted to prod me some more, and get this deal done for his client. I am such a fool, and I should have known better.

"I need to go. Have a nice afternoon, Mr. Langford," I say formally, super gluing the crack that appeared in my shield mere moments ago. He begins to speak and takes a step toward me, but I spin on my heel, open his office door, and stride out.

Leaving him and his demands behind.

6

BENJAMIN

She is fucking stunning, and just like the other night at the bar, my eyes are again glued to her ass. It's looking like a ripe peach for the picking in that figure-hugging black dress, and I'd love nothing more than to take a bite. She looks entirely different than she did on Friday night, not at all like Mrs. Doubtfire I've dubbed her as, and instead like a sexy Jessica Rabbit with curves in all the right places.

But the way she acted just now has me wondering what is going on beneath the surface. Clearly, she didn't want to see Jeremy Lucas. To be fair, I don't much like to see him either. He's a greedy asshole of a man and someone I didn't think I would ever have to deal with in my office. There was no denying she was shaking, and I saw a little vulnerability in her face. Her tough exterior fell momentarily, and I didn't like it. After witnessing her shine dulled slightly, I have a feeling this woman was only ever meant to sparkle.

Sandra appears at my open door, pulling me from my

thoughts. "Michael is free and waiting for you down in his office." I nod to her and straighten my tie, needing to adjust myself after having my hands on her again. After I got home from the bar on Friday, I am not ashamed to admit that I relieved the tension by visualizing her naked body underneath mine. *Emily Carr*. At least I know her name now.

I walk down the hallway toward Michael's office, still frustrated by what happened this morning. It was meant to be an easy one. The elementary school is so run-down that anyone in their right mind would be a fool to reject an offer of five million. But to also reject ten million, that was pure crazy. Michael is one of my best lawyers and only wanted me in the room because he knew Beasley would go off the rails if he didn't get his way. With both of us there, he was thinking we may be able to keep him in check, but it appears we were wrong. Jonathan Beasley is a slimy asshole, but a rich one. And he has us on a healthy retainer, so regardless of his character, it's one I wish to keep.

Michael's door is open, so I walk through and close it behind me as he looks up from his paperwork on his desk.

"What the fuck was that?" he says, and I shake my head, not the only one who found this morning's meeting totally unexpected.

"Who was she? Do you know her?" he asks me as I begin to pace his office.

"I met her Friday night at the bar. Had no idea she was a lawyer," I answer him, my mind running into overdrive.

"She's not," Michael states, and my eyes flick to him in a silent request for more information.

"Or she isn't a practicing lawyer, anyway. She is a teacher at the school." He turns his computer screen around to show me the research he has already done on her. My eyes flick to the screen, and I see a picture of a smiling Emily Carr staring back at me. It is from the school website and says she is a teacher of kids with special needs.

"Fuck me." I run my hands through my hair. I am totally confused. This woman is making minimum wage as a special needs teacher in a run-down elementary school on the wrong side of town and still owned the meeting like a pro.

"Yeah, from what I saw today, she can hold her own. The school can't afford a lawyer, so they obviously are using the resources that they have."

"They are not interested in selling," I say to him as I take a seat in the chair opposite him.

"I know, but Beasley wants that property…"

"Get a file together on her. We need to know everything about her. How long she has been at the school, where she lives, her history, get everything you can find," I tell him in a rush, my mind containing a whirl of questions.

"Already on it. What do we do about Beasley?" Michael asks, rubbing his chin.

"Well, maybe he can't get what he wants this time?" I murmur, knowing that Beasley will never rest until he gets exactly what he wants.

"Hah. You can tell him that. It is better coming from

the boss than me," Michael says, lifting his palms in surrender.

"What was Jeremy Lucas doing here?" I change the subject, knowing full well the slimy prick wasn't here to see me. I don't have a lot of time for Jeremy, but he is extremely well connected and one of those people you need to keep on your good side.

"He was meeting with Clive about a merger he is considering."

Clive is our merger specialist, specifically in relation to international acquisitions, with a focus on China and Asia Pacific. He's one of the best in the city, so it is understandable that someone like Jeremy Lukas would want his input.

"Please tell me we are not doing business with him," I groan, really preferring that we stay well away from the asshole who has a reputation for undercutting and conducting underhanded business dealings.

"He spoke with Harrison, so I am guessing that is now something you need to discuss with him," Michael responds with a smirk. I rub my hand down my face, and we get to work figuring out a plan of attack to get our client the school property he desires.

AFTER DOING my own research on Emily Carr, I have to say, I didn't find much. She is a ghost, and aside from her bio on the school website, I found nothing. Michael is still digging, which is why I now find myself outside William Heights Elementary School.

Walking through the glass doors to the front office, I stop short in the tiny foyer. It is much more compact than what I was expecting, and although colorful with kids' artwork strewn everywhere, it is smaller than my bathroom in my penthouse. My cell buzzes in my pocket and I don't even bother pulling it out to see; I already know it is Sasha. Her calls are now increasing. I used to get a few a week, all I would ignore. But now it is a few a day, with messages in between. It is starting to get really annoying.

"Can I help you?" an older lady behind the front desk says, eyeing me warily. I am in my crisp Prada suit; my polished black leather shoes reflect the overhead lights, and my dark hair is styled to perfection. I look out of place in the suburbs, let alone a school like this that is in desperate need of a good paint job and heavy mainte-nance work.

"It's okay, Margaret, I will take it from here," George says, appearing from the office at the side. It seems the old guy does have a voice. He didn't use it earlier in the week at our meeting and let Emily do all the negotiations at the table.

"George," I say and extend my hand with a nod in greeting.

"What can we do for you?" I am surprised when he takes my hand and his grip is strong. He doesn't appear to be the weak old man I thought he was.

"Well, I wanted to come by and look at the school and was hoping to chat with you or Emily some more."

"Our position hasn't changed," he says, his stance solid.

"I understand that, but I wouldn't be doing my job if I didn't try," I offer.

He nods in understanding.

"Emily is still in class. Perhaps we should go down to her room and you can see the good work we do here. Might make you understand our position more."

"Happy to," I say, and I follow him down the corridor.

"We have close to eighty kids here, and five different rooms. Most are for general studies, so the kids here are able to get a solid education before moving on to the local middle school down the road. We offer them free schooling, meals, and additional extracurricular activities, such as weekend swimming lessons to help them engage and thrive, which unfortunately, doesn't always happen in this community." I nod, listening to the information George is giving me, interested in the business of education and filing away anything he says that I may be able to use against him later. As I look around the small hallway, I notice peeling paint, scuffed walls, and cracked floor tiles. It really needs an overhaul.

"However, Emily teaches our special needs class. It is a group of about ten kids, varied in ages and disabilities," he says, coming to a stop outside a classroom. This is not entirely new information, as from the school website, I know she is a teacher for kids with special needs. I can't say I have spent a lot of time with kids who need extra support, or kids in general, but I assume it has to be a hands-on role.

"Let's go in and see what they are up to," George says as his eyes pierce mine, watching my face as he opens the door. Immediately, I am hit with noise. Kids talking over the top of each other, and as George holds the door open for me to enter behind him, I already feel a headache coming on.

Looking around the classroom is different from what I expected. Colorful art covers the walls; a small sensory space is set up in one corner, and then a quiet reading nook filled with soft cushions and rugs in the other. There are desks, but not individual ones, rather one large one in the center of the room, where a group of kids currently sit together, some coloring and others using clay or Play-Doh or some such craft supply.

My eyes roam the room until I spot her. She's sitting next to a young boy, and I think they are doing some type of dance or movement, but then I realize that they are signing. She has a big smile on her face and her long hair is up in a ponytail, some strands falling out around her face, and my fingers itch in my pockets to tuck it behind her ears. It looks lighter here in the bright afternoon sun, and even softer than I recall. My dick jerks in my pants as I remember her in my office earlier in the week. I was so close to claiming her lips with mine and it took all my willpower to stay professional around her.

"Good afternoon, class," George says, loud enough for everyone to hear, as well as signing it, and all the small heads turn in our direction.

I look at Emily, the shock that I am here in her space evident by the look on her face. At least I got her back for the surprise of having her in my office. I would say we are now even.

"This is Mr. Langford. Please say good morning,"

George continues, and the kids say good morning in a variety of different tones and grunts.

"Good morning," I say to all of them, my hands still in my pants pockets, giving them a small nod. But they have no interest in me, their focus going back to the tasks they were doing before I arrived.

I watch as Emily signs something to the young boy and then stands, walking over to us. Her eyes question George, and I see him shrug in response. She stalks straight up to me and grabs my elbow, and as much as we are on opposite sides of this business deal, I do like her manhandling me as she guides me back toward the door. Her head barely reaches my shoulder, so I feel huge next to her, but I also have the desire to fling her over my shoulder and go caveman on her. Eddie was right, she isn't my usual type. The girls I date are much taller. I have never been with a woman who is a little pocket rocket like Emily.

"What are you doing here?" she hisses, not happy to see me, and I smirk, liking that I can ruffle her feathers.

"I wanted to check out the school, to see the work you do here." Her face softens a little, and I think I might've won her over. We have met on two occasions now and both times she has been a pain in my ass. Now, though, I feel that she may be starting to open up and let me in and, maybe, just maybe, give me a nugget of information I can use against them in order to get this school for my best client.

"Cut the bullshit, Ben. We both know you are here to case the place, look for clues or loopholes."

And apparently, I was wrong. She is just as difficult

today. She has a blatant distaste for me, that much is obvious. But I can't help but be that much more intrigued by it. I hate it and love it in equal measures.

"Well, while I am here, why don't you show me around?" I say through gritted teeth, trying to push aside how infuriatingly sexy I'm finding her to be.

She huffs out a breath like I have just asked her for a kidney and turns to survey her class.

"I will leave you two to it, then," George says with a sly grin and nods to me before walking back out the door.

"Fine, come on." She sighs, her eyes sparkling as she spins around, grabbing my hand and pulling me back into the classroom farther. Her hair flies out in my direction, and I shove my other hand into my pocket again so I don't do something stupid like reach out and touch her.

"Class, Mr. Langford is going to be sitting with us for a while. He is really excited to meet you and get to know you some more." After dropping my hand, her face is now lifted with a fake smile as the boy she was signing with earlier walks up beside me.

He pulls on my suit jacket to get my attention, and I look down at him. I am tall, so I must seem enormous to a little boy who can't be any more than five or six years old.

When he signs something to me, I shake my head, feeling bad I can't understand him. "Sorry, little buddy, I don't know sign language."

"He just asked how tall you were. He loves basketball and really wants to play in the NBA when he grows up," Emily says as her face lights up when she looks at him.

"I'm six feet two inches." His eyes flick to Emily, and she quickly moves her hands. He must understand because he looks at me, wide-eyed, and his smile takes over his face before he dances off back to the corner, where he was playing with Emily when I arrived.

"Gavin, let me help you with that," I hear Emily say and look over to see her helping a bigger boy, this one perhaps closer to twelve or thirteen, but he is enormous for his age. Supporting most of his body weight with a walking stick, he walks to the back of the room, one leg not quite working as well as the other. She gets him settled at another workstation, and as she does, I notice a young girl sitting on her own, so I make my way over.

"Hi there, what are you reading?" I ask her as I squat down in front of her.

She answers without looking at me. "*Cinderella*. It is my favorite fairy tale." Her voice is cute, her blond locks moving a little as she speaks, shimmering in the sunlight.

"*Cinderella* is a great story," I say as I look down at the book in her hand and sit stunned for a moment when I realize there are no words or pictures on the page, but rather little bumps of braille. She lifts her head, then and I see the most beautiful round face, with blue eyes that appear glassy and not focused on me or anything else.

"Rosie, Mr. Langford loves a good fairy tale. Why don't you read him a page?" Emily suggests as she comes up behind me.

"Sure!" the little girl says in excitement, and I watch in amazement as she begins to tell me about the horrible stepmother and stepsisters, all the while her face tilts toward me as her tiny fingers run across the page in front of her.

My heart clenches in my chest as I take her in,

completely happy to be reading to me. I grind my teeth and stand, taking a step back, remembering that I am a top city lawyer, here for one purpose and one purpose only—to make money. And the only way to make more of it is to get this deal done for our best client and not become distracted by cute little children or sexy teachers.

No matter how good the latter one looks in those jeans.

7

EMILY

I saw his face soften while sitting in front of Rosie, and although I am biased, if she can't make him melt, then no one can. There is something about cute little girls that can pierce a man's heart right through. But Ben is not my friend, and I can't get too close to him, even though my body betrays me each and every time we are together.

"Seen enough now?" I ask him, crossing my arms across my chest and raising my eyebrows. My attitude is firmly back in place, because I know that he is wasting my time. Waltzing in here, expecting to find out all our secrets. He is a total Neanderthal, just like I predicted at the bar. Although the thought of his hands around my waist has my skin tingling from the memory.

It has been a long time since a man touched my body, and even longer since I enjoyed it, so sue me if I have daydreamed about him over the past few days. Although seeing my ex at his office was what my nightmares are made of, and that moment brought back many horrible memories. It only reminded me why I prefer to just give men in suits a wide berth.

"You do amazing work here, Emily, but I do need to get back to the city. Walk me out." As usual, it is an arrogant demand, not a polite request. I roll my eyes and call for Sarah in the classroom next door to keep watch of my students for five minutes as I walk Ben back down the hall, about ready to kick him out myself.

"You know, with ten million dollars, you can do a lot of good for those kids," he says, almost accusing me of not putting their best interests first in this decision. It is his lame attempt to make me feel bad for not taking the money that was on offer.

"The school is old, but we have everything we need, and the kids are thriving. If we sold the school, of course, ten million would go a long way, but we would all have to move farther away to purchase another property that would be big enough for our needs, and then spend more time and money renovating it to get it just right. The whole process could take over two years, and what are these kids meant to do during that time? Then, after a short while, businessmen come knocking again, offering another ten million for the property so more condos can be built and it becomes an endless cycle? We've thought this over. It wasn't a rash decision, Ben." When he doesn't say anything, I decide to throw in my own guilt trip.

"You know, if you would like to leave a donation to support their education, then please speak to Margaret at the front desk. She can organize that transaction for you." I know it's difficult for men like him to part with their money.

Selfish assholes.

I watch as his jaw clenches, clearly not pleased that I made such a suggestion, and we continue to walk down the hall. I don't understand these men. Never have and never will. They have millions, literally millions of dollars in their bank accounts, and the thought of sharing some of that wealth with others less fortunate makes them irate. Sure, many of them do it for a tax write-off, just not many of them do it out of kindness. To help their fellow man. But spending it on penthouses, European vacations, or supermodel girlfriends seems perfectly reasonable.

We reach the foyer, and he stops, turning to look at me as he runs his hand through his dark hair and sighs.

"You're not going to take the offer, are you?" he says, and I shake my head.

"Not even if he offered twenty million?" he presses, and again, I shake my head.

"The kids have been here for years. This is a safe space for them; they are secure and happy and their learning for the past few years has been better than ever. To move them, no matter how seamless the logistics are, is only going to be detrimental to them and their families. We just can't put them through it," I say, making one final attempt to try to get him to understand.

He nods, although I can see his mind working, and I know I haven't gotten him over the line.

"You know my client is not going to stop until he has the property. You need to prepare yourself for that." Even though it is not threatening, it is a warning. I nod in understanding. George and I know this is not going to be an easy fight.

"See you around, Doubtfire," he says, taking a few steps backward toward the door, a smirk pulling at the corners of his mouth.

"See you, Neanderthal," I reply, my lips matching his, before he steps out the door and gets into a shiny black Bentley that costs more than I earn in a year.

I shake my head, not sure what our next move should be, but hurry back down the hallway to my class. They are my priority.

I'M HOME in my tiny two-bedroom apartment, trying to resist the urge to throw the glass in my hand at the wall in frustration. I have just put Rosie to bed and opened my emails to catch up on some paperwork for another grant I am applying for, when I see a new email from Langford Law sitting in my inbox. They are asking George and me to attend another meeting in the city, this time with the mayor of our area joining us. No doubt, their client has waved a fat check in the mayor's face, and they are now using him to put the pressure on. I am not a fortune teller, but I can see him increasing our monthly property fees, taxes, and probably implementing some new law that we will now need to find the money for. If Mr. Beasley is paying the mayor to enforce new fees on our school to intimidate us or blackmail us, then it is a clear case for the anti-corruption watchdog. I may be an elementary school teacher, but I know slimy tactics by greedy businessmen when I see them, and Jonathan Beasley is exactly that.

My cell rings, George's name lighting up the screen.

"Hi, George, did you get the email?" I ask, already knowing that he did.

"Looks like another trip into the city for us next week, Em. I will get Sarah to cover your class, assuming you are still willing to represent the school on this?" He sounds tired and stressed, and I hate that.

"You don't even have to ask. You and the school have done so much for me; of course I will do whatever I can to keep it in your hands."

"Alright, I will talk with you tomorrow to formulate a plan."

"See you then," I say and then hang up and flop back onto my sofa with a defeated sigh.

We both know that this is an uphill battle. Money and power win every time, and I am a testament to that fact. But I need to fight for George, just like he fought for me.

When I first met him and his wife Glenda at the women's shelter, I knew we all had a connection, and clearly, they both felt it too. As volunteers, they ensured everyone was well looked after, but after they offered me a warm coffee, the three of us spoke for hours while Rosie slept beside me, and under the clause of confidentiality, I told them everything.

That night changed my life. It was the night I learned the importance of compassion and of helping one another. I was so worried about what I was going to do with my life and how I was going to support Rosie. But Glenda and George took us in. They turned their basement into a large studio apartment for us, and Glenda managed to get me a teacher's diploma scholarship at the local community college. Because of my high grades in college, I was able to breeze through most of the formalities and finish it in record time.

From there, I was offered a position at the elementary school they owned, and when Glenda passed away last year, a little glimmer went out in my life as well. We were all heartbroken. Still are.

I lean my head back against the sofa and look at Rosie sleeping in her room from where I sit.

We live a simple life now. A safer one. I help her learn and I try my hardest to save our money so we can be secure. As I rub my eyes, my cell phone pings with an incoming text, and I notice right away it is from a number that I am not familiar with.

> Neanderthal: Don't say I didn't warn you, Doubtfire.

I smile despite myself, and I don't hesitate to reply.

> Doubtfire: Bring it on, Neanderthal.

For added color, I include an angry face emoji. Juvenile, I know, but it portrays how I am feeling right about now.

> Neanderthal: Take the money, it is not worth the fight.

But that is where he is wrong; it is totally worth the fight. George and the kids are worth it all.

Doubtfire: See you soon. Be ready for us.

Neanderthal: I can't wait.

I close my cell and throw it on the sofa next to me. The stupid grin on my face tells me I am enjoying this way too much. I like our banter, and I also love to push his buttons. And surprisingly, the work is making me feel alive, especially since it is the first act of competition I have had with a person over the age of twelve in a long time. I start to formulate a plan in my head, because I know I need to play dirty—it is the only language these men understand. Looking the part in a conservative black dress is not going to cut it this time.

8

BENJAMIN

I grab the paperwork from my desk and rush out the door. My head is throbbing from the incessant messages Sasha continually sends. It is slowly driving me mad. That, on top of my heavy workload, has me nearly bursting a blood vessel today. There're a million things to do and not enough time to do them.

Michael, Jonathan Beasley, and the mayor of William Heights are all in the boardroom, and Emily and George will be here any moment. I stalk past Sandra, making my way down the hall, just as the elevator opens. Emily steps out, and I stop dead in my tracks. Holy shit.

Long gone are the casual teacher clothes and the messy ponytail I saw last week. It has now all been replaced by her signature shiny, long blond hair, glowing skin, big round eyes, and pouty lips all complemented by a slight flush to her cheeks. Her curvaceous body is encased in a red dress, one that's still appropriate as a corporate look, but she's making it so much fucking sexier. My pulse races at the thought of unzipping her dress, just to discover what is hiding underneath. If I had to guess, black lace underwear is what I would find.

Her eyes meet mine, and I watch her smile grow from across the foyer. Not a smirk, not fake, but a genuine full smile. She pays no attention to Natasha or Naomi or whomever it is who sits at our reception. As she confidently strides toward me, I wait, with my breath caught in my chest, for her. We look directly at each other—everything else is mere background noise—and as infuriating as she is, this look she gives me makes me feel powerful. My eyes scan her face, and I drink in her sparkling blues. Then, just for another moment, I let my eyes wander for a bit.

"What are you staring at, Neanderthal? Haven't you seen a woman before?" she asks with a quirked brow, standing right in front of me, her hands on her hips, clearly toying with me. I half think about grabbing her by the hand and leading her to my office and fucking her on my desk. The thought alone is making me hard, but I clear my throat and get a handle on myself.

"So glad you could join us." I remain professional as I pull open the conference room door, and she steps through. I shake George's hand, and then he follows. I take a breath, catching the hint of lavender, and I wonder how the hell I am meant to concentrate on this fucking case with her looking and smelling like that. For once, I am glad Beasley is Michael's client and he is running point on this.

"Emily! Great to see you again," Michael says, but I don't miss the look he gives her, and jealousy coils in my stomach. I watch him and the other two men with him devour her with their eyes, pissing me right off. She smiles and shakes their hands, ignoring their ogling. *She knows how to play the game. I totally underestimated her.*

"Fuck," I mumble to myself as I take a seat opposite her and George, with my team now outnumbering them, four to two.

"Thank you for joining us again. As you know, my client here, Mr. Beasley, is extremely keen to purchase the school property, and we have since discovered that Mayor Simplot also believes that new condos would be beneficial for the community," Michael states, kicking off the meeting straightaway—not here for small talk.

"Oh, is that right?" Emily says, and I sit back and watch everyone in the room like a hawk.

"Well, Emily, I know the school does wonderful things for many kids in the community, but developments like this don't come into the community very often, and from what I understand, Mr. Beasley is offering a fair sale price, which would only benefit the kids."

"Hmm... I see." Emily nods again, and I don't know how I know, but she has something on us.

"Look, you need the money, and I have it. Let's just stop playing dress-up because we all know you have no idea what you are doing and don't have experience dealing with the top end of town. Just go back to the kids and look after them and leave the big business to us men, darling."

My fists clench in my lap as our client tells Emily what he really thinks of her. I have a sudden urge to punch the stupid idiot in the face for speaking to her like that. I wait for her explosion, but it doesn't come. I watch her as she takes a measured breath.

"What my client means to say—" Michael starts.

"I understand perfectly what Mr. Beasley is saying, and with all due respect, Mr. Beasley, you don't know the first thing about me. So let me just make this really easy for you. We do not want your money; we are not selling the school, and Mayor Simplot, if you begin to make city decisions to financially ruin the school because you are being paid handsomely to do so by Mr. Beasley here, I will take the recording I have of this conversation and submit it to the anti-corruption watchdog."

Checkmate.

"Jesus," Michael says under his breath, but loud enough for me to hear.

"You little bitch! You can't do that!" Beasley yells and jolts up from his seat, looking like he is about to jump over the table and strangle Emily. I stand up, ready to end him if he even thinks to get any closer to her.

I grit my teeth together. "Michael, why don't you take Mr. Beasley to your office to discuss things," I suggest, and Michael grabs Beasley by the arms and practically drags the seething man from the room.

"Emily, George, I certainly didn't mean that the city was not supportive of the school; you know that we are," Mayor Simplot starts stuttering, trying to shovel himself out of the hole that he began to dig when he agreed to even be in the room this morning. I am not privy to it, but I am sure Beasley offered him money to be here, and Emily seems to have the same conclusion, hence the recording.

"We know exactly where your support lies, Harold. Don't worry about that," George spits out in reply, disgusted.

The mayor stands and nods to them both, then promptly walks out of the room with his tail between his legs.

"Em, I am going to go chat with Harold. I will see you at school later," George says sternly and walks out the door with purpose.

"Well played, Doubtfire, well played." I cross the distance and stop in front of her.

"Thank you for keeping your client on a leash. I thought he was going to jump over the table at one point there," she says to me, half-relieved, half-joking. I notice her hands shaking slightly, making me frown.

"Beasley is a little entitled..." I say as I open the door to the conference room for us to walk out, and I put my hand to her back, wanting to soothe her.

"Just a little," she murmurs sarcastically, and I smirk, glad to see her now relaxing into my touch.

As we step out of the conference room, I hear the familiar voice that pierces my ears like nails down a chalkboard, and my body immediately stiffens.

"Ben! Darling," Sasha says as she steps into our conversation, and I don't miss Emily's eyebrows as they arch in question.

"Sasha, what are you doing here?" I demand, in a tone that implies that she isn't welcome. Because she isn't. My stress levels have peaked again. I really need to put a stop to this. It is getting out of hand.

"I came to take you for lunch!" she says, flicking her

long locks over her shoulder and pushing her breasts out at me. I cringe at her over-the-top flirtatious behavior, as I see Emily stifle a laugh out of the corner of my eye. It is then that an idea dawns on me. A crazy one. I don't even pause to think about the words before they tumble from my mouth.

"Sasha, let me introduce you to Emily... my *fiancée*." Sasha's smile falls, and Emily goes rigid in my arms. Turning to her, I meet her gaze. She's looking at me like I've lost my mind, and maybe I have. But desperate times call for desperate measures.

"W-what?" Sasha stutters, glancing at Emily, then to me and back again.

"Yes. Darling, this is Sasha Davies," I say to Emily, my eyes pleading with her to act along with me, and I don't miss the mean glint in her eye before she relaxes into my arms.

"Lovely to meet you, Sasha," Emily says, her smile now wide, and my arm wraps around her waist, presenting a united front.

"But, what, I mean, when..." Sasha's not even able to string words together.

"Sasha, we ended months ago. I know you will find someone just as wonderful as I have. Everything happens for a reason, it seems," I say, pulling Emily into my side even closer. I like the way she feels, tucked against me, like she was always meant to be there. How I ever thought Sasha was it for me, I have no idea. Looking at her now, in comparison to Emily, there really is no contest.

"Well, um... congratulations!" Her voice rises with emotion, her smile fake as they come. "I don't want to keep you, and I just remembered I had somewhere to be..." she says to me before walking back to the elevator with the fastest steps I've ever seen her take. Her freshly blow-dried hair does little to hide her bright-red cheeks or the heavy scowl that now adorns her brow when she faces us again before the elevator doors close.

Emily doesn't wait a moment longer, grabbing my hand and pulling me down the hall. She brings us right into my office, not dissimilar to how I had her last week, and I bite my lip so I don't laugh out loud at the situation we've found ourselves in.

"Hold his calls, Sandra!" Emily says as she pulls me past my assistant, then the door to my office closes on Sandra's smile, amusement radiating from her. This will be her entertainment for the day.

In the safety of my office, I slump on the sofa as Emily paces the room. I am surprised she went along with me. I said it half expecting her to slap me and walk away.

"Start talking," she demands, throwing my own words I said to her in this very office last week back at me.

"Sasha is my ex who is not taking no for an answer. Sorry, it just slipped out." It's a poor excuse, but it's the best I can do. I didn't even consider the ramifications before I threw both of us under the bus. I didn't think any of it through.

"Just slipped out?" she almost screams, her face now contorted in panic.

"It's fine. Take a breath. No big deal," I say, standing, my hands raised like I am taming a wild beast.

"No big deal! Are you kidding me? You are Benjamin Langford. You being engaged is a *very* big deal!" she says, bewildered as she gapes up at me. Yeah... I may have forgotten about my status for a second there.

"Fuck." Grabbing my hair and pulling it, I rack my brain, wondering where the hell my thoughts go around this woman. It is so unlike me to react this way. I am strategic. I plan everything. I am thorough with my work and with my life. This is totally out of character. Not to mention what this will mean for business. I can already see Beasley's face turning a bright red in anger for being engaged to his current enemy number one. Now I might be panicking too.

"It is probably already trending on social media!" She isn't wrong. I have literally just dumped us both into a shitstorm. I sit on the sofa, thinking for a beat. I have to come up with something. Emily continues to pace back and forth before me, and the longer I look at her, I'm determined to not retreat out of this deal. She felt way too good in my arms.

It comes to me then. My eyes flick to hers, and almost as if she can sense it, she looks at me suspiciously.

"What?" she barks.

"Let's pretend," I say carefully, wanting to ensure I position this right. My mind is working in overdrive now, bringing the plan together. I still don't know how to combat Beasley, but I will have to work out something. Figure it out as we go. He isn't going to like it, but I am a professional, and I keep my private life private. I can move off working the case directly and just leave it to Michael, if need be.

"Pretend?" She stops pacing and looks at me, her brow crumpled, her gaze hard.

"Yes. You will be my fake fiancée for a few months, and I will do something for you in return," I offer, confident my idea will work.

"Have lost your goddamn mind?" I try not to take her response personally. Any other woman would jump at the chance to be engaged to me. Apparently just not this one.

"It could be a perfect plan..." *Perfect* might be a stretch. Sitting up straighter, I lean forward, setting my elbows on my knees as I look up at her.

"It's a terrible plan," she retorts with an exasperated huff.

"Well, okay. Maybe just perfect for me, then. Being with you will most certainly get Sasha off my back. What can I do to make you say yes to this? Whatever you want, just say the word." Maybe I shouldn't give her free rein, but I'll do just about anything. She finally stops working a dent in my overpriced rug, coming to stand directly in front of me, hands on her hips.

"How about start with this... What even are the terms of this fake fiancée agreement?" Emily asks, making me acutely aware of her intelligence. Relaxing back, I cross my ankle over my knee, allowing me to get a better look at her power stance.

"Give me one month. Dinner one night a week and one weekend night, photos, maybe a work function. We will need to spend time together. I need her to see us out and about, being romantic, and then I am sure she will get the picture and leave me the hell alone."

"The whole city will get the picture!" Emily seethes, her hand going to her head like she has a migraine before it falls and her hands land on her hips once more. With a deep inhale, she steps even closer to me, forcing me to look up again from this position. "As soon as we end this charade, won't she just come crawling back to you again? How are you so sure this will work? That it will even be worth it?" I wave her off before she's even finished with her questions. This has to work, and now that I have made the offer, I really want Emily to say yes to me. The rest I don't even care about anymore. She basically growls at my dismissive action, then narrows her eyes on mine.

"And what exactly do I get in return?" There we go.

"Like I said, *anything*," I say, my eyes not-so subtly grazing over her body, taking in the small rise and fall of her perfect breasts with her quickened breaths before my eyes rest on her face to see her smirking.

"Anything, huh?" I nod, albeit a bit hesitantly from the look on her face, acutely aware that I am now signing a deal with the devil. One of my own making.

"I want the school," she states, leaving no room for misunderstanding. I give her an incredulous look.

"Anything but that. I can't just sign over multimillion-dollar deals. I have a duty of care to my clients." If anyone heard that I didn't represent my clients with one hundred percent integrity, the whole firm would crumble. And as the CEO, I am not about to be the one who lets that happen.

"Okay, let's circle back to that. How is this going to look to them? Have you even thought about how that could play out? We've been in the same room together, in front of him. Don't you think that's weird? We certainly didn't act like we were engaged." Her hip pops as her arms cross over her chest as she stares down at me like I'm a royal idiot. Which wouldn't be totally incorrect, considering every question she's asking is one that hasn't crossed my mind on my own.

"I will work it out, offer them full disclosure. Lay my cards on the table. I will tell them you are it for me and leave it to Michael to manage the client, just like he has been doing," I offer, then internally wince, knowing that I now need to inform my brother so Harrison can be aware of what is happening. The realities of my deal are now starting to seep into my bones.

"Fine. Here it is. Wednesday afternoons, you will volunteer at the school for art class," she states, and I nod my head easily. That isn't too bad. I will have to shuffle meetings, but surely art class is only for an hour tops, and I can work in the car while in transit.

"On Saturday mornings, you will assist with swimming lessons at the local pool," she says, and again, I nod. I can cope with that too.

"Anything else?" I ask, searching her face. There's got to be more. She hasn't asked for much, and to be honest, she could ask me for anything but the school—money being the obvious thing many women want when with a man like me, that and a bump in the society rankings tier. I wonder what she really hopes to get out of this.

"Just... no planned media interviews or articles. I will do this fake engagement. I can hide from the paparazzi, but I want to stay out of the media as much as possible." I hear vulnerability in her tone, so unlike how she usually sounds. It's another thing that is different about her. Any other female would be Instagramming our every date from start to finish for the world to see, yet this one doesn't even want to be seen with me.

"The paparazzi will always try to get a shot. But I will protect you the best I can. You have my word." And I mean it. I will keep her safe. Nobody will ever touch this woman on my watch.

She nods, her eyes pinning mine, an unspoken truce running between us.

"Then I guess it's a deal," she says, extending her hand for me to shake on it.

"Deal," I reply, grabbing her soft hand, our handshake firmly sealing our fate.

Without another word, she turns and grabs her bag to leave, and I can't resist. "So can I call you wifey?" I smirk at her, and she rolls her eyes. As I open my office door, Sandra struts up to us.

"Ben, Harrison called and said to remind you of your midday appointment. He is meeting you there." Harrison, Tennyson, Eddie, and I have a weekly lunch at the corner bar down the street. Nodding to Sandra, I look at Emily.

"Let me walk you out," I say and wave my hand in front of us. Together, we make our way to the elevator, and I turn to her. She stands next to me, her head tilted upward to meet my gaze, her long hair falling down her back. Right now, she looks like she did at the bar, and I like her head back, looking up at me like this. I am about to say something that I really shouldn't even be thinking, like how much I want to march her back to my office and strip her of her fucking red dress, but I clench my teeth together.

Being in a fake engagement is not ideal, as the press,

of course, will have a field day. But the more I think about it, the more I am sure this is what will keep Sasha off my back. Plus, I will get to spend more time with Emily and maybe find something that can help my client purchase the school he so desperately wants.

The only problem is trying to keep my hands to myself. Because whether I want to believe it or not, Emily is the only woman who has grabbed my attention in months, and the only one who I am itching to touch but can't.

This is going to be the hardest month of my life.

9

EMILY

There have been many difficult occasions in my life up until this point, but being in close contact with Benjamin Langford in this elevator is one of the hardest. My *fiancé*. I am scared, I am not going to lie. I am dancing very close to the flame that continues to haunt me, even to this day. But I would do anything for George and the kids, so putting myself out there to try to win this case is the least I can do. Even if it means portraying a fake fiancée to one of the city's most well-known bachelors. I could tell he hadn't thought through his offer. Not as well as he should have. His client is going to be angry, and that thought alone was enough to get me to agree to this stupid idea. Because if his client is focused on that, they might drop the case altogether, and then we'll have a chance of keeping the school.

With his tall frame standing next to me, our arms touching slightly, my senses are in tune with his aroma as the delicious scent of fresh woods after a heavy rain fills my nose. My fingernails dig into my palm, and my heart races. *It has been way too long since I have been with a man; I am losing my mind.*

It is lunchtime, so the elevator from the top floor is a slow journey, stopping at each floor as more and more people pile in. As it gets crowded, I shuffle slightly, pressing into Ben. His arm brushes mine before it comes around and rests on my lower back, not unlike he did moments earlier in the boardroom. It isn't unwelcome, not unwanted, but a little bit surprising and very calming.

"You okay there?" he whispers down to me, his warm breath skirting across my neck, sending small shivers down my chest. I look up to catch him smirking.

"I am great. It was a successful meeting, and I have an amazing fiancé, so I couldn't be happier," I smart back, and he smiles. I don't miss the genuine look in his eyes.

"Glad I make you so happy, darling." With that mocking endearment, our new arrangement vibrates between us, the tension growing heavier in the small space.

The elevator stops at yet another floor, and a few people get out, but his hand remains firmly set on me. I don't move either, content to stand close to him, feeling almost protected. A feeling I crave and have never experienced. I guess I need to get used to it. We will need to be seen as a united front when we are in public, and I need him to see the school and the kids as real humans doing amazing things. Maybe that way, he will at least try to get his client to see a different point of view and leave us alone—if his client doesn't fire him first, that is. Just before the doors close, Sasha dashes into the elevator, and I feel his body stiffen. I don't miss the way she looks at him with possession in her eyes. I wonder what she has been doing in the building all this time; she left Ben's office at least ten minutes ago. Maybe she has another boyfriend or something.

"Ben," she purrs, obviously over the shock at our engagement news as she walks straight up to him like they didn't just see each other moments ago. Unlike earlier, I can't help but notice how beautiful she is. I look like a dowdy schoolgirl next to her. She might as well be a model straight off the runway. A flash of both jealousy and disappointment courses through my body. Jealousy, because these two have history, and disappointment for thinking Ben is different than any other man. But I smile, nonetheless, looking like the happy fiancée I am supposed to be, instead of the broke single mom that I am.

"Sasha," Ben says with a curt nod and in a tone which indicates it really isn't that good to see her again.

Then she looks at me and raises her eyebrow. *She is challenging me.* She is aware that he is engaged, but is not abiding by girl code and is going after my fake fiancé anyway. I look away, not wanting to be involved, already regretting the deal I just made. This is the last thing I need. To be in the middle of their lovers' tiff. I close my eyes and take a breath, sorting my racing mind, pushing away any stupid thoughts I have of how good I feel being close to Ben and realigning my brain to think of George and school, the only reason I even agreed to this stupid arrangement. Ben's grip around my waist tightens, clearly expecting me to run, which is exactly my plan as soon as we reach ground level.

I watch the lights on the elevator as we descend, and I'm thankful that we stop on no other floors. Out of the corner of my eye, I see Sasha reach out and touch Ben's tie, then she leans in and whispers something to him. I want to scratch her eyes out with Rosie's braille pen that I have stashed away in my handbag.

The elevator dings, and as soon as the doors open on the ground floor, we all start to pile out.

"Doubtfire..." I hear Ben grit out as I escape his grip and walk swiftly out of the elevator.

"See you later, darling," I say in my best fake fiancée tone as I give him a little wave and force a smile to my lips before walking away from them both quickly. That is one helpful thing about being small, the ability to disappear in crowds, and I'll use this to my full advantage today.

Along with the rest of the people, I walk at pace through the foyer, my heels clicking across the polished marble as I head to the double glass doors. Once outside, I take a left, eager to get straight to the subway and back to school.

I make it halfway down the street before I stop when I see a homeless man sitting on the sidewalk.

"Hello," I say to the man, bending down a little to get closer to him.

"Hello, ma'am," he replies with a kind smile.

"Are you in need of anything? Is there something I can get for you, or would you like me to call the local shelter to see if they have a space tonight?" I offer. I know what it is like to have nothing. I never had to live on the streets, but Rosie and I jumped from shelter to shelter for a time. That was before George took us in, and so while I don't understand exactly what this man is going through, I know a little of what he may be feeling.

"No spaces in the shelter tonight, they're all full, but I will take a dollar if you have it," he quips with a shrug, squirming where he sits on the hard sidewalk.

I nod. There are far too many homeless people and never enough spaces. If I ever win the lottery, that is the first thing I would do. Build a massive shelter, with all the support systems in place, so it becomes a hub for people like this man, for people like me, who need support at a time when there is none.

"Sure thing. I'm Emily, by the way," I say as I grab my purse.

"I'm Dale."

"How long have you been out here, Dale? On the streets?" I ask as I fish around in my purse to see what money I have.

"Most of my life, Emily, most of my life." I nod at his confession. Homelessness is a hard position to break, and some people never survive it.

I find twenty dollars in my purse and hand it over.

"Thank you, Emily. You have fed me for a week with this." He reaches out to grab my hand. It is my last twenty. Something I was keeping to take Rosie for a milkshake after school this week. But we don't need milkshakes. I am sure I have some ramen at home and maybe we can make a quick trip to the library to see if they have any new braille books we can borrow instead.

I squeeze his hand. "Anytime, Dale. I wish I could do more. Be safe." I stand and turn around to head to the subway, but instead step straight into a tall, hard chest as large hands encase my waist to keep me steady.

Ben was standing right behind me the entire time. He is looking at me now, admiration in his eyes, and the air leaves my lungs as they drill into mine.

"What's that look for? Haven't you seen anyone do a good deed before?" I say with a quirked brow, trying to brush off the surprise.

"I have. I've just never seen a guardian angel quite like you," he says, his serious tone something new. His eyes glisten as they look into mine, a few seconds passing as we quietly take each other in as people rush all around us. I feel his hand lingering, caressing my waist just slightly.

"I have to run, but I will see you next week for art class. Text me the details," Ben says, almost snapping us out of the moment as he lets go of my waist and turns, walking in the opposite direction. But he takes one last look between Dale and me before he does.

Dale walks up to me then, and we both stand together, watching Ben until he disappears into the crowd.

"Ben's a nice guy," he says to me, and I whip my head around to look at Dale.

"You know him?" I ask, shocked that Ben knows the local homeless man.

"Yeah, Ben gives me twenty dollars every morning, along with a coffee from Starbucks. Makes my mornings better," Dale says, smiling, and I can't help but smile in return.

Ben is just full of surprises.

10

BEN

I rush into the bar and head to our regular table at the back, surprised to see my brothers already there waiting. Even though it's busy, I can still spot them from a mile away, usually because there is always a table of ladies constantly nearby. Such is the life of billionaire bachelors like us.

"Sorry, gents, had a meeting," I say as I take a seat at the table with them.

"About time. I have to be across town in an hour," Harrison says, straightening his tie, and I see a table of his staff behind us, their heads buried in their phones and laptops, clearly waiting for the governor to take him to his next appointment. My older brother is well loved in Maryland, and his hard work doesn't go unnoticed by the masses.

"Glad you could spare us an hour, your excellency," I mock, and he thumps me in the arm before he grabs his water.

"What took you so long?" Eddie asks, eyeing me questioningly. I am always on time; usually I am the one waiting for them. It is one of my annoying traits. I like to be punctual, and I expect punctuality from everyone else. My eyes flick to Tennyson, already seeing him downing a whiskey and wondering how many he has had. He went to New York a few months ago, and ever since, he hasn't been himself. My brothers and I have talked at length to both him and each other, but he keeps telling us he is fine.

"Chasing women, brother?" Tennyson pipes up, and I smirk. He isn't exactly wrong.

"Just finishing up a meeting with Emily," I state, wondering where the waitress is, because I need a drink.

"Who's Emily?" Harrison asks, and I am relieved when the waitress delays my answer. The four of us order quickly, because not only does Harrison need to leave, but the rest of us need to get back to the office to finish our financials for the month. As we order, I see the waitress eyeing Tennyson, but he is doing a good job of ignoring her, something she doesn't seem to like. I can only assume he has had sex with her, but can't remember her name, so he is ignoring her, hoping this awkwardness of their meeting will melt away and never be spoken of again.

The waitress leaves without saying a word to Tennyson, and I raise my eyebrow to him in question. But he doesn't pay any attention, as the boys are focused back on me.

"So, who is Emily?" Harrison presses, and I pick up my menu again, pretending to peruse it.

"Why are you so quiet? Has your tongue been busy

doing something else, Benny boy?" Tennyson uses my kid nickname, and I throw a punch, hitting him in the arm.

"Ow, what the fuck, man?" He rubs his arm dramatically, and I run my hands through my hair to try to pull myself together.

"Again, who is Emily?" Harrison repeats to me, as he takes a sip of his water.

"She is the woman defending the school case I'm working on at the moment. The property Beasley wants to own in William Heights," I explain, acting like I didn't just want to fuck her in the elevator. I take a deep breath and my brothers all wait, knowing I have more to add. I'm not sure how to deliver the news. It is by far the most outrageous thing I have ever done, so I just blurt it out. "And I am not chasing her. She is actually my fiancée." The waitress saves the day again, bringing me my beer, and I take a quick drink.

Harrison almost spits out his water, Tennyson grins in delight, and Eddie's eyes are wide as he stares at me, unmoving.

"What?" Eddie and Harrison ask in unison, shocked.

"*Fake* fiancée," I confirm before I proceed to tell them about my deal with Emily.

"Red flag. You are a fucking Langford. You cannot be running around town with a fake fiancée," Harrison grits out. He takes our reputation very seriously these days since becoming governor, and I support him on that, but his immediate reaction to me being engaged, fake or not, has my jaw clenching.

"If it is just fake, why did you hit me?" Tennyson asks, rubbing his arm again.

"Just a reflex, sorry," I say with a laugh, not sorry at all.

"Nope, not work related and not very fake at all, by the looks of it," Tennyson says, leaning back in his chair like the cat that got the canary.

"Again. What the hell is going on? A fake fiancée? How is that ever going to work?" Harrison continues, and I can basically see his thoughts racing behind his eyes.

"Sasha's calls have escalated. She just came to visit me in the office, and I needed to find a way to get her off my back once and for all. Emily was there, and the idea flew out of my mouth before I could rein it back in. I talked with Emily after, and we came to an agreement. We will go out a few times so Sasha can see us together, maybe to a few events and business things too. Once Sasha is off my case, Emily and I will go our separate ways." My stomach feels like lead as I talk through the plan out loud. I don't like the sound of us going our separate ways.

"What does she get?" Tennyson asks, looking skeptical.

"She just wants me to hang out at the school and help some of the kids with their swimming. Nothing major," I say, shrugging, because she could have asked for so much more.

"So you are not paying her?" Harrison asks, surprised.

"No, I am not fucking paying her," I spit out. I refuse to pay a woman to spend time with me. In any capacity.

"She didn't ask for much..." Eddie adds, leaving an accusation out there.

"My guess is that she wants me to embed myself into the school and the kids so that I can make this Beasley deal go away," I tell them. It's pretty obvious what her intentions are.

"Nothing Beasley does goes away," Harrison murmurs over the top of his drink. He knows as well as I do that when Beasley wants something, he will stop at nothing to get it.

"So you're telling me that you have met a woman, who has agreed to be your fiancée, but has asked for no money, and is getting no personal gain whatsoever?" Tennyson asks as he sits back in his seat, eyeing me.

"Me with the kids. That is all she wanted."

"Mom is going to have a fucking field day," Eddie says, and all four of us take a swig of our drinks. Our mother is a force unknown to us. After almost fracturing her relationship with Harrison, she has quickly moved on to me. The longer I can keep this news from her, the better, because I am sure when she finds out, the other side of the world will hear her explosion. Especially since she and Sasha get along so well. Sasha has probably called her already, because my phone is suddenly very quiet.

Mom was the one to introduce me to Sasha, having met her at a fashion charity function and deciding that a woman like her would be the perfect match for me. That should have been the biggest red flag of it all. I usually ignore all my mother's ideas, but she wore me down, and so Sasha and I went on a date. Then another, and another, before we became semi-serious. Mother was off my back, and I escaped any further issues. The drama that ensued after Harrison met Beth is seared into everyone's brains except hers, and that is something I didn't want to experience.

I sigh and rub my hands over my face. "I'm so fucked. She is a pro in our meetings, yet a special needs teacher. I can't wrap my head around it. I have been thinking about her ever since I met her at the bar the other week."

"Wait, are you talking about the nun?" Eddie asks, now sitting forward, engrossed in the conversation.

"The one and only." I sigh, taking another swig of my drink.

"Fuck, so you like her, then? This is not just a business deal?" Tennyson pushes, clearly intrigued as well.

"She isn't your usual type..." Eddie starts. Here we go again...

"What, you mean tall, tanned, and from a magazine?" Harrison interrupts, and all three of my brothers laugh and cheer their drinks, mocking me and my past relationships.

"Fuck off, you assholes," I murmur. Eddie made this point at the bar the other week, and I don't need to keep hearing it.

"She is stunning..." Tennyson says, nodding at Harrison. "In a sexy librarian kind of way." I need to clench my fist under the table to ensure I don't punch him in the arm again.

"Maybe I should meet her if she isn't your normal type, Ben. Then maybe after your fake fiancée deal ends..." Tennyson continues, knowing I am the jealous type after my debacle with Sasha.

"Don't finish that sentence," I spit at him, and he laughs in my face, taunting me. He loves pushing my buttons.

"You know you really can't get involved with her; it

could undermine the case," Harrison says, looking at me seriously. The thoughts about how this affects work became secondary and now I am still scrambling to figure it out.

"I'm not planning to. Besides, Beasley is Michael's client, not mine." While that is true, I still own the firm, and the only way to get this past Beasley is to be upfront and honest, informing him in writing.

"He is the largest client of our firm. You can't fuck this up," Harrison warns, and I nod because I know. I know I shouldn't go near her, shouldn't touch her, but fuck, I want to. I make a mental note to work with Sandra this afternoon on a letter of information. Might as well get it done today and deal with the ramifications from there.

"I saw Sasha just now in the elevator. Again," I say, trying to change the subject.

"Oh, how did that go?" Tennyson asks, keen to get the news.

"She whispered in my ear that she misses me and wants to get together. And this was after she knew I was engaged..." I say, not feeling all that good about having my arm around Doubtfire while Sasha was whispering in my ear. I tug at my tie and crack my neck.

"Fuck her," Tennyson spits out. If there is one man who hates cheating more than me, it's Tennyson. Sure, like me, he is a playboy, but he has never cheated, preferring to keep things nonexclusive with his women, and it has worked well for him so far.

"Don't ever go back there, man. It's not worth it at all," Eddie says, shaking his head. None of my brothers liked

Sasha. They hated it when I brought her along to work dinners and other functions.

"So are we going out tonight, then?" Tennyson asks. He is always on the prowl, and most Friday nights I join him.

"No, not tonight," I say, not meeting his eyes.

"What, so you don't want Sasha, and this Emily means nothing to you, so what's holding you back? We can go to The Latin Rose bar downtown. It's private. Discreet. No one will bat an eyelash that you are there." He prods me, knowing the answer, just waiting for me to admit it.

I shrug my shoulders. "Just got some work to do tomorrow," I say, acting nonchalant.

"Bullshit. What work?" Eddie fires back, and it is now two against one as Harrison watches the dynamics, playing his part as older brother well.

"Fuck, you're giving up on a Friday night out in the city because you now have a fake fiancée. She must be hot as—" Tennyson starts up again.

"Don't finish that sentence unless you want my fist in your face this time." The two boys holler in laughter.

"Just don't fuck up Michael's case," Harrison repeats. He is laughing now too, but Beasley is our best client. If we lost him, it would be a big hit to our bottom line.

"I'll try not to," I say with a smirk.

"Hey, what's the deal with Jeremy Lucas?" I ask Harrison, hoping like hell he doesn't become a client.

"Ahh, I heard he is trying to invest in China. Needs some advice."

"Are we bringing him on as a client?" I'm eager to

learn more about the man who Emily was hiding from last week. In his position as governor, Harrison has a lot of connections and knows everyone. As former CEO of our law firm, he also offers our services to his connections when need be.

"I gave him some free advice. He has a whole team of lawyers, so he doesn't need any more, but I like to keep him on our good side if I can." Harrison's response is one of a politician, but I know he doesn't want Jeremy Lucas anywhere near our firm either so we are all on the same page.

"He is an asshole, if you ask me," Tennyson says as he finishes his drink.

"What do you know?" I prod. Tennyson manages our construction business, and he, like Harrison, knows a lot of people.

"I know that he doesn't pay his bills, shortchanges everyone, and thinks he is unbeatable. Not very well liked, and to be honest, I would keep him at arm's length. He has a violent streak." That last comment is sobering.

"If I know anything, it is that getting into business with a man like Jeremy Lucas is a bad business decision. We will stay well away from him, boys, but keep him on our good side when possible. I don't want any trouble following us around," Harrison advises, and I nod. None of us want to be on his bad side, or any side, for that matter.

He doesn't seem to play well with others.

11

BEN

I am running late again, which I hate, as Ralph drives me to William Heights. It is the first school art class for me this afternoon, and then I have swimming lessons this coming Saturday. Emily will come into the city with me this week for dinner, our deal starting to feel more official.

I still have no idea if my plan is going to work, especially considering Sasha has been sending me numerous messages this week. It appears the fact that I am engaged has only heightened her interest and she is nothing if not persistent. Emily, on the other hand, has only texted a few times to organize the logistics of today and that is it.

The next step with Sasha will need to be a legal one, but I hope it doesn't come to that. I could call this whole thing off, given that she seems more intense than usual, but I have taken a shine to this suburban spitfire, and I want to take this time to see what makes her click.

The car pulls up to the school, and I pack my laptop away. I have a million other things that I need to be doing today, and painting primary colors is not one of them, so I am not in the best of moods as I walk through the reception. Margaret's familiar face smiles up at me from the front desk, looking like she must be expecting me.

"Straight down to room twenty-two, Ben. They are waiting on you," she says as I put my cell phone in my pocket and try to ignore the constant ringing. Sasha *again*.

I strut down the hall to the sounds of kids yelling and laughing until I get to Emily's room and push open the door. The kids are dizzy with excitement, smiles lighting up their faces, as Emily runs around the room, getting paints and brushes and paper organized for them.

My cell phone vibrates against my leg again, and I am reminded that I need to be a million other places other than here.

"Miss Carr, I need the bathroom!"

"Miss Carr, is the paint ready?"

"Miss Carr, can I draw dinosaurs today?"

The kids all talk over each other, the hum of their chatter growing louder with their anticipation. Clearly, art class is the best one, but it is already giving me a migraine.

I take a few steps farther into the room, and Emily looks up at the movement. Her eyes soften and a small smile comes to her face that makes me feel glad that I came. My smile reflects hers automatically.

"Oh great, you're here!" she says, throwing me an apron that has old paint splotches on it from across the room. I look down at my new navy Prada suit. I came severely unprepared for this.

"Fuck," I murmur, looking down at the apron in my hand, and the whole class stops. You could hear a pin drop as I lift my head and see what has everyone's attention and realize they are all looking straight at me.

I gaze around the room, seeing that all ten pairs of eyes are on me, and they all have a look of shock on their faces.

"You said the bad word..." little Rosie whispers to me. Shit, they all heard me swear.

"Oh no, you are in trouble now," the older boy whispers as his eyes dart from me to Emily and back again.

"Mr. Langford!" Emily berates me in her school-teacher tone, and for some reason, my dick really likes it.

"We do not speak like that in this classroom!" she says, a small glint in her eye as all the kids look around at anything but me.

"I'm sorry, Miss Carr, it won't happen again," I grit out to her, equal parts annoyed and turned on as my cell phone continues to vibrate against my leg.

"Mr. Langford, can you put on your apron and assist me with the paint, please?" She can't be serious. This suit costs five thousand dollars. Even with the apron, that's not happening.

She stands there, watching me, her hands on her hips, waiting for my response. When she doesn't get one, she lifts her left hand and wiggles her ring finger, reminding me of our deal and also of the box I have in my other pocket.

I sigh, having no choice but to concede as I take off my jacket and lay it on her desk in the corner. Rolling up my sleeves, I then put the apron on and walk over to her to see nothing but delight in her eyes.

"You're enjoying this, aren't you?" I ask, unable to hide the amusement from my tone as I help her grab the large bottles of paint from the cupboard.

"Thoroughly," she says with a smile. With a grunt, I walk the bottles over to the center of the table, setting them down. I survey the table. Paints, brushes, water, and paper all adorn the space, while Emily gets everyone organized in their aprons.

"Mr. Langford, can you help me?" a small voice peeps out, and I turn to see Rosie leaning against her walking cane, not far away. I walk up to her and grab her hand.

"Sure, Rosie, what do you want to paint?" I ask as we make our way carefully to the table. When she reaches out, I help her place her small hand onto a chair for her to sit.

"I want to draw my family," she says with a big smile. I watch her for a beat, smiling myself. She is without sight, but one of the happiest people I have ever met.

"Okay," I say, not knowing the first thing about painting. Stick figures are as far as my creative flow extends.

"Can you get my special paper, please?" she asks, and I look around the table before I spot a small folder with paper inside. Rosie's name is written on the front.

"I've got it," I say, reaching over, grabbing the folder, and putting it near her. I open it and look at the paper. There are raised marks on every sheet. Each one with a small descriptor on the top. I've never seen anything like it, and I am quiet for a moment as I take it all in.

"So you have a few different pages here..." I offer,

feeling stupid that I had no idea blind people could paint and there was this type of thing on the market.

"If you put my brush in the paint, then onto the paper, I can do the rest," she says confidently, and I admire her tenacity.

"Sure, here." Placing her brush onto the plate of paint, I guide her to the paper with the invisible, raised lines. Her brush follows her fingers as they feel for the lines on the page, and I see a stick figure with long hair come to life.

The paint is a bit messy, but probably better than I could do. Her fingers are also coated, but I have noticed her sense of touch is really what is working here. She is feeling her way, feeling the paint, the paper, all of it.

"Who is that?" I ask, amazed at her ability.

"My mommy," she replies as she continues with a smaller version next to it.

"And who is that one?" I ask, but then my phone vibrates. Pulling out my cell and seeing it is Sasha again, I turn off my phone and shove it back in my pocket.

"That's me!" She giggles, and it is contagious so I laugh too.

She puts the brush down then, and I look at her. I can see more raised lines on the page for other people, but she isn't painting them.

"Do you need some more paint?" I ask, curious as to why she stopped.

"No. That's my family, me and Mommy. My daddy is a bad man. He hurts my mommy, so we don't see him anymore," she whispers to me, and I sit, stunned for a moment, that this little girl is telling me this.

It isn't totally surprising, as there are single parents everywhere, but it must be hard to be a single parent to a special needs child. And to also have a father who hurts her mother, that is something I have never had to navigate. My heart beats harder in my chest for a minute for this little girl, wishing I could take any of her worries away.

"Let me go and put this on the drying rack." I grab the wet painting, giving her a fresh page before I go, and I see her get busy starting her next masterpiece. I peg her painting onto the rack in the corner, and my eyes flick to the opposite side of the room to Emily.

She is helping the older boy again. Like last week, she is supporting his entire weight as he maneuvers across the room to what appears to be the bathroom.

"Ben," she says, her head turning back to me as she struggles to lift the boy and hold him up. He is tall and sturdy and leaning against her small frame. He almost towers over her. "Watch the class while I help Gavin to the bathroom," she says, and I am stunned that she needs to help the kids to the bathroom as well. Her role as a teacher extends well beyond what I thought.

When I head back to the table, one of the kids is very excited and lifts his brush into the air just as I am coming behind him. Bright-green paint licks up my pants and the side of my shirt with a splash.

"Shit!" escapes my lips before I can catch it.

Stalking over to the sink, I start the water and grab some paper towels. Wetting them, I try to remove the paint, but only succeed in spreading it around, making a bigger mess than what was there before.

"Dammit." I throw the paper towel into the bin and turn off the taps in a huff. Turning around, I stop short as I see every child in the room looking at me, still and quiet as mice. Again. They are scared stiff at my outburst, the fright in their eyes evident. I close my eyes and take a calming breath, trying to rein in my inner frustrations. It's just a suit. But really, did I have to wear the new one?

It is then that Emily and Gavin come out of the bathroom, and upon seeing the kids looking my way, her head turns to me too.

"What did you do?" she asks, putting the boy in his seat and walking over to me. The kids go back to quietly painting, and she looks down at my suit, noticing the green now covering my clothes.

She rolls her lip, trying unsuccessfully to hide her smile.

"Next time, wear old clothes to art class, Ben," she says, grimacing through a laugh.

"I have ruined a brand-new suit!" I hiss at her, and this causes her to laugh even harder. *Fuck, she is beautiful.*

"Go ahead, laugh. You are in my town soon. I'm taking you out to see how you like being somewhere you are not used to," I grit out, even though I'm quite enjoying seeing her smile. She looks up at me, her eyes sparkling. My anger subsiding, I pull out the box from my pocket.

"I got you this." I open the jewelry box and show her the engagement ring I purchased for her. A large solitaire diamond. It glistens in the overhead lights. Even though it is a fake arrangement, I tried to find something that I thought she would like. It is simple, but classic, large but proportional.

She gasps as her eyes take in the ring. "It's really beautiful, Ben..." she says in awe before looking back up at me.

"Are you sure you want the first engagement ring you buy for a woman to be for a fake engagement?" she asks me, and it is something that I hadn't thought of before.

"I am not sure I'm marriage material, Doubtfire, so I'm more than happy to put this on your finger." I grab her left hand and push it onto her delicate finger. Once it's in place, I find myself pressing a kiss to her hand. Not something I had planned, but it feels natural, and as my lips touch her skin, I feel a little remorseful that this is fake.

After the shitshow my father left behind when he died, I never thought I would get married. But there is something about Emily that has me faking proposals and ruining expensive suits that never would have happened a few weeks ago.

12

EMILY

I have no idea why I agreed to this, but had you asked me a month ago what I would be doing, a date with a billionaire from the city was not what I would have said. Sarah and Allie are both over to help me get ready and are going to stay here tonight to look after Rosie. She just finished reading *Cinderella* to Allie in bed while I ran around my small apartment, getting ready.

Opting for a little black dress, something I got on sale at the local thrift store, I don't scrub up too badly. I look at the wall clock nervously, seeing it is seven p.m., and he said he is sending a car to get me at seven p.m. sharp.

"So tell me, where are you going again?" Sarah asks as I check the contents of my handbag again for the fifteenth time.

"He didn't say. He just said dinner," I reply, not paying her a lot of attention as I double-check I have money for a cab to get home from the city, assuming that is where we are going.

"You can relax and enjoy this, you know," Sarah says,

coming up to me and putting her hand on top of mine. I take a big breath and sigh.

"It has been a long time since I've been on a date, and to be honest, I really never thought I would go on a date with a man from the city again." Even though it is purely a business arrangement, I am still unsure if I am doing the right thing.

"I know, and I also know that all men in suits are the devil in your eyes, but just go and enjoy yourself. Get to know each other and have a little fun." She slips two condoms into my bag, and I bark out a laugh.

"He is our enemy, Sarah. I am only doing this for the school. I'm sure I will be home by midnight, so don't worry about that," I say in reply, my cheeks heating at the suggestion.

"Well, you know Allie and I are staying here overnight so... you know... if you don't make it home until breakfast tomorrow, we don't mind," she adds with a wink, and although I have no intentions of anything other than dinner, I appreciate her advice.

Before I can say anything further, there is a knock at my door. "That must be the driver. I will see you guys later," I say to both Allie and Sarah, then tiptoe into the bedroom to place a kiss on Rosie's head as she sleeps, closing the door behind me. I walk to the front door and open it, only to be greeted by a large white-shirted chest that takes up the entire doorframe.

"Oh! Hi?" I say, stepping back, a little startled, not expecting Ben to be at my door.

"Expecting someone else?" he quizzes me, and I don't

miss the appreciative gaze as it sweeps over my body, heating me from the inside out.

"No, just your driver." Sounding unaffected around him is only becoming more difficult, I'm noticing.

"Here, these are for you," he says, thrusting a packet of Milk Duds at me.

"Ahh... thanks?" I say it as a question, my brow furrowed.

"I saw you eyeing them in my office the other day, and I thought you might like them." He shrugs like it is no big deal. But to me, it warms my chest that he noticed.

"Hi, I'm Sarah," Sarah says, coming up to introduce herself, and he shakes her hand.

"Hi, Benjamin Langford." Could he be any more formal?

"Hi, I'm Allie!" Allie yells from the kitchen, where she is not so subtly drooling over my date. Ben waves and gives her his trademark sexy smile. I think I see her physically swoon in response.

"Okay, well, now that we have all met, it's time for us to go." Putting the candy on my bench, I walk to the door, wanting to get this over with as I gesture for us to leave.

"Don't rush home. We have everything covered. Enjoy yourself!" Sarah makes sure to say as she pushes us out the door, encouraging us to leave.

"Thanks, girls, I owe you," I say, walking out and closing the door behind me.

"They seem like good friends. Your roommates?" Ben asks, taking my hand unexpectedly and walking me out to the car. It should feel odd, but it doesn't. My hand sinks into his like it is exactly where it is meant to be.

"Just friends. We are all teachers at the school," I offer as we walk down the stairs. I don't mention Rosie. He doesn't know she is my daughter, and he doesn't need to know. This is a business arrangement, no personal details required. And I plan on keeping it that way.

"You look nice—different from last time I saw you out of work hours." I think back to when we first met at the bar and cringe a little at the memory of my attire.

"Thank you... I think?" My eyes crease in mock confusion, and he gives me his grin. My heart makes a movement it hasn't in a long time when he looks at me like that.

"You look good in anything, Doubtfire," he says quietly as we reach the car, and he opens the back door of the black Bentley I notice he drives to the school. Sliding into the seat, his driver gives me a small smile, and I take a deep breath. This is already pushing me well outside my comfort zone. An expensive car and a driver do not belong in the life I live. I swallow quickly and take a few more deep breaths as Ben circles around the trunk and enters the other side.

"So, where are we off to?" I ask as he gets settled next to me, just as I feel my stomach rumble.

"To feed you, by the sounds of it," he says, laughing once again and grabbing my hand.

"I haven't eaten all day! The kids were crazy today," I say, my hand slipping into his all too easily.

"Crazier than usual?" he quips, raising an eyebrow.

"Every day I learn something new. Like today, Gavin, the oldest boy in my class, told me he wants to be a gamer. So we spent time looking online at the gaming industry. Did you know those professional gamers earn well over fifty thousand dollars a year!" I say, my eyes wide, still in shock that you can actually get paid for sitting around and playing video games.

"Some even more than that, I believe. How old is he?" Ben asks, seemingly genuinely interested in my day and my kids, so I prattle on about them for the entire car ride. I need him to see them as people, to understand each and every one of them.

"So Michael has no hearing; Rosie has no sight, and Gavin has lost some mobility of his leg?" Ben looks at me in disbelief as the car stops in the city.

"Yep, the rest of the class have varying learning difficulties or impairments, so it is super busy, but I am all they have." I shrug as he sits next to me, rubbing his chin, looking deep in thought.

"We are here, sir," the driver states as he gets out of the car, opening my door, and Ben runs around the back of the car again.

The first thing I notice is the noise. The car was super quiet, but now that we're in the city, the streets are busy, cars, taxis and buses all vying for a piece of the road. The second thing I notice is the smell. Rubbish, pollutants, varying foods now infiltrating my senses, the fresh air of the outskirts now a distant memory.

Ever the gentleman, Ben offers me his hand again, and I grip on to him, a little unsteady on my new stilettos. I am thankful that I don't fall on my face. We make our way quickly into the restaurant, and I look around tentatively as soon as we enter. It is beautiful. Exactly the kind of place a billionaire would take his date. White linens, candlelight, small tables, lounges, and shiny flooring.

The staff scurry around as soon as they see us, and we are promptly seated at a table to the side toward the back. We are within sight of most patrons, but a little secluded, which I appreciate.

My eyes are darting everywhere, and I can feel my shoulders tensing up near my ears.

"You okay?" Ben asks, and I whip my head back in his direction to be met with his deep eyes staring right at me.

"I am absolutely starving." The words rush out quickly as I smile. Fake it till you make it, isn't that what they say?

"The wine you ordered, sir?" A waiter comes promptly to the table, his uniform pristine and stature straight.

"Thank you," Ben says, nodding, his eyes not leaving me even for a beat.

"None for me, thank you." I put my hand over the top of my glass, preventing his pour.

"You don't drink?" Ben asks, sitting back a little.

"I do, just not much, and not on a school night ever," I say, grabbing my glass of water and taking a gulp, feeling extremely parched at the moment.

"So the champagne I saw you sipping at the bar?" he prods, leaning forward, his hand on the table, resting there for only a second before he grabs mine again.

My eyes flick to our connected hands for a beat before they trail back up to his face.

"Many people are watching us tonight, so we've got to put on a show," he says with a wink as he lifts my hand, the big diamond glistening, and kisses it softly, his eyes never wavering from mine.

"That night at the bar was my once per year trip into the city with my friends. I had exactly two glasses of champagne before I left for the night. My limit is two. Any more than that, and I cannot function the next day." I offer him a tidbit. Might as well get to know each other better while we are here.

"Okay, no alcohol. I got it," he says, placing my hand back on the table, but keeping it in his.

"So, have all your ex-girlfriends stalked you after you broke up, or just the beautiful supermodel-like ones?" I ask, knowing that a woman like me is so far removed from what a man like Ben would usually date, it is almost comical.

"This one in particular is hard to get away from. But now I have you. You're my secret weapon." Winking at me again, he raises his glass and takes a sip of wine.

"I will try my best to beat them all away from you. Wait until she hears how fantastic you are at swimming lessons. My ten kids are very excited to have the extra help in the overcrowded, unfunded, public swimming pool." I smile wide then, knowing that he is going to hate it.

"You underestimate me, Emily. You think I can't handle the heat you bring?" he teases, his thumb now rubbing over my hand.

"Oh, I know you can't." I laugh lightly, enjoying the way his eyes light up with our banter.

"Bring it on," he challenges with a wiggle of his eyebrows.

"You got it," I say with a wink of my own, just as he moves my hand in his, and our fingers intertwine, just like that of true lovers. Nothing has ever felt more right, and I need to repeat the words in my head to not get carried away with this. *It is fake. It is all fake.*

13

EMILY

Ben sits relaxed opposite me. His eyes have been glued to me all night, and I have caught him a few times checking me out. As our fake date goes on, he is smiling more, his handsome features keeping me on edge.

"You know, whenever I go out for dinner, I am usually rushed, talk about work, check my phone constantly. But tonight, I haven't looked at my phone once; our work talk has been minimal, and I could sit here with you for as long as you'd let me," he says, his honesty flowing out of him, making him even better-looking than he was before. And it's because I feel the same.

"Well, I can't say tonight was too painful for me either," I quip, our eyes now openly devouring each other.

"Were you expecting it to be?" he asks, sitting forward, keen for my answer.

"Honestly? Yes. But you have surprised me," I say with a grin. The feeling is odd, but this level of flirty happiness, borderline giddiness, is something I haven't felt for years.

"Some people think I am a lot to handle. I know I can be intense, especially with work. But I have a feeling that you could manage everything I bring." He is flirting and not even trying to be subtle anymore. This is a game we have been playing all night, and I am thoroughly enjoying myself.

"Hmmm, well, I am good at handling problems. I am an excellent multitasker, and I have fantastic negotiating skills..." I may not work in a fancy office, but those skills I need on a daily basis with my class. And I can guarantee he'd be a bigger pain than my job has ever been.

"Are you saying I am a problem, Miss Carr?" he teases, using his lawyer voice.

"You are a very big problem. The biggest!" I laugh then. It's amazing to me how any tension or nerves I had about tonight, or Ben, have all disappeared.

"I can assure you that I am big. But I don't see that as being a problem." The air catches in my chest, and I feel my cheeks heat as he quirks a brow. With his eyes on mine, his posture softens. When he smiles at me this time, it's genuine, almost as if he is laughing at himself for his flirty comments, before he clears his throat.

"Are you ready to go?" he asks with a sigh, like he actually doesn't want to leave at all. Although the restaurant is still busy, we have been here long enough. But if I didn't have to work in the morning, it'd be the perfect night to continue.

"Sure, let me just run to the restroom." I give him a

smile and walk through the restaurant to the back, feeling his eyes on me the entire way.

I do my business, check my lipstick, and take in a breath. I feel so good right now, and as I look at my reflection, I see a strong capable woman staring back at me. And real or fake, I have a handsome, eligible man waiting for me, who if he decides to kiss me good night, then I am going to let him. With a final tuck of my hair, I grab my bag and walk out, feeling on cloud nine.

I only make it three steps through the darkened hallway before I feel a rough hand grab my arm, twisting me around. I wince in pain at the grip and come face-to-face with a very angry Jeremy. My heart immediately starts pounding, nerves shaking my limbs, as my flight-or-fight kicks in. But I need to be strong. I am not the weak young woman I was when I first met him, and I am not bowing down to his commands anymore. So even though I am scared out of my mind, I pull on all the strength that George has instilled in me over the past few years and stand my ground.

"What the fuck are you doing here?" he spits out, not letting go of my arm.

"None of your business," I hiss back. There is no one around, but I am trying to be quiet and not cause a scene.

"*You* are my fucking business. What are you doing with him?" he grits out, and I look up at him, his face red and distorted, teeth grinding together. It makes me sick.

"I don't need to explain anything to you. Let go of me, Jeremy. You're hurting me." I try to pull myself out of his hold, but am unsuccessful as his hand only tightens. His stare is murderous, and I can smell the whiskey on his breath.

He has always wanted me, even after everything he's done to me. His stalker behavior has eased over the years, but never truly gone away. I left with Rosie years ago, and while he wants nothing to do with her, his own blood, he still wants me. I have no idea why, but perhaps because I am the only woman to have ever left him. It is like a game to him, something he has to win. It isn't because he loves me, because you don't treat someone you love the way he treats me.

At this point, I know I will have bruises from his grip. It has been a while. Months since the last ones left my body, so I knew it wouldn't be long until he turned up again. I guess seeing me here in the city, on a date with a Langford, no less, expedited the timeframe. At least Rosie doesn't have to be around to witness it this time.

"Let go of me," I say again, my voice pitching a little higher as I now start to panic, not sure what to expect from him next. This is the problem; he is just so volatile and unpredictable.

"Get your fucking hands off my fiancée before I break your fucking arm myself," Ben says in a growly tone I haven't heard from him, coming up behind me. Grabbing Jeremy's hand off me, I yelp in pain and hold my arm to my chest, rubbing it to try to ease the sting.

"Don't fucking touch me," Jeremy spits, flinging his arms away and stepping back from Ben, who looks murderous and like he is about to totally lose it. "You have no idea what you have gotten yourself into, Ben, no fucking idea," he adds before spinning on his heel and walking away.

I sigh and close my eyes, embarrassed, exposed, and frightened. He is such an asshole. I hate that this is a part of my life.

I feel Ben move in front of me, my eyes still shut. "Are you alright?" he asks, concerned, and I nod.

"I'm fine," I say with a small smile, finally looking up at him. As fake as this date is, I really didn't want Ben involved like this. I feel guilty. This is something I should have told him about before jumping into this agreement. But how do you explain to someone that being close to me could have serious consequences for your health, because my ex is a crazy abusive maniac.

"Come on, let's go," he says, wrapping his arm around my waist protectively, and I continue rubbing my arm until we step outside and get back into the car.

We settle into the back seat while Ralph drives me home to William Heights. Ben leans over and takes my arm in his gentle hold, looking it over.

"What do you need?" he asks me softly, and I almost choke on my unshed tears at the question. Those kinds of words from a man are entirely new for me, and I feel a flood of relief at hearing them. Knowing that it is possible for someone to care enough to ask.

"I'm fine." I keep my answers short, because I am fragile at the moment, and I don't want to break down in front of him. My poor friends will get that version of me as soon as I walk in the door at home.

"How do you know Jeremy Lucas?" he asks, looking

serious, and I sigh again, still not knowing what to tell him and what to keep to myself. I think for a beat.

"He is my Sasha," I say quietly and look into his eyes.

Ben doesn't need to know the full details. He doesn't need to know that the night I caught Jeremy cheating on me in his office, he pushed me down the stairs, which sent me into preterm labor. The fall and impact are what caused Rosie's vision impairment. He doesn't need to know that from that night onward, Jeremy's infatuation with me grew and his jealousy at having to share me with our new little girl overshadowed everything. In the end, after years of abuse, physically, mentally, and financially, I offered him a deal. I'd walk away with nothing but Rosie. I wanted nothing from him, not a home, not a car, not any money or child support. It was a deal he couldn't refuse, because I could have taken millions from him, and he is very motivated by money.

But he also doesn't like to lose in any capacity. So, he had me followed. He's watched me struggle over the years, and he shows up regularly, still verbally abusive and physically at times. He is not someone who plays by the rules at all. I left quietly without taking a cent, so therefore, he thinks he won. Got the best of both worlds —kept his money and kept me on a leash. But in reality, I know I won, because I got Rosie, my everything. I walked away with the clothes on my back and Rosie in my arms and that was like winning the lottery.

Ben runs his hand over my arm in a light caress, the sympathetic attention he's giving me in complete contrast to the man himself.

"He shouldn't be touching you like that," he states, his

jaw tight, and I nod quickly, scared to say anything. If I do, my eyes will overflow, and I don't want to cry. I have shed gallons of tears, and I promised myself no more.

He puts his arm around me then and pulls me across the leather seats to him. I sit in his embrace in the back seat of the car, feeling safe and protected. We drive through the streets, both of us lost in our own thoughts. Ben doesn't push me for any other information, and for that, I am grateful. But the calmness within me fades as my mind drifts back to Jeremy. Now that he knows that I am engaged, and to who, he won't stop until he's won.

And I refuse to be his prize.

14

BEN

She is right. I fucking hate this swimming pool. There is so much chlorine in this water, I think I have lost the first layer of skin from my body. My eyes are red and raw, and my fingers are all wrinkled— because I have been in this steam-infested pool with half the townspeople for the best part of an hour—and while Gavin, who I am trying to assist, is having a great time, I feel a migraine coming on from all the squeals that bounce around this poorly made structure.

Yet my eyes keep flicking to Emily. I haven't seen her since our date during the week, but I have thought of nothing else since. We had a great time, and I was really looking forward to extending the evening further, at my place, with her naked, but that thought soon got cut off when I caught Jeremy Lucas with his hands on her. Even now, my blood is boiling just thinking about it, and I have a million questions I want to ask her. But she is a private person and didn't seem to want to elaborate, so I let her be. She was shaking like a leaf, and I could see her trying to be strong, so it was all I could do to hold her all the way back to her place. Even then, I didn't want to let her go.

Today, I watch her in the pool next to me, smiling and playing with the kids without complaint. She is in a conservative black one-piece suit, not at all like the string bikinis every other woman I know owns. Yet she is sexier than all of them put together.

"Going okay?" Emily asks, catching my eyes and gliding up to me. Rosie is doing a great job of doggy-paddling to the side of the pool and back, lost vision not deterring her one bit.

"You do this every weekend?" I ask her in disbelief.

"Every Saturday," she confirms, standing next to me. The water where I stand covers me from my waist down, and as my eyes trail down, I get to see her fantastic breasts semi submerged, teasingly so.

"Why do you need to do it? Can't their parents?" I ask as I maneuver Gavin around again and watch him as he glides to the side to meet Rosie, the two of them swimming and playing together now.

"Their parents have to work. Many work seven days a week to support their families. The kids come with us every Saturday morning, learn a new life skill, and spend time with their friends outside of the classroom environment." I can hear the passion in her voice. She loves these kids.

"So you work six days a week with these kids?" I ask, admiring her commitment. Lots of people I know work long hours, as it is common in the city, but most of us work behind a desk, and weekends in the comfort of our own home, none of us combatting ten special needs kids in a warm, germ-infested swimming pool.

"It's not work if you love it, Ben. What about you? I am sure you work, what fifty-sixty hours a week?" she prods, her hands skimming across the top of the water, her head flicking back and forth between me and Rosie.

"Try seventy or eighty. I work pretty much all day and all night," I offer, never having really thought about my hours before, although my brothers and mother all tell me I work too much.

"That's a lot. What do you do for fun?" I watch as she dips her body into the water, pushing her head back so her hair falls out of her face, then stands back up, her hair now long, straight, and wet down her back. Her face is fresh, natural, and without a blemish, glowing from within. Fucking beautiful.

I clear my throat.

"Golf with my brothers," I offer, even though it takes me a moment to think of something. But I never miss a game with them.

"Wow, sounds enthralling," she says sarcastically.

"What? Golf is one of the best sports in the world!" I offer, feigning offense.

"Golf is boring, Ben. What else do you do?" she pushes with an expectant wave of her hand.

"I have no time for anything else. Work, golf, and then go out with my brothers every week for drinks," I murmur, noticing for the first time how boring that all sounds.

"Well, now you can add swimming to your weekly

activity list," she says with a playful smirk, tilting her head at me. "Want to race?"

"What?" I laugh, my smile stretching across my face on its own accord, mirroring her own.

"Last one to the far edge has to buy lunch?" I look to the far edge and back to her.

"Deal!" I say, but she is already off, her body gliding ahead of me before I bolt into action.

"Shit." I am so focused chasing her that when I touch the edge, there is no doubt in my mind I have won. Until I come up for air and see her already there. I pant, trying to catch my breath, and she looks at me and laughs.

"You beat me?" I ask, offended.

"It was easy. You're too slow." Her grin is a mile wide, and I love it.

"Too slow, huh?" I ask her as I glide closer, my hands wrapping around her waist before I hoist her up with ease and throw her three feet into the air back across the pool.

"Arghhhh, Ben!" she screams in laughter as her body floats through the air, crashing into the water with a splash. I wade toward her, watching her pop up, her wet hair spread all across her face.

"Bit wet there?" Grinning, I grab her waist again with one hand, pulling her up to me. We are on the deep side now, so her feet have no chance of touching the bottom.

"Oh my God, you are crazy," she splutters, laughing breathlessly, trying to brush her hair out of her face. I hold her to my body tighter and hear her intake of breath as our skin touches under the water.

"I've been called worse," I murmur as my other hand comes up, and I help her brush her hair out of her face. Her hand grabs on to my shoulder, wrapping around my neck, her other resting on my chest. I should move us to shallow water so she can stand, but I like having her in my arms and her hands on my body, so my feet remain rooted.

Her body relaxes into mine after a few beats, and I bring my hand down from her face, letting it wander down her back, to her waist. The two of us are silent as we come down from laughing, but my heart is thudding in my chest, my dick following suit.

"We don't have to put on a show here, Ben. No one really knows you here," she whispers, her eyes searching mine.

"I know." I smooth my hand up her body, skimming across her hips and bringing it higher, my thumb almost brushing against the side of her breast before I drag it back down again. I like feeling her, touching her soft, warm skin, and now that I have started, I am finding it difficult to stop. Our faces are so close, I can feel her breath on my lips... All it would take is for me to lean in slightly, and I could taste her.

"*Miss Carr!*" one of the kids yells out her name, and we both jolt and look over in time to see Gavin sitting on the edge of the pool deck.

"I need to go to the bathroom!" I huff a laugh, and Emily smiles.

"Back to work," she says, then goes to push off, but I grip her waist, her body easy for me to manhandle as I keep her in my hold and walk us to the shallow end toward Gavin together.

"You stay. I'll take him," I offer, getting us to the edge to meet Gavin, yet my hands on her body remain under the water, away from prying eyes.

"You sure?" she asks, now standing and watching me with uncertainty. Her hand trails down my arm, and I reluctantly remove my hands from her body. Rosie swims over to her then, Emily grabbing her up on her hip. I have noticed the two of them are close.

"Don't worry, Doubtfire. I've got it." I give her a wink before I lift myself out of the pool and lean over to help Gavin up. My eyes flick to Emily, and I don't miss as her gaze lands on my body without shame. I may not be the fastest, but I work out regularly. My body is taller and more solid than most. What I lack in speed, I make up for with strength, and now, standing half-naked in front of her, she sees it. Even though I hate this steamy swimming pool, I will come again just to see her, touch her, and be in her presence. Because this may be one of the best days I have had all year. It was the fun I've been missing.

15

BEN

"**F**ore!" I yell as my golf ball flies into the air and straight across the fairway onto the complete opposite hole.

"Shit. That is the worst hit I have ever seen in my entire fucking life," Tennyson remarks as I stand in shock, wondering how I shanked the ball so bad. We have nearly finished eighteen holes, and I have had a shit game.

I turn around, looking at my brothers. Eddie passes over a hundred dollars to Tennyson, and my eyes crinkle as he pockets it.

"Are you betting on me?" I snarl, just as Harrison looks up from his cell phone from where he is sitting in our golf cart.

"Easiest hundred dollars I have ever made," Tennyson quips, and I shoulder check him on my way past.

"You alright?" Harrison asks me as I slump in the cart next to him, our two younger brothers joking around at the tee bed before they take their shots.

"Fine." I rub my hand down my face.

"You don't look fine. What's going on?"

"I bought her a diamond," I say too quickly, not realizing how much I needed to get it off my chest since I slipped that ring on her finger. I underestimated the impact something like that would have on me. I never really thought too much about the act before, but as I slid it over her knuckle, the seriousness of the act hit me hard.

"Shit, a real one?" Harrison asks, his eyebrows lifting as he searches my face.

"A few hundred grand real," I murmur.

"A few hundred grand? Have you lost your damn mind?" Harrison rears back like he has been slapped.

"I want the best for her," I say with a shrug, not really thinking about the money.

"She is your *fake* fiancée! The ring could have been fake too! You will never see that ring again, you know that, right? She may have said she only wants you to spend time with the kids, but now she has a quarter of a million on her finger, so clearly, she is getting something very worthy out of this deal." Harrison groans before sitting back in his seat, a look of shock on his face.

I love my brother. He has always looked out for me, and I know this is just his protective instinct kicking in. She never asked for it, though. I didn't even talk to her about it before I bought it for her. It was my decision, and mine alone, and I wouldn't change it.

"It looks good on her." I shrug, almost laughing at the look Harrison shoots me.

"A quarter of a million looks good on anyone. Just look at our mother," he grits out, reminding me we have family dinner with her again this week. These monthly dinners creep up quicker and quicker every month.

"Are you coming to dinner this week?" I ask, wondering if the governor can grace us with his presence.

"Yes. Are you bringing your *fiancée*?" he questions teasingly, his tone lighthearted again.

"Fuck no, I will not subject her to our mother. I learned firsthand from you what a special kind of hell that will be." I grimace, thinking back on Harrison's own journey of bringing a woman into his life. Those wounds are still not fully healed. Not by a longshot.

"Well, just be ready for the onslaught. No doubt she will know all about her second-born son being engaged by then. It is already starting to come out. My media team told me they saw something in *Society News* this morning."

"I have a feeling that Sasha probably already told her. Mom has been blowing up my phone. I feel like a storm is brewing," I say, taking a deep breath. I don't care about the media. They write things about us boys all the time. But I feel bad for Emily. I know she wanted to keep this as private as possible, even though there is nothing private when you are with a Langford.

"I hope you know what you are doing, brother?" Harrison asks, raising his eyebrows at me.

"I've got no fucking idea," I quip, as Eddie and Tennyson finish taking their hits and the golf cart moves to find our balls.

"I'm taking her out for dinner again tonight." Harrison is quiet for a beat. After our last date, I wasn't sure dinner in the city again was a good idea, but Emily was happy to come, and this time, I am not letting her out of my sight.

"Where?" he asks.

"Mario's," I say, having booked the best table, one that is a little secluded, but also visible for those who really want to poke their noses into my business.

"That makes a statement," he says, side-eyeing me.

"I need people to see us, but she doesn't want media attention. Mario's is one of the only places in town where media can't access but where the who's who of society go."

"You do know Mom is not going to make this easy on you." Harrison's words bring me back to reality with a thud.

"I know. I hope she learned her lesson with Beth, though, and leaves Emily alone." I again rub my eyes, the stress of my situation burying in my shoulders. I have no idea what I am doing; I am just trying to make this work for both of us.

"And Beasley needs to buy that property," he pushes.

"Mm-hmm," is my only response.

"No. Ben. Beasley needs to buy that property. If not, you need to find him an alternative to focus on very quickly, because otherwise, we will lose him a client."

"You're the fucking governor. Don't you think we should be investing in schools instead of tearing them down?" The words are foreign to me as they leave my lips. Progress is progress, I have always believed. Progress makes our construction and real estate businesses a lot of money. But we are not total assholes. I don't particularly want to kick kids out of their school, but I have never given it as much thought before as I am now.

"Of course we should be investing in schools. Education is very important." Harrison nods in agreement.

"Well, do you think we should be turning this one into condos?" I continue, using him as my sounding board.

"I have no idea about this particular school, Ben. But progress happens. I am sure there are other schools nearby," Harrison says, and I don't understand how he can be so calm.

I say nothing. The memory of green paint on my Prada suit is distant, but the visions of Emily struggling to take a boy to the bathroom, of grabbing Rosie's hand to help her paint, and for slipping that ring on her finger like a promise, are very vivid.

Harrison sighs, seeing how much this is affecting me. "Send me the details. My team and I will look over it. See if there is anything that we can help with."

"Okay, thanks." I nod, grateful he might be able to help me with this situation.

"And Ben?"

"Yeah?"

"Be careful. This has potential to blow up in your face if you are not." Harrison's voice is stern as he gives me his warning.

"Don't worry, I will look after Beasley," I mutter, my thoughts swirling.

"I'm not worried about Beasley." I look at him, confused.

"I'm worried about you," he states seriously. He is visibly concerned, I'm just not sure why.

"I'm fine. It's business," I say with an unenthusiastic shrug as Harrison eyeballs me.

"You were a mess after Sasha, and I have a feeling that Emily is already more than just business." When I start to shake my head, he gives me a look that says I'm full of it.

"She is my fake fiancée. A few dates, a few weeks, then it will be nothing," I offer, trying to act like it is, in fact, nothing. Merely another business transaction. The whole thought of it curls my stomach.

"A diamond worth a few hundred thousand is not nothing. Just be careful," Harrison warns again.

"I'm always careful." With every business decision I make, I look at all angles. I assess things carefully; it is why I am such a good lawyer.

Except this one. This decision flew out of my mouth before I thought about it for even a second. My eyes flick to Harrison, who is looking at me like he knows exactly what I am thinking.

16

EMILY

Sitting on the soft leather seats of this pristine black Bentley, I look out the window, and not for the first time, I question my decision. I really wanted to immerse Ben into life at the school, to try to get him to see how wonderful it is and what we would be losing if his client bought it. The idea of being his fake fiancée, I gave little thought to at the time, and now as I drive into the city for our second official date as an engaged couple, I wonder what the hell I am doing.

He is Benjamin Langford. Literally from one of the wealthiest families in the country. His older brother is our governor. He could have hired a myriad of women to fill this role, yet here I sit. Like the schmuck, I am.

I am nervous, I won't lie. Our last date ended so badly that I almost didn't agree to tonight. But Jeremy knows now, so there is no more hiding it. I just need to deal with the consequences, whenever they come. Because they are coming, I can feel it.

The city lights fly past the car window as we drive

down the streets. I listen to the soft jazz music that Ben's driver Ralph has on while I twist the large diamond around and around on my finger. It is beautiful and bigger than anything I would have imagined for myself. And because of that, it is not practical, so I can't wear it to work. I live in constant fear of losing it, so I hope he has it insured. It feels heavy, matching the feeling I have in my stomach.

It has been a long time since I have come into the city regularly for pleasure. My pounding heart and sweaty palms are evidence of that. I take a few deep breaths, trying to find some inner calm, my stomach a whirl of knots. I hope I can eat my food tonight and try to find some enjoyment. Sitting across the table from Ben is something that many women would only dream about, I am sure. The whole situation leaves me with butterflies, proving that I am not immune to his good looks either, regardless if he is an arrogant jerk most of the time.

"We're here," Ralph says, interrupting my thoughts, and I look out the window as we pull up to a pristine city skyrise. I look down at myself, glad that I borrowed a nice dress from Sarah. I am relieved that I actually look like I belong, even though I know I don't. Not anymore.

Ben comes into view as he walks out of the building foyer. He is sure, steady, and wearing one of his many suits, looking so sexy that I almost melt into his leather seats. My eyes are glued as I watch him make his way to the car, open the door, and slide into the seat beside me. Taking another deep breath, I try to steady my nerves.

"Doubtfire," he says smoothly in greeting, a smirk lifting his lips as his eyes meet mine.

"Neanderthal," I reply, tempering the smile threatening to break through.

"You look stunning." His words leave me breathless for a moment, before I realize he is probably already in character, ready for the biggest act of our lives.

"This old thing?" We both know this is not my normal attire.

"Old or new, you still look beautiful," he murmurs, and my eyes flick to him. His compliment catches me off guard. Our banter is long gone, as is the air in the back seat of this car.

"I got you this," he says, handing me a card.

"Oh. What is it?" I ask, opening it up and pulling out some paperwork.

"A full golf membership at the club my brothers and I go to. You tease me about golf being boring, so perhaps we can play a game so I can prove you wrong." He raises his eyebrows with a smile growing on his face, and I can't help but laugh.

"Sounds like a challenge," I say, no chance of the smile being wiped from my face anytime soon.

"If you don't like it, you can drive the cart, but I have no doubt you will be a natural at that as well." I let his observation sweep over me. He can be sweet sometimes.

He grabs my hand, lifting it up close, and surveys the sparkling diamond that adorns it. Then he's threading his fingers with mine.

"Are you sure you are okay with this? There will be a lot of eyes looking at us tonight." I swallow the rising bile in my throat. This is a terrible idea, I know it. But I need to save the school, and aside from this agreement,

I haven't a clue how to do that. So I will take my chances.

"I am a woman of my word. You have stuck to the deal so far, and so will I," I say, squaring my shoulders, determined. When you have nothing, the only thing you can rely on is your word. And I take mine very seriously.

"At least my suit will stay one color tonight," he quips, his lips quirking up a little, and I smile. *The kids.* Just the thought of them brings a smile to my face and any remaining tension is broken again. I'm doing it all for the kids.

"Just don't wear Prada next time." Why he would ever wear a designer suit to art is beyond me.

"Why the hell do you have lime green paint in art class, anyway? What happened to primary colors?"

"The lime green glows in the dark. It is awesome, and the kids love it. Why stick to primary when you can have a rainbow, Ben?" I ask, almost in challenge, to try to get him to see that things are not always as simple as he thinks they are. His jaw clenches, but he remains silent.

"So, my darling, did you have a good day today?" I ask, pouring on the act, trying to let it sink into me. Reaffirming this is just pretend and not actually a real date. Aside from our date last week, it has been years since I went on a real date, and I can't let myself get confused. I need to remain focused. Laser-like vision on the end goal. He looks at me, smiling at my change in subject. Our hands remain intertwined, him holding them on his lap.

"Work, work, and more work. You? How are the kids?" he asks, pushing the questions back to me like the talented lawyer he is, and whether he realizes it or not, his thumb is strumming across my hand, caressing my skin lightly, giving me goosebumps up my arm. I force myself to not think about it. He is obviously getting into the act, making it feel more natural, so I try to ignore all about the warmth spreading across my chest, and make small talk.

"Well. We had music today, along with story time at the library, so it was busy."

"Music?" he says, cringing. "How does that not give you a headache?" His shoulders lower, his body relaxing. *I like that talking to me relaxes him.*

"It does. But it's worth it. You should hear it when we do choir!" He squeezes my hand as he chuckles, making me smile. Then he's bringing it to his mouth and kissing my fingers. The move startles us both as we lock eyes, and he freezes, my hand midair near his lips. *What is going on?* My heart thuds out of my chest. *This all feels too real. Too good.*

The car stops after traveling the short distance to the most expensive restaurant in the city, and Ralph jumps out to open the door. I watch Ben swallow, his grip on my hand still firm as he lowers it slowly.

"You ready?" he asks, breaking our stunned silence. He looks at me questioningly. This is the moment. This is the moment I should say no and get back to my suburban apartment, lock the doors, and pray this whole nightmare will go away. But as I take another deep breath, I catch his woodsy cologne, and as his eyes pierce mine, I put on my mental armor.

"Ready," I reply, pushing my shoulders back and getting my bearings.

Ralph opens the door, and Ben steps out, waiting outside the car for me, then he grabs my hand again. I haven't been to this restaurant before, but they are all the same. The last time I was at a place like this was with Jeremy. The memory sends a shiver down my spine.

"Cold?" Ben asks as we walk into the restaurant, and he drops my hand, placing his around my lower back and tucking me into his side as we start this game of being life partners.

"I'm fine," I say as I lift my head high, ready for the parade through the restaurant.

Ben speaks to the maître d', and we walk through the bustling room, weaving between tables and waiters. I don't miss the stares we get and the quiet murmurs that now fill the air. Ben must feel me stiffen because he squeezes my waist. I feel his thumb again, rubbing so slightly against it, caressing my skin, which puts me at ease. Even though it should have the opposite effect.

When we reach our table, Ben pulls out my chair, and I sit, remaining elegant, pulling from all my history as I feel every pair of eyes in this restaurant on me. I take a sip of the water on the table, looking at Ben, who is far too calm and charismatic, sitting opposite me, as he pays no attention to the looks we are getting and instead orders us a bottle of mineral water. I realize he's not choosing the wine tonight, knowing it isn't my drink of choice.

"I have been meaning to ask you..." he begins, leaning back in his chair, looking into my eyes.

I raise my eyebrow, waiting for the question he is pondering. He opens his mouth to speak, but before he can, a woman comes up to our table. Looking up at her, I see that it is Sasha, and even though I have only seen her twice, she is becoming an extremely annoying thorn in my fake relationship. I watch with interest as she completely ignores me.

"Ben, how great to see you!" she gushes, and Ben sits forward, grabbing my hand on the table, his thumb again moving across my skin almost absentmindedly.

"Sasha. How can I help you?" he asks in a cold and somewhat distant voice.

"Oh, I just wanted to say hi," she says sweetly, her lame excuse falling from her lips. She still hasn't acknowledged me, acting as though I am not here at all.

"I was speaking to your mother the other day..." she continues, and I get the feeling that these two must have dated for a while if she knows his mother. Ben sighs like the whole conversation pains him.

"I thought as much," he murmurs, the smile that was on his face moments ago falling away.

"She was very surprised to hear that you were engaged!" Her eyes finally flick to me, a small smirk pulling at her glossy lips.

"Yes, I guessed she would be," Ben grits out, not adding to the conversation with unnecessary information.

"She seemed to think I was incorrect about that fact." I can't believe the audacity of this woman.

"Well, this diamond on Emily's hand would prove otherwise," he says, lifting my hand and kissing my finger. I give him a small reassuring smile, deciding to help end Ben's misery.

"Sasha," I say to get her attention, and she looks at me

as though I am a piece of dirt on her shoe. "It's so great to see you again. But if you don't mind, my fiancé and I are having a romantic dinner for two. If you can leave us to it, that would be great." My tone holds a little more venom than I was expecting. But seriously, he is my fiancé, as far as she's concerned. Take the hint!

I see Ben bring his other hand to his mouth and stifle a grin, clearly pleased that I stepped up to the job of possessive fiancée. Sasha looks like I have slapped her.

"Ben, save a drink for me at the end of the night. We both know I am the kind of woman you need to be with, not..." She doesn't finish the sentence as she looks at me, her silence speaking volumes about what she really thinks. She looks back at Ben, flashing him her pearly whites and giving him a shimmy of her big breasts that are barely contained in her skimpy top. Turning, she gives me a brisk nod with fire in her eyes before she retreats. I have a feeling that won't be the last I see of her.

Ben lifts my hand to his mouth again. This time, he kisses me on the inside of my wrist, and my heart skips a beat as tremors run down the inside of my arm. His smile is cheeky and causes me to laugh at myself.

"Seriously, where is the girl code in this town?" I mutter, wishing he was kissing my wrist because he wants to, but knowing it is all just for show. Sasha's no doubt hiding somewhere in the restaurant, still watching. So I grin and gaze lovingly at him, playing the part.

"So what were you going to ask me?" I tilt my head, ready for his question.

"Rosie and George. You seem pretty close to both of

them?" he asks, and I remain still. That is not the question I was expecting.

"Yes, we are close. George is wonderful. He's a fantastic boss and an even better friend," I say, smiling, thinking of him and wondering what he and Rosie are doing at the moment.

"And Rosie?" This is where I should tell him that she is my daughter. It is on the tip of my tongue, but I can't get it out.

The waiter comes to my rescue with our food, and I steer the conversation to safer territory.

"So your mother knows we are engaged, then? I bet that will be an interesting conversation for you?" I ask, before stuffing my mouth with the softest gnocchi I have ever eaten.

"Everything to do with my mother is interesting, and not in a good way," he says, clear resentment in his tone.

"She can't be that bad. She raised four boys; that is a hard life for anyone!" I only have Rosie, and she leaves me exhausted most nights. I can't imagine raising four children.

"She didn't really raise us. I mean, she was around, and when I was younger, she was great. But we each had a nanny, and private boarding school as we got older, then we were off to college. None of us were around her much, to be honest," he says, cutting into his steak, and I have food envy for a moment.

"What about your parents? Do you see them much?" he asks, and I feel my heart grow heavy.

"No. They passed when I was younger. I bounced around relatives throughout my teens before hitting college." Thinking back, I am not sure how I would have survived if I hadn't met Jeremy. I met him fresh out of college at a city bar. He is a decade older and was having drinks with colleagues. At the time, I was living with friends, starting my career journey with various internships and trying to see what fit. He flew in, treated me like a princess, and swept me up so fast I didn't know what hit me.

Until he did.

"I'm sorry to hear that, Emily." The look in his eyes isn't one of pity; it's of comfort. If only I could experience this from a man I was going to be with for real. Feeling tears burning the backs of my eyes, I decide to move on to safer topics than my past.

We are able to chat effortlessly for the entire rest of the night, both of us forgetting that this is a business arrangement as we find some common ground. The date passes too quickly, and I am surprised to have actually enjoyed myself once again. My cheeks hurt from smiling and laughing so much. Now as I take my full belly to freshen up in the ladies' room, I smile at my reflection, wondering if I should have stayed away from the city as long as I have. I am sure both Sarah and Allie would love to come here, and I imagine a lovely girls' lunch at this restaurant one day. That gnocchi was seriously the best.

I wash my hands in the sink, already excited to get back to the man who waits for me at the table. A few women walk in, each of them running their eyes over me, probably assessing if I am worthy of such a man's attention. I can feel my tough exterior starting to crack and my heart defrosting, and I know I can't let it. But it's seeming impossible to avoid.

Pressing my dress down, I pull my shoulders back. He is my fake fiancé; he is using me to keep his former girlfriend away, and I am trying to embed him into the school culture to try to save it.

That is it.

I am firm and confident as I stare at my reflection before walking out of the bathroom. I hold my breath and look around anxiously before making it exactly two steps until I see him and feel off-kilter again. He stands off to the side, waiting for me. His hands are in his pockets, his legs crossed at the ankle, leaning against the wall. I come to a sharp stop as our eyes openly devour each other.

"Ready to go?" he murmurs as he pushes off the wall and walks to my side, looking like every woman's dream man. His hand automatically slides around my middle, like it was always meant to be there, fingers gentle but firm as he pulls me close. It feels so good. Like he is keeping me with him. Safe, tucked into him, like he never wants to let me go.

"I'm ready." The words leave my mouth breathier than I was planning, and I watch his eyes as they move from mine, down to my lips, and back again. The bathroom door opens behind me then, and I see Ben's eyes flick up to whom I assume are the two women who followed me in earlier, before looking back at me.

"Let's give them something to talk about," he whispers, his face lowering to mere inches from mine.

"This wasn't in our agreement," I whisper back, my heart pounding harder in my chest.

"I'm a lawyer. I am making an adjustment to our original agreement," he taunts, his face edging even closer.

"Well then, I want something in return too," I say quietly, my hands already running up his chest of their own accord. The need I have to be close to him is almost suffocating.

"What do you want?" he murmurs, his nose skimming my jawline, my nipples peaking against my dress at the sensation. My legs weaken a little as his grip around my waist tightens.

"We have a school excursion in a few weeks, and we need volunteers." We're sharing breath at this point, our lips hovering over each other's.

"Done," he growls without hesitation before officially closing the distance. In this darkened corner of the restaurant, Ben kisses me like he means it.

His soft lips massage lightly against mine, but with purpose. I swallow a moan at the feel of him, my grip on his lapels white-knuckled as our bodies press together, not an inch left between us. His hands spread over my back, keeping me close, before one lowers a little, skimming over the curve of my ass. This is the first kiss I have had in years, and it ignites a deep feeling of longing within me. It should feel weird, like it isn't meant to work, but it does. Oh, it does.

When Ben pulls away slightly, we're both breathless, and I can feel his warmth breath on my cheek as his lips move to my ear.

"They're gone. Let's go. I want to take you somewhere," he says, his voice low and deep, rumbling through my body. My skin prickles with an undercurrent of arousal. He stands tall, fixing his suit, and as I look behind me, the women who I guessed were there moments ago are gone, and I wonder when they left. Together, we walk out of the restaurant before finding Ralph standing by the car outside, waiting for us. We are halfway across the sidewalk before I turn my head and look down the street and stop short.

"Wait," I say, both Ben and Ralph looking at me before turning to see what I am staring at.

"What the hell is he doing out here so late?" Ben mutters, and we both walk down the sidewalk to meet the homeless man who is curled up, sitting out in front of a nearby bank. It isn't freezing, but it isn't entirely warm either, and it will get cooler as the night progresses.

"Dale? What are you still doing out here?" Ben asks, the two of us dressed in our finery as Dale sits in torn jeans and a mismatched sweater.

"Ben! Good to see you," he says, smiling up at us.

"Dale. Is there somewhere you can go tonight?" I ask, concerned about his well-being.

"Not tonight. The shelters are full," he mutters with a shake of his head.

"What do you mean, full? How can they be full?" Ben asks, astonished, and understanding washes over me that Ben really has no idea how other people live.

"What about the one off Louis Drive?" I ask, trying to work through my mental file cabinet and think of all the shelters I know. Ones I have used.

"Full," he says with a sigh.

"What about the one down on Silver Street?" I ask again.

"Full," he states, his mood now getting lower.

"What about on Commander Drive?" I ask about the small one I know. It is not as well-known and it's a little farther out of the way so it is less busy. Ben is looking between the two of us, concern etched into his brow at our conversation.

Dale's eyes light up. "I didn't try that one," he says.

"Let me call them." I don't wait for an answer before I fish out my phone and hit the number that is stored in my cell. I turn my back to talk, leaving Ben and Dale to chat and am relieved when I hear they have a spot.

"I got you in tonight," I tell him, my smile wide, and see Ben watching me as I deliver the news.

"Really?" Dale says, his eyes lighting up at the news.

"Yes, all free for you tonight. It is a small shelter, so everyone forgets about it," I say, giving him a look to tell him that he may be able to spend more than one night there.

Ben's eyes remain on me, curiosity burning in his stare.

"Thank you, Emily. Thank you," Dale says as he stands and collects his plastic bag of belongings.

"See you around," he says, as Ben and I stand there looking at his retreating frame.

17

BEN

"**L**et's go," I say, grabbing her hand and leading her back to the car, where Ralph remained waiting for us. I have been on edge since following her to the restrooms, not wanting her away from me for one moment. I haven't seen Jeremy Lucas since our last trip out for dinner, but I sure as shit am not giving him any leeway when it comes to Emily. I have no idea of their history, but I know he is exactly that. History, and he needs to stay there.

My steps are swift, and I can hear her heels on the pavement as she almost runs to keep up. I feel tense, like something is crawling up my back. How the hell does she know all these shelters in the city? How am I oblivious to the fact that they are all full? The energy humming through my body from the kiss earlier has set me on fire, and that mixed with the conversation just now has me taking it out on the pavement under my feet.

"Slow down," she says just as we get to the car, and I hold the door open for her and watch her slip into the back seat as I chat with Ralph, telling him the new destination. I don't miss his surprise as I slide in next to her.

As I sit in the back seat, I am immediately greeted by her soft lavender scent as it wraps around my chest. I was astonished seeing her with Dale just now. I see Dale all the time. He permanently sits outside our offices; that is his spot. My brothers and I always offer him money, and at times we have ensured he has somewhere to go, especially during the winter. Every other woman I have been with looks at him like he is disgusting. Including my mother.

But not Emily.

As Ralph starts to drive, I stretch my arm up and over the back of the seat, trying to get my jumbled feelings under control. The flame that simmered under my skin before kissing her has now turned into a raging inferno, and I want to strip her naked and see the ecstasy I know I will find buried deep inside of her. I try to push the thoughts aside. Harrison's voice strums in my head to *be careful.*

I shouldn't be touching her at all and that is what pisses me off the most. I need her school to keep my client happy, so getting caught up with her is the last thing I need to entertain. But as I sit here in the back seat, I watch her looking out the window at the passing lights, and I feel at peace. There is no one around to see us. No spying eyes, no Sasha to flaunt Emily in front of, yet I want to touch her. This fake engagement we have entered into was one of the stupidest things I have ever thought up. But I would do it all again in a heartbeat to have my lips on her again.

"Where are we going?" Emily asks, turning to look at me in question, obviously confused that we are not heading to the highway to take her home.

"I want to show you something before I take you home," I say, giving her a small smile, which she returns.

"Okay. As long as it isn't another fancy restaurant. I have never eaten so much in my entire life," she jokes, as her other hand rests on her tummy, and her head falls back against the seat. She is so beautiful. I chuckle then, her eyes sparkling in delight.

"Tonight was the first date I have been on where the woman has eaten pasta. You continue to surprise me, Doubtfire," I say as I look across at her. It is true; most women I date push a salad around on their plate, have their face buried in their phone, and drink too much champagne. Tonight was a refreshing change, just like our first date.

"Carbs are an essential dietary requirement; I have no idea why anyone would purposefully not eat bread or pasta. They are my life blood," she mocks with a smile, one I want to swallow with a kiss.

The car makes a right turn and her body slides across the seat, coming right up against me. My arm is still lying across the back seat, so she fits perfectly into my side. Our eyes remain on each other, and she goes to move, but my other hand moves on its own accord as it rests on her bare knee, keeping her close.

"Ben?" She whispers my name, her breathy tone shooting through my veins and straight to my cock. I like having her close to me. Just like at the swimming pool, I am feeling greedy, my hands not only wanting to touch her, but almost needing to.

"We're nearly there," I respond, wanting her to stay cupped into my side. Squeezing my fingers on her knee, I lift my hand to her face and grab her jaw, strumming my fingers up and down her jawline, my internal battle to pull her lips to mine on repeat in my mind.

"Where are you taking me?" her voice purrs out, our faces so close I can nearly feel her breath on my skin.

"Somewhere I have never taken anyone before." Her eyes crinkle in question. I move my hand back to her knee, and then I feel her. With her hand resting on top of mine, I bite on my back molars, waiting for her to push my hand away. Instead, her fingers curl around mine, and I turn my hand, cupping hers and holding it tight on her knee.

We are so focused on each other that neither of us realizes the car has stopped until Ralph opens his door and steps out. The slam of the door shutting is the only thing pulling us apart.

My grip on her hand remains because I don't want to let her go. Our eyes remain locked, unspoken words sitting in my chest, as the two of us look over each other, searching for answers that I don't think either of us have yet.

I swallow, trying to collect myself before I pull away, her hand falling to her side as I open my door and step out, the cool night air slapping my face. Standing outside, I straighten my jacket. *What the hell am I thinking?* I crack my neck before reaching in and offering her my hand, trying to be the gentleman, when I really want to be anything but.

She grabs it without hesitation and steps out to join me, and I watch her expression as she looks around. Ralph is nowhere to be seen, and I smile when I see her eyes widen when she takes in the view.

"Wow…" she says, her feet moving slowly toward the millions of lights off in the distance, her heels crunching on the gravel underneath her feet.

"Where are we?" she asks in wonder. The city lights twinkle and shimmer like stars, the whole scene mesmerizing.

"My estate," I offer, almost cringing when I say it, because it is all a little obscene, even if it is my sanctuary.

"What?" she asks, turning to me in shock. I watch her eyes darting around, trying to see anything. But there is darkness all around us, the sparkling city lights all framed by tall trees on either side.

"I have an estate just out of town. Here on the hill is the best view of the entire city. My house is just over there." I point, and she turns to look.

"The view is amazing." She forgets all about my home and looks at the lights again. The city is so small up here. It looks almost tranquil, like we are sitting in the stars.

"Let's go up to the pavilion."

I just sent Dale off to a fucking shelter while I take Emily to my fucking pavilion. I never thought too much about the financial divide before, but tonight it is sinking in deep. Grabbing her hand again, because I just can't stop fucking touching her, the stress leaves me for a beat when I feel her warm hand in mine.

She follows my lead as we walk the small gravel walkway that is now lit up that leads to my outdoor room, where I have brought no date ever before. She is the first woman to ever set foot inside the gates of my estate. Aside from my brothers and a few friends, I keep this place just for me. I spend the majority of my time in my city penthouse, as it is much easier for work that way. But I need the space, and the fresh air, and this estate gives me that and more.

"This is beautiful. Really, I can't stop staring at it all." She smiles up at me, her face illuminated as we head up a few steps to where I have a large lounge with big fluffy pillows to relax on. The small kitchen is tucked away at the back, along with a fire pit that remains unlit because I wasn't planning on bringing her here.

It is cool, because there are no walls, only four large columns at each corner. But through the darkness, we can see the shadows of my entire estate. Still, the city lights are the main attraction.

"I come out here to think. When I need space." I find myself opening up to her a little more as we take a seat, fully facing the lights. She kicks off her heels and tucks her legs up on the sofa, sinking into the soft, luxurious fabric. The move would ordinarily annoy me, but tonight it feels oddly comforting and extremely domesticated, and I am glad she feels at ease in my space. I am glad she feels at ease with me.

"Well, thank you for sharing this with me. It's truly breathtaking, Ben."

I relax next to her, my hand automatically resting across the back of the sofa behind her. My fingers dangle down, caressing her bare shoulder, running patterns across her skin. She looks up at me and the back of her head settles against my arm. The position is not dissimilar to what we were in moments ago in the car.

"It's beautiful, Ben. Really, really beautiful. I can't stop saying it. I could stay right here and look at this every night and never get bored," she says, tilting her head to look up at me before she looks back out at the view.

"It really is," I say, but as she gazes out at the lights, my eyes remain on her.

18

EMILY

L ike the gentleman he is, Ben dropped me off at my apartment after our date, the memory of our searing kiss scorched into my brain. We sat for nearly an hour in his pavilion, staring at the city lights, his hand rubbing my bare shoulders. It was both the most relaxing and most romantic date I have ever had. Now, days later, the diamond on my finger is not feeling as heavy, and I find myself wearing it more and more. I slip it from my finger and place it in my jewelry box before walking back to the kitchen. The dirty breakfast dishes do not need the extra sparkle this morning.

After our date, pictures started appearing online. I am not identifiable in any of them, luckily, due to the soft restaurant lighting and the semi-private table we had. Even if I was, here in the suburbs, no one expects a schoolteacher to be engaged to one of the city's most eligible bachelors. While my life hasn't really changed, I know Ben is getting hounded.

"Mom! Have you got my goggles?" Rosie yells from the bedroom as I am cleaning our breakfast dishes in the kitchen. It is our usual Saturday morning ritual, which consists of a lazy breakfast of chocolate chip pancakes before I take Rosie to the public pool for a swimming lesson.

"Yes, Rosie, I have them in the bag already," I reply as I hear her getting her swimsuit on. I wipe my hands on the towel as my cell phone pings with an incoming message. I am surprised to see it is from Ben, and I swipe to view.

> Neanderthal: How do you take your coffee?

> Doubtfire: Good morning to you too, Neanderthal.

> Neanderthal: I'm at Starbucks around the corner. I'm bringing you coffee.

My body stills. Ben is supposed to meet us at the pool, not come here to pick me up.

> Neanderthal: ??? Coffee order please, Doubtfire. I'm holding up the line here.

> Doubtfire: Caffè Misto

I type back quickly before throwing my phone onto the dining table and rushing to my bathroom to ensure I don't look like the exhausted mother I am.

"Rosie, we are expecting a visitor," I yell to her so she isn't startled when the doorbell rings.

"Who, Mommy?" she asks, and I look around the door to her, my sweet, sweet girl. I step into her room and take her hand, walking her to the bed, and we sit on the edge next to each other. She looks just like me when I was young, and I am so glad she got none of her father's traits. I pray it stays that way.

"Mr. Langford is coming here so we can all go to swimming together today, rather than meeting us there," I say, holding my breath, wondering what she will say. We don't have visitors. Aside from George and the girls, no one comes here.

"Oh goodie! I can read him the rest of *Cinderella*!" she exclaims happily as she starts patting the bed, searching for the book in question. I leave her to it and quickly pick up a few items from the floor, brushing my fingers through my hair as the doorbell rings.

"He's here!" Rosie practically yells, grabbing her small walking cane and following me to the door. Apparently, Ben has a way with all females, not just me.

I open the door, and he is standing tall in the doorway, holding two coffees. Looking freshly showered, he's wearing a navy Henley top that shows all his defining muscles and blue jeans. He looks even better in casual clothes, and my hand grips on to the door so my knees don't give way and I don't fall into a heap on the floor. My eyes travel up and down his well-defined chest, then his strong shoulders, before resting on his Cheshire cat grin.

"Good morning, Doubtfire," he says as he passes me a coffee.

"Doubtfire? Who is Doubtfire, Mommy?" Rosie pipes

up from behind my legs, and I see Ben's eyes widen slightly, shock evident on his face.

"Rosie, come and say good morning to Mr. Langford." I take her hand and lead her next to me and in front of him. This should be interesting. His surprise visit unearthed my secret, So I'm not sure what to expect. I stand rigid in the doorway, waiting for him to make an excuse and leave.

"Hi, Mr. Langford!" Rosie says merrily, looking as cute as pie in two ponytails, standing next to me.

"Ahhh..." Ben starts, and I see his eyes flick back to me and then take in my apartment behind us. His face has paled slightly, and his eyes look panicked.

"Hi, Rosie," he says, looking at me, his eyes questioning. "You live here?" Ben asks my daughter but looks right at me.

"Sure, I do. Just me and Mommy," she says innocently, and I'm feeling sick that I didn't tell him earlier.

"Just you and Mommy?" he asks, his gaze flicking to mine again.

"Sorry, I should have told you," I say quietly as I watch him taking in the information before Rosie cuts me off.

"You smell nice, Mr. Langford!" Rosie says, and I agree with her as I breathe him in.

"Call me Ben, Rosie. Mr. Langford is an old man's name," Ben says, smiling at my daughter, his shock disappearing from his face.

"But aren't you old, Ben?" she says without missing a beat, and I giggle.

"Some days I feel very old, Rosie," Ben replies, his grin now matching hers.

"Okay. Mommy, I am going to finish getting ready for swimming." With her cane in hand, she walks back into the apartment. We have lived here for long enough now that Rosie knows the floor plan front to back. I haven't moved any furniture, decorations, or changed a thing since we moved in, wanting to keep it consistent for her to remain as independent as possible.

"Come in," I say as I sweep my arm into the apartment and step back from the door. "Thank you for the coffee delivery." I take a small sip as I walk into the kitchen and lean against my kitchen counter. As Ben enters into my space, he seems to take up all the room. I have never had a man in my apartment, if you don't count George, anyway. My apartment is small, and for us two girls it is just fine, but here now with Ben, as tall as he is, it looks almost comical.

Ben pierces me with his eyes. "So you're Rosie's mom?"

"I didn't want to say anything, not at first. I wasn't sure about you, me, or this agreement, or..." I say, starting to talk too fast, waiting for him to run. To make any excuse to get the hell away from me and my daughter. I am still surprised he turned up here at all. Given it is only nine in the morning and he traveled from the city, he must have been up early to get here.

"Stop. It's fine, and I understand. I'm a little shocked, but it kind of explains why you two are so close. I just thought she was the teacher's pet. She looks like you," he says, taking a sip of his coffee and coming closer. He stops right in front of me, looking down, his eyes asking all the questions his mouth has yet to say.

"Her father is not in the picture. Hasn't been for a very long time." I offer the only information he is going to get.

"Good to know," he says, leaning in closer. Every inch he moves, my heart beats a little faster.

"I am still trying to find my footing with this whole fake fiancée thing," I say on a breath, visuals of Ben with Sasha in the elevator coming to my mind. My thoughts must be clearly displayed on my face because he looks serious for a moment.

"Me too," he admits as he grabs my hand, noticing the ring is gone. He looks at me with a scowl.

"I am not wearing it swimming! What if I lost it?"

"Good point." Lifting my finger to his lips, he kisses it softly. Confusion swirls around my body, as does the warm feeling in my chest. We haven't spoken since our city date. The incredible kiss we shared has played on repeat in my mind for the last few days, wondering what the hell I was thinking. But with him now standing right in front of me, here in my kitchen, I don't feel remorse, but rather the desire to do it all over again.

He watches me intently, and I feel heat in our exchange as his fingers brush back the wisps of hair that have fallen around my face. He drags his fingers along my jaw and down my neck, and a trickle of goosebumps follow his touch as the fire within me grows stronger.

"There is no one here, Ben... we don't need to pretend," I whisper, reminding him that we are not on show. Even though the last thing I want is for him to stop.

What is it about this man that makes me equal parts giddy and equal parts want to rip his clothes off. I felt it the moment we first met at the bar and the feeling has only intensified with every interaction we have had since. He looks at me like I am the most important person in the world; it's almost domineering, but in a positive way. His fingers scorch my skin and heat pools in places it hasn't for a very long time.

I watch as his Adam's apple bobs, the spark between us now near electric. This is not what I thought my Saturday morning would consist of.

"I know, and I don't care," he murmurs as he leans in, and like my body is disconnected from my brain, I lean toward him too. I'm lost in his eyes as he looks down at me, his lips coming closer to mine with every breath.

"I'm ready! Are you ready, Ben?" Rosie appears again, excitement evident in her tone, and we jump apart like two teenagers caught by their parents.

He looks at me, and I smile. "Sure thing, Rosie, but I am not swimming today." I narrow my eyes in confusion.

"That pool took the top layer off my skin last week. I can't do it two times in a row," he murmurs to me, and I roll my lips.

"Next time, can you bring your swim trunks? I want to pair up with you instead of Mommy for a change." Rosie is beyond excited now at us having a house guest and has clearly pushed me out of the way now that Ben is her new favorite friend.

"I think I would like that, Rosie. Next Saturday, I will bring my swimming trunks so I can join you."

Rosie giggles, and I raise my eyebrows at Ben, but he simply shrugs and smirks back at me.

"Okay then, let's go!" Grabbing our large swimming bag that is overflowing with towels and clothes in one hand, I take Rosie's hand in the other. I don't know why, but I just can't master packing. Bags, suitcases, anything. I always shove things in and hope for the best; my swimming bag is clearly evidence of this.

Ben holds the door open and takes the bag from me as we walk out, the whole thing feeling oddly domestic.

We hit the sidewalk and I feel Ben's hand on my back, the warmth and protection instant. Rosie and I start walking toward the bus station. The swimming pool is not far away, but too far for us to walk, so we normally take the nine thirty a.m. bus, which puts us at the pool at nine forty-five, and we are in the pool by ten.

"Where are you going?" Ben asks me. He has stopped walking and is looking around the street.

"The bus station," I reply simply.

"We catch the nine thirty, Ben. Come on, we will be late!" Rosie says, and I know we need to hurry up because Rosie hates to be late to anything.

Ben reaches for my hand and begins to pull me toward him and in the opposite direction. "I'll drive," he says as he leads the way, holding my hand, and Rosie follows behind me.

"Stop," I say as I halt mid-stride. "Ben, we need a car seat for Rosie. We have to take the bus."

He thinks about it for a moment, frustration crossing his face before following us back to the bus stop, where we catch the nine thirty just in time. My hand remains in his grip for the entire trip, his thumbs skimming my skin softly. I watch him without his notice, as he is looking around constantly before his eyes land on me. When our eyes connect, he stares at me for a beat before his lips curve into a large smile.

And if I didn't know better, I would say he is actually enjoying himself.

19

BEN

I sit here on the damp plastic chair, shrieking kids filling my ears and hot chlorinated steam hitting my face. I caught a bus for the first time ever, and even though it wasn't entirely unpleasant, it was yet another thing I wasn't prepared for. Public transport is not something I have ever had to rely on, and I am frustrated that I couldn't bring us. I have already emailed Sandra to purchase me a car seat for Rosie, and I will be driving us from now on. Although having Emily close to me for the entire trip was worth it.

I watch a mix of kids and parents flailing around in the water before my eyes rest back upon the woman who has been front and center in my mind for the past month. If someone had asked me a few weeks ago what I thought I would be doing today, watching my fake fiancée swim at the local pool with her daughter would not even enter my mind. But I can't deny the ferocious feeling I have when I am around Emily; where it comes from, I have no idea. The fact that she has a daughter threw me for a second this morning. Now not only do I have a fake fiancée, but also a fake stepdaughter.

As I sit watching them, I remember Rosie's painting at school and her telling me about her dad being a bad man. The memory makes my stomach sink like I swallowed lead. This woman, who is smart, sexy, and caring, is also a single mom. I can now see where she gets her resilience, and my protective nature has flared up even more for both of them.

My eyes remain firmly on Emily, who's currently laughing and playing with her lookalike daughter and some of the other kids from class. I have no idea what I am doing. I have no idea what even possessed me to make her my fake fiancée, but as I look around the perimeter of the pool, I see every man's eyes are on the same woman, and I know now that I have stepped into her world, it is going to be hard to leave.

"Cute kids, aren't they?" a familiar voice breaks me from my thoughts, and I sit back and look up at George.

"George," I say as I stand and extend my hand to shake, before he drags a seat over to me and sits down.

"You are on the wrong side of town today, Mr. Langford," George says matter-of-factly, not looking at me, his gaze resting on the kids with Emily in the water just in front of us.

"Well, I thought it would be nice to get to know the place," I say, my eyes drifting to Emily again as she holds on to Rosie's waist and helps her float and kick from one end of the pool to the other.

"She's delicate, you know..." he continues, and I turn my head to look at him. "She comes across tough, but she has been through a lot. She doesn't need another man to use her and treat her like trash once she's no longer of use to him."

I nod in understanding, but don't reply. My curiosity has already been piqued about Emily's history, and that comment is only adding to my interest. I want to know everything about her.

"Hi, George. Rosie, George is here now," Emily says, placing Rosie's hand on George's shoulder.

"Hey, Grandpa George!" Rosie squeals from beside me, dripping with pool water and pulling off her goggles. Emily is behind her, grabbing towels from the bag next to my feet, so I pull it closer and get one for her too. She wraps Rosie in a towel first as she chats with George, and I wrap Emily in a large towel as soon as she's done, covering her sexy body in that mesmerizing one-piece from everyone's eyes but mine. I stand closely behind her, my chest almost touching her back. My palms rub up and down her arms on top of the towel, the need to have my hands on her at an all-time high. Leaning down, my mouth mere inches from her ear, I still smell her lavender scent rising above the chlorine, making my mind abuzz.

"I prefer you without the towel, but for the sake of public safety, best you get changed," I growl in her ear. If another man looks at her, I will lose my mind. I don't miss the goosebumps that appear down her neck at my words. I like that she is as affected by me as I am by her. I let my hands run down her arms until they settle on her waist, taking the towel with me to close the gap as she leans back into my chest.

She chuckles as she glances up at me, whispering

over her shoulder. "Everyone is in a swimming suit, Ben. No one is looking at me." Now she is just pushing my buttons; she knows it, and I know it.

"Every fucker in here is looking at you. You are the most beautiful person in this germ-infested place, and right now, I am about ten seconds away from throwing you over my shoulder and taking you home to show you exactly what I want to do to you." The declaration of how I'm really feeling has her eyes widening and mouth slightly agape.

"Better close that mouth, because looking at me like that is not helping," I say as I move my hips a little so she can feel what she does to me.

She gasps at that, before she closes her mouth, her cheeks tinting darker, and then she surprises me by purposely bending over to grab her bag off the ground, pushing her backside right into my pelvis. I clench my fists together at her sides and swallow down the groan rumbling deep in my chest.

"Come on, Rosie, let's get changed, and then we can go out for lunch," Emily says, standing back up and taking her hand before looking at me. Her hair is wet, her body dripping, and my knees are weak as I stare down at her, my balls swollen and no doubt blue. The two of them walk down the hall to the changing rooms, leaving George and me standing next to each other, watching them go.

"So, how did your chat go with Mayor Simplot?" I ask, prodding for information. I feel like I get whiplash, the moment the words leave my mouth. The deep sinking feeling in my gut gets deeper as I move the conversation to business. To what this visit should be all about instead of what I wish it was—spending time with Emily.

"Simplot is as slippery as a snake and only looks after himself. The school will never be at the top of his agenda."

I nod. "You know Beasley will not stop. When he wants something, he will stop at nothing until he gets it." I feel the need to warn him. I need them to understand that this is not me. This is not my decision. I am just representing my client. My *best* client. I have to do this.

George nods. "We will try our best, and our position won't change. But I am worried for the kids, for the staff, for Emily," he says, looking at me pointedly. "The school is a very big part of many people's lives. My late wife and I started it over twenty years ago and have seen many kids thrive who would ordinarily slip through the cracks. We do a lot of good, we help a lot of people, and Emily and I promised my Glenda that we would take care of it."

George is stern, and I have to admit it has been a long time since I have spoken to anyone so passionate about something that wasn't bringing them millions of dollars. Being around him and Emily is refreshing.

"He is one of our firm's biggest clients, George. We will try to offer you the best deal we can, but you know how these things work..." Keeping my hands in my pockets, I feel sick, but big business always wins. But he already knows. He knows that Beasley will play every underhanded trick in the book to get that property. He knows he will lose. There really isn't much I can say, as we are on opposite sides here. George and Emily against Beasley and his contacts and money and my firm. My eyes flick back to the hallway to see if the girls are coming, but it is still vacant.

"I understand. So, you're here today to see Emily personally, or are you here on business?" George asks me, straight to the point, and I need to think about my answer. I go with the truth.

"Both, George. Both." I sigh, already feeling like a bastard for even admitting it.

"Well, thanks for being honest. Can I give you some advice?" he offers, looking at me in a way that I feel that my father would if he bothered to give me any fatherly advice when he was alive.

"Best you leave now and not get too attached to Emily, because if your firm wins, I can guarantee you that you will lose. We all will." His warning sends a chill down my spine, his eyes serious as they hook on to mine. He doesn't wait for a response as he walks toward the hallway, just as Emily and Rosie exit the bathrooms, and he takes Rosie's hand.

I let his advice sink in before walking over slowly and joining them.

"Ben, come for lunch!" Rosie practically jumps as I get near them and reaches out her other hand for me. I look at it, and then my eyes flick to George who is staring me down. But like the idiot I am, I still believe I can have my cake and eat it too, so I take her hand. When I meet Emily's sparkling eyes, the weight is immediately lifted.

I am not sure what will happen, but swimming lessons and lunch on a Saturday may just be my new favorite thing.

$\sim$

THE FOUR OF us have lunch at Mona's, a local diner not far from the pool, and I must admit, the food is pretty good. Everything is homemade on-site, no mass-produced sandwiches or day-old pasta here. I watch as Emily takes care of Rosie, putting her needs first. I have been watching her for the past five minutes help feed Rosie her soup, something warm after the swim, but I am in awe as this woman feeds her blind daughter while her own lunch goes cold. She's the kind of mother every child should have, one I didn't have the fortune of experiencing. George and I have both finished our meals, while Rosie is only halfway through, and Emily hasn't started at all.

"Rosie, would you mind if I fed you so your mom can eat her soup before it gets cold?" I say, not knowing the first thing about feeding kids, especially ones that have no sight.

"Oh, you don't have to do that..." Emily starts and appears shocked that I am even offering.

"Here, let me do it." Leaning over, I take the spoon from Emily's grasp. My fingers brush hers, and her eyes meet mine across the table. I give her a small nod, wanting her to know I've got her, and she lets go of the spoon, letting me take it without argument.

"Ben, did you get soup too?" Rosie asks as Emily sits and watches our interaction with interest.

"Eat your soup, Doubtfire. We'll be fine," I mumble to her. I know she is hungry because I can hear her stomach agreeing from across the table.

She nods, not saying anything, and starts to eat her soup while Rosie and I chatter to ourselves, but I don't miss the glances she gives George, or the feeling of his eyes drilling into my back.

We finish in record time, as it appears I am a pro at supporting Rosie. I grab her wrist and fist-bump her once we are done, realizing that we beat Emily, who finishes up her soup a few minutes later and asks for the bill.

"Okay, Rosie, let's go!" George says, standing.

"Bye, Ben, I hope you come again next Saturday!" Rosie says excitedly, before her arms reach out to me, and I hold her to help her find her way. She takes a step in my direction and her little hands wrap around my neck as she gives me a hug. It is unexpected, and I stop breathing for a moment. She is so tiny in my arms. I've never held a child before. I get my bearings once again and give her a little squeeze before handing her over to her mom. Standing from my chair, I shake hands with George, once again feeling his disapproval in his grip.

"Rosie is having a sleepover at George's tonight," Emily explains as she pulls a small backpack from the large swimming bag. If Rosie is having a sleepover, then Emily is going to be home alone. She looks at me for a beat, and I swallow roughly. My thoughts have gone straight to the bedroom, hers obviously doing the same if the pink in her cheeks is anything to go by.

"Yes, we have a new audiobook to listen to. This one is *Beauty and the Beast!*" Rosie hugs her mom with a giggle, and we watch them leave.

"So you are on your own tonight then?" I ask Emily as

I throw cash onto the table for lunch, at which point, she stops, gathers it up, and tosses it back at me.

"My town, I pay," she says as she reaches into her purse and pulls out some cash to cover it. It feels weird; I always pay for everything. No woman has ever refused my money. Before I can protest, she answers me.

"Depends..." she says with a coy smile and a shrug, and we step out of the diner to begin our walk back to her place, no longer needing the bus with Rosie not with us. It feels weird to walk, as it is not something that would happen in the city. Ralph drives me in my Bentley everywhere I need to go.

"Depends on what?" I ask, playing with fire.

"If I get a better offer," she quips, a smile tugging at her lips. One I return easily.

With her swimming bag over my shoulder, I reach out my other hand and curl my fingers around hers. It has been a long fucking time since I did this. Walked hand in hand with a woman. Since Sasha, I have never been on a date with the same woman more than once, and never, ever have I held hands. But my body is itching for contact with her. I can't stop myself from wanting her.

"Does Rosie stay over with George a lot?" I ask, interested to know what support systems she has in place, especially since Rosie's dad isn't around.

"George is like a father to me. Rosie refers to him as Grandpa because we are all so close. He has done so much for me that I will never be able to repay him." She looks ahead, not meeting my gaze or giving me any more insight. She is smart. I have a job to do and so does she. We are fighting on opposing sides and so the "right" thing to do would be to walk away. But I don't. I can't. I am too far gone. All I want to do is get this woman home and show her exactly how much I want her. Her grip in my hand tightens, and I feel my heart thump in my chest the closer we get to her building.

By the time we approach her street, it is late afternoon. The whole day was spent together, and it still wasn't enough. My need for her has only grown stronger. Any city stress left my body the moment I saw Emily. When we finally reach her door, I am doing all I can not to grab her and never fucking let her go. I wait as she unlocks the door, walking through, and I stand watching her, my eyes dropping to my favorite sight.

"Are you coming in, or are you just going to stand there looking at my ass all day?" she sasses, smiling through a laugh, and I know I shouldn't, but fuck it. This is happening. I drop the swimming bag on the floor at her front door and grab her around the waist, spinning her around to face me.

"I can't help it. You have an incredible ass," I grit out, thankful to have my hands on her. But I'm almost at my breaking point.

"Really? Tell me what else you like," she teases me, and little does she know how hot the flame is burning under my skin. Every word that leaves her plush lips stokes the fire within me.

"God, your body is fantastic," I start, as my hands mold along her muscles, smoothing lower and pulling her to me. "Your eyes, your smile, your laugh... fuck, my list is long," I murmur as I duck my head and run my nose up her neck, breathing her in.

"Ben..." she pants, her head falling to the side a little, opening up to me.

"I love the way your body feels against mine. I'm so fucking hard for you right now, Emily..." I whisper against her skin.

"It feels so good to be in your arms," she whispers back, and I pull away and look at her, to see that honesty written in her expression. Staring down at her, her eyes are lust drunk, her hair a little messed up, cheeks flushed. She is the most beautiful woman I've ever seen.

"I've been waiting all day to get my lips on yours," I growl, cupping her jaw with my hands and pulling her to me. Without waiting another moment, I lean in and capture her lips in mine. Her lips part in surprise, and I sweep my tongue across them, a little whimper sounding from her throat rewarding me to keep going.

Her hands come up and grip on to my wrists as she gives me the access I was waiting for, and I delve into her warm mouth with abandon. Her initial shock has gone, and she releases any tension from the day in a moan that shoots right down my body. She is now kissing me back just as feverishly, and like a bonfire, we erupt.

She pushes her front door wider with her hip and we stumble through it, our lips not parting, our legs and arms doing a dance to feel our way inside. We are in a frenzy, but it isn't happening fast enough. Bending down, I grab her ass, hoisting her small frame up my body, feeling electric when she wraps her legs around my waist. Kicking the apartment door closed with my foot, my palms mold to her ass as my tongue tangles with hers. I'm consumed with tasting every inch of her beautiful body. Right here, right now.

"Tell me where to go, or I am having you right here," I growl, my dick so hard, it's throbbing.

"Second door on the right," she pants as she pulls away from my mouth and starts to tear at my shirt, trying to get it off me. I grip her ass with one hand and help her with the other. We are frantic, the past month pure foreplay as we danced around each other, and now we can't stop, no matter if we should or not.

She may be my fake fiancée, but nothing about this is fake.

I find the room she indicated and see her large, perfectly made bed in the center, throwing her on it before kicking off my shoes. Unbuttoning my jeans, I stop when I see her in only her underwear—fucking black lace, just how I imagined it to be.

"Fuck. Do you know how long I have wanted you? To see you like this? You're like all my fucking dreams put together," I groan out as I stalk to her and pull her to me, my hands gripping around her bare waist. She smiles up at me in response, and like a silent call, my lips are on hers again. Standing next to the bed, she is on her knees on the mattress, and I let my hands wander. I roam her body, the feeling of her soft skin and her dips and curves causing all the blood in my body to rush to my cock, which is straining against my jeans.

"You are so fucking beautiful," I murmur like I am in a trance. Her hands mirror mine, running across my body, treating me with sweet caresses that make me shiver. We are both exploring, our eyes looking over the other in the moments our lips part, then going back for more. I see her perfectly curved breasts spilling full in her bra, the way her waist skims in before skirting out and showcasing her hips. The slide of her neck down to her shoulders, her pouty lips, and her bright-blue eyes, my favorite ones. I am enjoying her hands on me too much as they move from my shoulders, down my chest, before resting on the open zipper of my jeans.

I kiss her again then, wanting my mouth on her, needing to taste every inch as she pushes my jeans down, taking my underwear with them.

"Do you know how many times I have visualized you in black lace underwear?" I murmur to her.

"Probably as many times as I have thought about you naked," she says, a small smile gracing her lips that makes me chuckle.

With my hard cock freed, she wraps her hand around it, and my head rolls back as a growl escapes my chest.

"You be careful with that. He has a lot of work to do because I am making you mine tonight. And I plan on letting everybody in this building know about it," I growl into her mouth as I press a rough kiss to her lips, dragging them down her jaw to her neck.

I bring my hands up her body and wrap my fingers in her hair, struggling to understand how her body next to mine can already feel better than any of those that came before her.

"Are you going to just talk about it, or are you going to do something about it?" Even now, she likes to push my buttons. Huffing a laugh, I grab her around the waist with one arm and lift her before I join her on the bed and I lay her down. Hovering over her, I let my eyes wander again, looking at her splayed out on her back underneath me. I want to take my time and cherish her, but I also want to fuck her into the mattress so badly that the two thoughts are competing in my mind.

Her pouty lips part, her nipples peaking against the black lace fabric, and I reach my hand down and brush my fingers along the edge teasingly before pulling it down and exposing her breast. Leaning over, taking it in my mouth, I roll my tongue around her nipple, and then I pull the straps off her shoulders until they are both exposed, sucking on one while molding the other with my hand.

"Yes, Ben..." she pants, her back arching slightly, pushing her chest toward me, her hips moving, trying to find the friction we both want.

"Let me take care of you, Em," I whisper, her new nickname escaping my lips as they travel down her chest and pepper her stomach before I meet the last piece of black lace. My hands follow down her body, skimming her sides, until I feel the lace that runs across her hips, and I begin pulling it down. Slowly, I remove her underwear like I'm unwrapping my final gift. I see a birthmark on her hip, small and brown like a Milk Dud. A stamp of originality. Most women I meet would laser it from their body, so it is yet another reminder of how genuine Em is. My fingers caress her hips as I expose her to me, a sight that I will never forget. I hear her breath hitch a little, her fingers running up and down her stomach, waiting for my reaction.

"You look so pretty spread out for me..." I murmur, lost in the visual of her.

She glistens, her arousal for me appearing to be just as high as mine is for her. I pull the black lace down her legs and throw it on the floor before slowly kissing back up her leg, taking my time to taste her and feel her soft skin on my lips until I reach the apex between her thighs.

"Mmmm... Yessss... Oh my..." She pants and whimpers, writhing for more, as my lips tickle her skin. I am in heaven.

Her hands land in my hair, and I lick her, all of her, her flavor now embedded on my tongue, and wanting more. I am already addicted. I move my hands to the inside of her thighs and spread her legs wider, giving me full access to her center. I hear her breathing increasing, little pants now audible, and her hands dig into my hair even tighter, pulling a little, making me lick her, taste her, and fuck her with my tongue as if I've been starved, not able to get enough of this woman who turned up into my life totally unexpectedly. She moans, her hips starting to move against my mouth, as my tongue delves inside over and over, before I suck on her clit, repeating the motion, again and again. When her grip in my hair becomes almost painful, I know she is enjoying this as much as I am.

"That feels so good..." she moans as her body squirms. I want her to let go for me. She's so close, I can feel it.

"God, I am so hard for you, watching the way your body moves for me. What are you doing to me?" I murmur against her skin, my body aching for her. I bring my hand close and slip one finger inside her, teasing her slowly, curving it a little while I continue to lap her clit with my tongue. Fuck me if this is not the best Saturday afternoon of my life.

"Ben... Right there—I'm going to..." she pants out as her hips grind against my face faster, and I quicken my pace to match hers. Her body arches just before she shakes and shudders beneath me, whimpering like she's on the verge of something momentous.

"Ben... Oh my... Ben!" she cries out in pleasure, my name on her lips music to my ears as I smile against her clit. As she comes down from her high, I slow my pace and remove my finger, gripping her thighs and keeping them spread wide. My hands hold her in place as I lick every last drop of her, never wanting it to end.

20

EMILY

I pant, breathless, not sure why I ever waited so long to experience something that euphoric. Ben is much better than any of my battery-operated friends, that is for sure. That was one of the best orgasms of my entire life, and it was over much too soon.

"You're so fucking beautiful, especially when you come with my name on your lips," he says, crawling up my body before taking my mouth again. I taste a mix of him, warm coffee, and myself, and it has me moaning and ready for more.

He lies on top of me, resting his weight on his elbows on either side of my head, as I feel his long, heavy cock throbbing in need against my stomach. I was taken aback when I lowered his jeans. The confidence I had to take what I wanted is something new, but he makes me feel safe. Something I haven't felt in too long. It has been a while since I have been with a man and certainly have never been with a man so big. Jeremy was my one and only. He took everything from me, including my innocence.

This man's tongue is magic, and I already know that I will be craving him again. We shouldn't be doing this. We have very clearly stepped over the line with each other, but even though I know it is a bad idea, I can't stop these intense feelings I have for him.

"You okay?" he asks seriously, brushing a few strands of hair away from my face as his eyes meet mine.

"Never been better," I reply, a wide grin overtaking my face at how he's looking at me. There's something in his eyes that has me damn-near melting.

"Good, now I want to fuck you with my cock like I have wanted to since the night I met you," he says as his kisses move to my neck, hitting my sweet spot right below my ear that pulls a moan directly from my lips as my body begins to heat again. I am a moaning, panting mess underneath him in seconds; it is like he knows my body better than I do. My need for him is not sated, not even close. I could lie here with this man all evening and still not get enough.

"Ben..." I moan his name, not caring about anything else in this moment.

"I like it when you moan my name. I'm going to like it even better when you scream it," he says, not letting up on his assault. I shiver in response.

My hands roam over his body, wanting to feel every inch of him. He is strong. His muscles are firm, and it is evident that he works out regularly. I have never seen a man so defined and certainly never had one in my bed. Being with Jeremy was never like this. Jeremy always took what he wanted and never gave anything in return. His strength was always used against me.

When my hand reaches his cock, I wrap my fingers around his length and give him a small pump. As I do, he growls, a deeper sound than I've heard yet rumbling from his chest. That alone could probably make me come again.

"You keep teasing me like that, baby, and I can't be held responsible for what happens," he grits out, and my heart stalls for a beat. That word. In one little word my body feels like mush. Our nicknames for each other before this were cute, funny, a bit flirty, but Ben calling me *baby*, I didn't know how good that would feel. I smile against his mouth. The way he is working me over, I will be his baby today, tomorrow, and the next day.

"I think we are way past the point of responsibility now, aren't we?" I whisper, my tongue darting out, licking his lower lip.

"I need to be inside you." He speaks against my lips as he pushes himself into my grip. He is heavy and throbbing in my hand, making my body weak with need.

"I want that too." When he looks into my eyes, I nod, reinstating my desire. I've never wanted anything as much as I do Ben.

Quickly, he sits up and leans over the bed to his jeans, grabbing a condom from his wallet. I watch him as he grips and sheaths himself, and I swallow, wondering if I'll be able to take all of him.

"It's been a long time for me, Ben," I whisper, feeling delicate in his arms as he hovers above me, his gaze piercing mine. Vulnerability is sneaking into my nerves, something I hate.

"I'll go slow. I want to take my time with you," he whispers back, his lips touching mine. He is gentle as he kisses me, our tongues tangling in a slow and treasuring dance. I feel safe in his arms, as his hand runs down my stomach. His fingers circle my clit, spreading the wetness and making my body come alive, automatically reacting to his touch.

I feel him then, slowly pushing into me, and I completely surrender to every sensation. This is what I have been missing. I have been so busy being a mom and looking over my shoulder every minute of every day that I forgot what this feels like. I forgot what it feels like to be a woman. To be wanted. My breath hitches slightly as he presses in farther, inch by another inch, and my back arches like he commanded it. His mouth has now moved to my neck, to my sweet spot again, sending small shivers through me, my body not quite my own anymore. It is all his.

"Fuck, you feel so incredible, baby," he grits out, clearly trying to restrain himself, but I lift my legs and wrap them around his waist, opening myself up to take him deeper. We both groan as he bottoms out, his hips flush against mine, grinding into me. My hands grip his shoulders, and our movements find a rhythm that's making my head numb with pleasure. Slowly, he begins to edge out a little and then back in again. The pace along with his fingers on my clit and his mouth on my body create a perfect symphony. He is a conductor to my body, already knowing where my most sensitive spots are and how to make them sing. I have never had this before. I have never had slow and sensual, where the focus has been solely on me.

"Ben... everything you're doing is perfect. Feels sooooo good." I half whisper, half moan, my words almost a slur as my body moves automatically with his. His thrusts quicken as does his pressure on my clit and I feel the telltale build as my back arches more, my bare breasts pushing against his naked chest, the feeling of skin on skin only adding to my hunger for release. My fingers dig into his shoulders, and then I run them up into his hair, pulling him to me, not wanting any space between us. I crave his touch. I crave him desperately.

"Fuck, Em, you were made for me. This goddamn body, every inch of it, I can't get enough." He moans low and deep as he punctuates his statement with a punishing thrust that kicks off another and another, our skin slapping against each other as we both chase the massive high we know is cresting within our reach.

I feel it building. Even more powerful than before. Pushing my head back into my pillow, my moans and pants and whimpers are beyond my control. My body now belongs to Ben. I feel close, like I will explode from the pressure mounting within me, the feeling of him inside me igniting something I didn't even know I could feel.

"Don't stop, please, don't stop..." I beg, so close, my body chasing the feeling, meeting him thrust for thrust.

"I feel you clenching that perfect pussy for me. You take me so well. So. Fucking. Good," Ben growls, gripping my hip tight, and I know he is close. "Come for me, baby.

I know you're close. I want to feel you come all over my cock."

I don't know if it is the dirty talk or the fact that he can play my body like Mozart does a piano, but I let go with a scream, pulsing around him and my nails digging into his shoulders. I pant out his name, still reveling in the lasting pleasure with every one of his thrusts, and he follows me.

"Fuuuuck, Emmm," he moans, emptying himself in me, our hands gripping each other's bodies as we battle wave after wave. When we're both spent, he collapses on top of me, rolling off and onto his back beside me.

The two of us are quiet for a beat, our breaths heavy, both looking at the ceiling.

He takes a few deep breaths before he sits up, pressing a kiss to my cheek. Swinging his legs off the bed, he pads his way to my bathroom, where I hear him get rid of the condom before he comes back to me, crawling over my body, kissing me from my ankles, up my leg, across my hips, up my stomach, until he reaches my face.

"That was unreal," I say to him as he looks at me in what seems like wonder. I wait for his reaction. Being this close, there is no hiding anything, and I hold my breath, anxious for him to talk. He is quiet for a beat, and my chest grows heavy. *Was it not the same for him? Did that not flip his whole world on its axis?*

"Em... you're under my skin. I could do that with you all day and all night." His hand traces my cheekbone as he looks at me, my stomach fluttering. His touch is tender as he pulls me around the waist and drags me to him, spooning me, burying his nose in my neck.

"Well, you know what they say... tomorrow is never promised, and all we have is today," I whisper, and his hold around me tightens as he groans against my skin.

"We better make tonight count, then."

And for the rest of the day, until I fall asleep, he makes me see stars.

21

BEN

I roll over and groan. I'm tired. My muscles ache like I have run a marathon, and as I take a deep breath, I am sure I smell bacon and coffee. Opening one eye, I peek around to get my bearings. The room is not mine. There are soft throws and pillows, creams and soft pinks. I see a framed photo of Emily and Rosie on the bedside table and I smile as the memories of last night come to my mind.

My eyes adjust to the bright morning sun pushing through the window. Taking my time, I look around the room. It is so neat and tidy, plush and cozy, and nothing like my bachelor pad. She has a few knickknacks, a heavenly bed, and even though I'm sure this place was built in a time reserved for my grandparents, her touch has made the small space homey. I am surprised she is up after how much exercise we had. We devoured each other practically all night, and I had her two more times after we fell into bed yesterday afternoon, each time better than the last.

I lean over and grab my phone, my eyes widening when I realize it is already nine a.m. Scrolling quickly, I see a few messages from my brothers as they try to get in touch with me via our family chat. I am officially late for our scheduled golf game and their ribbing on where I could be if not with them has already started. This is a sleep-in for me, and I can't remember the last time I woke up so late. Rubbing my face with my hand, I get up, grab my jeans, and go into her bathroom to splash some water on my face.

Her bathroom is tiny as well, and I didn't pay a lot of attention to it last night, but in the bright morning light, I can see that I am so tall, my head almost meets the ceiling. I can barely fit in the room. She has perfect fluffy warm white towels, every surface is spotless, and I can smell her lavender scent everywhere I turn. I look at the shower and wish I was in it, naked with her, but as my cock starts to come alive at the thought, my stomach rumbles. We skipped dinner last night, preferring to eat each other instead, so I am famished.

Opening the bedroom door, I follow the aroma of bacon, and I spot her in the compact kitchen. She is busy cooking, stirring something on the stovetop while playing some soft music as her background. I lean against the doorframe, crossing my arms over my bare chest, and watch her from the distance. Her hair is up on top of her head in a messy topknot, stray strands framing her fresh face. As my eyes trail down, I forget where I am for a moment as my gaze feasts on her perfect peach in light-wash denim jeans. Her top is just as sexy. She's wearing a white button-down, the buttons open at the collar, showing off her glowing skin, delicate collarbone, and a peek of her lacy red bra underneath. I'm already ready to strip her down all over again.

The shrill ring of her cell phone interrupts my thoughts, and my eyes flick to her face. She doesn't look happy as she reaches over the counter and mutes the call without even looking at the screen. She still hasn't noticed me standing here as she multitasks. Eggs are in one pan, bacon in the other, bread toasting, as she pours juice, ignoring the phone.

"Can I help?" I ask as I push off the door, and she looks up at me. She smiles, and her eyes widen as she takes me in. My jeans are hanging low from my hips, and I walk over to her, her eyes on me the entire way.

"Morning," she says breathlessly as I stand in front of her.

"Morning, baby," I say, her new nickname falling from my lips. It feels as natural as breathing. I cup her jaw in my hands and kiss her good morning.

Her cell phone vibrates on the bench next to us, causing us to pull away from each other. She looks at the screen and scowls, rejecting whoever is trying to call her and pushing her phone away so she doesn't look at it.

"Everything alright?" I ask, intrigued at who is calling her early on a Sunday as she continues to run around the kitchen.

"Yes, of course," she says with a shake of her head, pushing the spatula into my hands. "Can you manage the bacon?" she asks, and although I am not sure if she is telling me the truth, I do as she asks.

She moves around the kitchen effortlessly as I take

care of the bacon, and it isn't lost on me that this feels oddly domesticated and yet totally normal. I usually hook up with a woman and sneak out the next morning or politely decline breakfast and leave. But not today. Today I am in her kitchen, using her spatula and cooking us bacon, and I have no desire to be anywhere else.

Her phone vibrates again. And like before, she looks at it and rejects it, sliding it away on the bench.

"Do you need to get that?" I ask, not wanting her to feel like she can't talk while I am here.

"Oh no, I just thought it may be Rosie, but it isn't, so it isn't important," she says, placing our breakfast on the table, and I plate up the bacon. Together we sit, filling our stomachs and sipping cups of delicious coffee.

Her phone vibrates another three times throughout breakfast, and each time she ignores it. If she needs to take the call, she could ask me to leave or step into her bedroom, but she continues to ignore it, and it is starting to piss me off. First, she didn't tell me about Rosie, and now I am wondering what else she is being secretive about. I don't like that feeling.

"So, last night was... um..." she starts, a small pink tint rising to her cheeks that softens me right to my core. I lean back, admiring her, grinning at how adorable she is.

"Unbelievable," I state, because it was, and I don't want her to think otherwise.

"I mean, we are fake engaged, I suppose..." she trails off, playing with her food. I can see the vulnerability clear as day on her face. She knows we both enjoyed ourselves, but she thinks that was a one-off of our arrangement or something.

"Let me be perfectly clear, Em. There was nothing fake about last night. That had nothing to do with our deal." I am firm in my words because I want them to penetrate. I have no idea what is happening and no idea what will happen. But I know what I feel, and I know I need to get this issue with Beasley and the school sorted immediately. She has quickly become so much more important.

"I have—" she starts to say before getting interrupted by her vibrating phone from the countertop. I watch her take a breath and sigh. Closing her eyes for a moment, it's like it pains her to hear it.

"Are you sure you don't need to get that?" I ask her once again, the tension in my shoulders rising, trying to give her an opening to take the call.

"No, it's fine." I am not convinced, but either way, she is not giving me any further information, so I drop it. I notice her smile is a little less vibrant now, her posture a little more slumped.

"So, you were saying?" I prod her, wanting her to talk to me.

"Oh, nothing... I forgot. Brain fog," she says quietly, rubbing her head. Again, I feel like she is not being truthful, and I don't like it, not one bit.

"I need to head home. I have to get some work done before a meeting tomorrow." I'm thinking a bit of space may do her some good, as much as I want to stay. Sitting forward in my seat, I take her hand, kissing each finger.

She brings her other hand up and touches my face, her smile genuine this time, and my heart stutters. This woman, with her perfectly messy hair, big blue eyes, and pouty lips that I just want to suck on, drives me wild.

Her phone vibrates again, and we lose our moment. She sighs, stands, and begins to clean the table, and I follow her lead. Rinsing our plates at the sink, I clear the rest of the things before I walk up behind her. My hands wrap around her waist, and I drop my head to her neck, inhaling her scent to keep it with me all day. Now every time I smell lavender, all I will think of is Emily. As my hands grip her waist, I pull her into to me, wanting to feel more of her. She leans back, resting her head on my chest.

She turns in my arms and faces me, and I don't miss the opportunity to kiss her. With a deep, slow, sultry kiss, I discover her mouth again, tasting her, devouring her, not able to get enough of her. Lifting her up, I put her on the kitchen counter, our connection not breaking as her arms wrap around my neck, and I pull her closer so she can feel exactly how hard she makes me.

This time, when her phone vibrates, I can't stop myself from handling the constant interruption.

"That's it," I say out loud, grabbing her phone and answering it without even looking at the caller ID.

"She's busy," I bark down the line and then hang up, not waiting to hear any response. Throwing it back on the counter, her lips are back on mine in the next second, which I greedily accept as a form of "thank you." We stay like that, kissing and touching, centering each other, for I don't even know how long.

"I'll go get my things," I say reluctantly against her

lips, because I really need to head back to my place, shower, and get my head into some work. She nods, and I grip her ass again to lift her off the counter before I give it a small squeeze and let go to gather my things.

"Did you get everything?" she asks me as we walk to the door.

"Yeah, but I want to take you with me too," I say as she opens the door, but I push her against it, kissing her again. If I don't leave now, I am going to fuck her up against this door.

"Jeez, guys, get a room," I hear a female voice say as another one giggles, and I pull back, looking behind me.

"Hi, girls," Emily says, smiling, as her two friends walk our way. A small blush tints her face again, and I smirk because I love that I can make her hot and bothered.

"Hi, Ben. Please, don't let me stop you…" Emily's friend Sarah says, winking at us as she slides past and goes into the apartment, flopping on the sofa. Emily is laughing now, and she looks radiant. Happy. I like making my girl smile.

"Uhhh. Hi?" Allie, Em's other friend, says as she awkwardly moves past us, giving me a small smile before following Sarah through the door.

"Bye, baby," I say, totally enamored and in deeper than I thought I ever would be. Giving her one more peck, I force myself to walk down the hallway and down the stairs. I hear her close the door, and my lips curl at the sight of the apartment complex in the light of day without distractions. The carpet is torn and worn; the paint is peeling; water damage can be seen in the corners, and the complex door doesn't even have a lock. I don't like leaving her here. The stark contrast between our lives is obvious, but as I walk out into the refreshing morning air, I get a whiff of lavender from the nearby garden. And just like that, I am back to thinking about Emily.

22

EMILY

"Please tell me you spent all night naked with that man?" Sarah asks the minute the door closes.

The stupid smile on my face tells her everything she needs to know.

"Go you!" she squeals, slapping me with a cushion as I slump onto the sofa next to her.

"So I thought it was all fake? He was practically sucking your face off just now. What the heck is going on?" Allie asks, intrigued.

"Arggghhh, I have no idea. What am I going to do?" I plead to them, because I can hide nothing. They already know everything. They know the diamond on my hand is a real gem signifying a fake engagement, the dire straits that the school is in, and the fact that there has been no man invited into my apartment ever. Until now.

"What, like you can't have a little personal fun while trying to save the world?" Sarah smarts.

"It's just... I mean, he is a Langford!" I say, the stark

reality being that he could afford to buy the entire community I live in, while I am still trying to work out how to pay for groceries this week.

"Yeah, but you have a big rock on your finger that currently says you are about to be one too," Allie points out as the diamond sparkles, creating rainbows on the wall when it catches the morning sun.

"It's all fake!" I sigh. But I immediately question that statement.

"Doesn't look very fake," Allie pushes, bringing me back to what Ben said this morning. That nothing about last night was fake...

"They were kissing, not committing their lives to each other. They are polar opposites, enemies at war, using each other for business gain, while also personal pleasure." Sarah purrs the last few words, but it is the first ones she spoke that hit the hardest. She is right. We are opposites. We are enemies, on opposites sides of the business deal he is trying to broker. While last night was amazing, I am hit with the stark realization that casual sex is probably what Ben does the most. And I played right into his hand, regardless of the sweet things he said before and after. But... maybe I shouldn't care? It has been so long since I have been with anyone; it is nice to feel a man's touch. Throw caution to the wind a bit.

"Don't look so grim. It is about time you had an orgasm delivered by a man," Sarah scoffs, obviously attuned to what I am thinking.

"And a Langford, no less!" Allie sings. I roll my eyes, and Sarah smacks her with the cushion.

THE GIRLS STAYED for a few hours today, and together we recapped last night's events. While Ben and I have entered into a fake engagement, the situation I am in is starting to feel very, very real. There is clearly nothing fake about the attraction we have for each other and although we are hot together, the feeling of foreboding that comes with our entanglement is real. One of us will lose, and I know it is not going to end well.

George called earlier and is keeping Rosie for another night, taking her to school tomorrow for me. Giving me the space to think and the break that I desperately need. To be honest, I think George likes to have company now that he is living alone, and they get along wonderfully. As I sit here in the quiet of the evening, it gives me time to digest the past twenty-four hours. Am I stupid for even entertaining getting involved with a man like Ben? A man who is my legal opposition? A man who wears a suit and whose family owns the entire state in which I live? Yeah. I think I may have lost my mind. But the stupid grin on my face won't leave, and neither will the butterflies in my belly or the aches in my thighs. My body is spent, all my strength gone, but I have never felt so alive.

As my head rests on the sofa, I enjoy the peace and quiet. I even had a nap this afternoon before I was awoken by the doorbell. A large bouquet of white roses arrived from Ben, plus a smaller one for Rosie. A shock, for sure. It was another first for me, a man sending me flowers. While Jeremy's constant calls this morning are somewhat new, I put it down to the fact that he saw me with Ben in the city during the week and now I am front and center in his mind. Which is what I was trying to avoid. It has been months since I have seen him, and his calls put a damper on my mood, but the flowers lightened it again.

I flick through the TV stations before heading to my bookshelf instead. A spicy romance is just the thing I am now in the mood for as I look through my collection. As I pull out a book that has been on my reading list for weeks, the doorbell rings, and I quickly skip to the door, wondering what it could be this time. I'm not really thinking clearly, still floating on cloud nine, and I realize my mistake the minute I open the door.

My heart all but stops, the air leaving my lungs, as he stands large and angry above me. Why I didn't keep the chain on and look before I opened the door, I have no idea. I am usually not this stupid. He barges through like he has every right to, pushing the door so hard it hits the wall, a small hole appearing where the handle smashes the plasterboard. Shoving me out of the way, my back slams against the door, and I wince as the other side of the handle slams into my ribs.

"Did your *fiancé* answer the phone this morning?" he seethes down at me, and I can smell the whiskey on his breath, even though I am a few feet away.

"None of your business. Get out!" I shout shakily, scared out of my mind, but trying to jolt him out of his drunken stupor. It has been a while since he's visited me, but the last time I was in the hospital for a week. He must have realized then that he took it too far, because he hasn't been around since. But Jeremy just can't let me go.

"Don't make me repeat myself. You need to call off this fucking engagement right now!" he yells, and I wish the slamming doors from out in the hall were people coming to help, rather than ignoring me and checking their locks. Jeremy is not their problem, though. He is mine.

"Go to hell," I spit out and brace myself for what is coming. I should know better; I should not answer back. I should run. By the time I come to my senses and begin to run from the apartment, he is already on me, and the last thing I remember thinking is that I am so glad Rosie isn't here.

When I come to, the apartment is dark, and my head is throbbing. I lie still for a moment, waiting for the pain to rush over me, and it does with a vengeance only a moment later, like a tidal wave. Silent tears stream from my eyes, not only from pain but from frustration and fear. I am so sick of being his punching bag.

The police have been involved multiple times, but he always has an alibi, always has friends who lie for him, and so the police charge him with a small misdemeanor and let him go. Jeremy has connections and he uses them well. Why would one of the state's wealthiest men drive all the way to William Heights for a woman? Especially when he can have any woman he wants in the city. He tells the police I am a scorned ex-lover. A gold digger, who just wants his money and attention and that I stalk him. There is nothing I can do without seeming like a crazy person, and no matter what, he gets to walk away without any consequences.

Jeremy's abuse started as soon as I found out we were

pregnant. I didn't find out straightaway, and then the thought of not keeping the baby was not something that even entered my mind. I was in love and in a long-term, committed relationship and beamed happily at Jeremy when I told him the news. He was ecstatic initially, and we started planning for our new arrival immediately. It also helped that my hormones were elevated, and the need to be with him in the bedroom increased throughout most of the pregnancy—something he loved.

But after I started to show, he no longer wanted to be with me. He began working late and on weekends, he would snap at me at the drop of a hat, tell me he no longer wanted the baby. He wanted to go back to what we had before. But we couldn't. I couldn't.

Then it all started to crumble.

After calling the police each and every time, I don't bother anymore. There is nothing they can do. After three serious beatings and a few altercations in between, I have learned to put my head down and stay off his radar as much as possible. In the early years, I moved from shelter to shelter, then I lived with George for a long while until I could get on my feet. When Jeremy didn't find me, I thought I was safe. But he somehow found out I was in William Heights. I assume it was through financial records, since there's no doubt in my mind he has people who investigate that kind of thing. I was naïve to think otherwise.

This is the first time he has been to my apartment, though. All the other times have been when he has asked to meet under the pretense he wants to talk about Rosie, or when he has caught me on my own while walking near George's house. I have been to great lengths to ensure he couldn't find me here. The lease to this apartment is even in George's name. But with money comes power, and again, I shouldn't be surprised. I feel stupid because I knew. Deep down, I knew this would happen. That the moment I met someone else, he would come back. When Ben answered his call this morning, trouble started brewing. I was stupid to think I could have a relationship with someone new. I'm damaged goods. Fake or real, Ben needs to run far, far away from me. I could ruin his reputation for life.

I blink a few times and lift my hand to my face, feeling the dried blood. Looking around, I see that my head hit the edge of the door as more blood is splattered there as well. I roll onto my side, grimacing, and grab my ribs as they twinge. He must have given me a few kicks to the torso while I was out as well. Getting on all fours, the pounding in my head is intense, and I grab on to the kitchen counter to pull myself up, albeit shakily.

I pause then and control my breathing, trying to keep my lungs from exploding in pain, and I hear my phone buzzing in the living room next to the sofa where I was lying earlier. I step slowly toward it and look at the screen. My heart drops when I see it's Ben, and I let it go to voicemail. It is nearly nine p.m., so I estimate that I have been laid out for at least a few hours. My eyes fill with tears, the full impact of my situation coming to the surface. I don't even know how I can get myself out of this. My eyes flick back to the cell when Ben leaves a message, and more tears glass over my vision. For the first time in years, I felt alive, I felt like myself. Don't I get that life? Don't I deserve it? Why can't Jeremy just move on?

Groaning, I slowly walk to my bathroom to try to clean myself up. As I turn on the light and look in the mirror, the sight is not a pretty one, but not the worst it's ever been either. There is a small cut above my eye, and the swollen skin around it is turning a dark purple blue. It has been without ice, so I need to get that sorted to hopefully lesson the pain and swelling from here on out. I know the drill. I have been through this before.

Unbuttoning my shirt, which is now stained with blood, I throw it on the floor. There is no major bruising on my body, which is good, since that means no internal bleeding either... I hope. There's a little redness, again nothing that some ice can't fix. All in all, it is painful, but I have been beaten worse, and I am just glad I lost consciousness. Otherwise, it may have been a different outcome. He doesn't like when I fight back.

I run the water, grab a washcloth, and start to clean myself up, then change into my sleepwear for the night. Walking into the kitchen, I grab the ice packs—the many I have stored for this very reason—and sit on the sofa to call George.

It is late, so he will be startled, but I can't teach tomorrow. The kids won't like to see my bruises, and although I can hide it from Rosie, the others will tell her, and I don't want her to worry about me.

"Em, what's wrong?" George asks the minute he picks up the phone.

"I can't come in tomorrow. Jeremy came today," I say,

grimacing and trying to breathe through the pain. My hands are shaking, my nerves totally shot.

"Okay, let me rouse Rosie, and I will come get you and take you to the hospital," George says, already knowing how this has gone in the past.

"No. Let her sleep, please. I'm fine, a bit bruised and sore, but nothing ice and painkillers won't fix. I think the kids may not like my new color, though, so I will stay home tomorrow. If you can bring Rosie home after school, that will be great," I say, feeling bad I am putting more of a burden on George. He is stressed enough about the school as it is.

"I will have Sarah cover your class, and I will come over in the morning. Did anything happen to make him visit?" George presses. We have both been grateful that I haven't heard from Jeremy for months, and I stupidly thought that maybe he had stopped for good.

"Ben stayed over last night. Jeremy was calling incessantly this morning, and then Ben answered. He isn't happy about the engagement either," I grit out, leaning back on the cushions, trying to get comfortable.

"He is a bad man, Em. We need to try to get you away from him. You shouldn't have to deal with this." I can hear the anger in his voice.

"I am sick of running, George. I'm sick of hiding. Wherever I go, he will find me. He has the money to do anything he wants, and I can't compete with that. I can't disappear from that." My body is fraught with trembles, tears running down my cheeks. I hate him for making me feel this way. I hate him.

"He will stop... he has to stop," I say again, not really

believing it. Now that he knows Ben is in my life, I know he won't stop. The only saving grace is that at least he won't touch Rosie. He never has, and he prefers to act like she isn't even alive, to ignore her entirely. It is me he wants. And it is me he can't have.

"He will stop when you are dead, Em, then what?" When a new round of sobs flows out of me, George takes a breath, then softens his tone. "I'm sorry. Are you sure you don't need the hospital?"

"I'm fine, George. Can you please just look after Rosie? I don't want her to know he was here."

"Maybe we need to talk to someone else, find a lawyer or something." It isn't the first time he has mentioned this.

"I can't afford a lawyer, and besides, what can they do? Jeremy has never been charged. Again, it is his word against mine." I sigh, taking a deep breath to calm myself.

"What about Ben? He could help. That big law firm could do something good." I shake my head, even though he can't see me.

"I can't get Ben involved in this. I have only just met him. I can't put this on him; this is the last thing he needs to get involved with," I say, already feeling guilty for even having this issue while being with Ben.

"You need to move back in with me. At least I can be with you, be a deterrent now that he has been to your apartment," George presses.

"I just... this apartment is my first step into independence. It is my first attempt at having a real life, one where I can just be me. I don't want to continue to run and hide. I don't want him to have that control over me.

Damn him. I want to just live my life." Living with George is safer and makes sense, but I don't want to change up my whole life again, and Rosie's, because of Jeremy's actions. I know there's another way.

"Why don't you think about it. You know my door is always open to you and Rosie. I love having you both here," George says, and I know. We love being there too.

"Thanks, George. For everything," I say before hanging up and lying back on the sofa, ice on my face and on my ribs. And that's where I stay, all night, until I watch the sun come up the next morning.

It has been a few days since I saw her. I have called her and texted, wanting to come over or take her out, but every time, she has been busy. I also don't want to come across as needy, but I want her, preferably with me, underneath me, every night. Although the traffic was a nightmare on this Wednesday afternoon, I have made the trip to the school for art class again. The urge I now have to see my girls hums through my body. I clear my throat, trying to get a grip on these new emotions, as Ralph dodges through the cars.

My girls.

Emily has been under my skin since the moment I met her, and I can't wait to see Rosie for our next install-ment of *Cinderella*. I haven't been around many kids before. My brothers and I are not really family people, ever since Dad died and broke our fantasies of what a true family means. But Rosie is a cutie, and she's making herself a home in my heart just as much as her mother.

It is all fake, the devil on my shoulder shouts into my

ear, and I grind my teeth. I need to keep perspective. She is my *fake fiancée*. I hear Harrison's voice in my ear from our phone call earlier. All my brothers and I were on a call to lock in our next golf day when I told them all about Rosie and how I spent the weekend with Em. Tennyson laughed, Eddie sighed, and Harrison had nothing but disbelief in his tone. That was quickly followed by an email from Beasley this morning, reiterating his push for this property and having concerns for my choice of fiancée, stating that we will talk about it at our next meeting. I have my team scouring for an alternative, hoping that I may be able to convince him to buy somewhere else, but the feeling in the pit of my stomach tells me that he won't change his mind.

Harrison hasn't had any luck either, but had renewed enthusiasm for the project once he learned more about Em and Rosie and my feelings about them. His team have spent hours reviewing protocols and chatting to the mayor since. Although it seems his hands are tied at this point. It is a commercial decision; there is nothing the state can do.

I rub my eyes as we pull up to the school. The afternoon sun is streaming down, and I see it in a new light. It is bright, colorful. The laughing kids can be heard from the moment I walk into the school foyer, making me smile, where I see the same woman at the front desk.

"Good morning, I am here to see Emily Carr." Keeping it professional, I grab the sleeve of my shirt and fix my cuff link that probably costs more than this woman's entire wardrobe. She lifts the phone and calls someone, relaying that I am here.

"You can go down. Emily is in the room on the left."
Nodding to her, I head down the familiar hallway,
hearing shrieks and laughter from the kids in the other
classrooms as I pass. I was going to bring flowers, but I
thought it may not be entirely appropriate. I haven't
thought until now how difficult it is going to be to not
touch her when I see her. Approaching her room, I open
the door and knock a few times as I enter. I see the same
kids as I did last week, and this time George is also in the
class, appearing to be assisting Emily.

Her hair is down around her face, her ass looking way
too good in those jeans she is wearing, as usual. She looks
up when she sees me and her smile is bright, and I can't
help but smile back just as wide. *Fake, fake, fake.* I quickly
look at George, who has concern etched into his brow,
but I offer him a brief smile, and he nods at me in return.

I grin like a loved-up fool and am grateful my
brothers aren't here to witness how much of a sap I have
become. I didn't have time to dress down today, so I have
worn an older suit, one that if paint gets splattered, it
won't matter as much, although I may stick to coloring
today.

She walks up to me in the effortlessly sexy way she
does, looking straight at me, her head angled upward,
making me feel like I am the only person in the world
who matters. That is the biggest turn-on with her; she
makes me feel like I am everything. I feel invincible.
Stopping right in front of me, my stare falters as I see
slight bruising around her face and a small cut above
her eye.

"What happened?" I ask her, my eyebrows pulling

together as I gently touch her face, pushing the hair back so I can see her more clearly.

"Oh, just a silly accident. I fell at home. I'm okay," she says, smiling as she takes a step away from me, pulling her hair down back around her cheeks like she is shielding herself from me, and I don't like it.

"How are you, Mr. Langford?" she asks a little louder in her schoolteacher tone, but before I can reply, I hear Rosie.

"Ben? Is Ben here?" she asks excitedly and comes walking over with her cane out in front, doing a good job of dodging the chairs and desks around the room.

"Hi, Rosie," I say as she comes up to us, my eyes flicking between Rosie and Em, still concerned with Emily's face. "I was hoping you could read me another few pages of *Cinderella*." Bending down to her level, she reaches out her hand and rests it on my shoulder. She is quiet for a beat before she whispers, "Can I touch your face, Ben?" My eyes flick up to Emily, who looks shocked, and her eyes look a little glassy.

"Sure." I grab her hand from my shoulder and place it on my cheek. Remaining still, her little hand pats my cheek, my nose, my eyebrows, and although she can't see me, I have a feeling she knows exactly what I look like now.

"You have a big nose!" She giggles, breaking the tension. It is a small gesture, but again, my cold heart defrosts a little more. These two women will have me completely melted if I am not careful.

"It is a very handsome nose," I jest, and she laughs again.

"Let's go find *Cinderella*," I say, then take her hand, and we walk toward the reading nook in the corner of the room, but not before I sneak a quick kiss to Emily's cheek. I see her neck blush slightly, and I smirk. But my thoughts are quickly brought back to the discoloration beneath that blush, and it turns my stomach.

After a few pages of *Cinderella*, I sit with Rosie and look around the room. George is helping some of the bigger kids, while Emily is sitting with two smaller boys, reading to them. Her facial expressions are hilarious, and the boys are a giggling mess by the end of the book. The school bells ring, and the noise level in the room increases as each child, including Rosie, starts packing up their things and walking out of the class to be collected from the front office.

As Emily is busy helping the kids out the door, I walk across to George.

"George," I say and extend my hand.

"Can't stay away, huh?" he says with a small sigh and shakes my hand. I begin to help him put the chairs on top of the desks, the whole ordeal reminding me of when I was at school, although the chairs are a lot smaller than I remember.

"I was hoping to take Emily out next weekend, in the city," I say to George. I'm not really asking his permission, but I want to let him know my intentions. That I'm serious about this.

George stops and looks at me, his expression stern. "I'm not sure that is a good idea..."

"I will take good care of her, I promise. You don't have

to worry." I try to make light of it, but his face doesn't even twitch.

He sighs again, and I watch as his gaze moves over to Emily before resting back on me. "I will have Rosie, that's no problem, but just protect her, Ben. Please." I'm confused at his response, but I file that away for another day as Rosie and Emily come back into the room.

"Rosie, Ben has done all our work for us!" Emily says with a little clap. She walks over and curls into my side, and my arm instinctually wraps around her waist as I kiss the top of her head. This is what I like. She fits, she just fits perfectly. She is perfect.

"Thanks, Ben, I hate doing the chairs," Rosie adds, smiling up at us.

"Come on, Rosie, I think I have a lollipop in my office," George says, taking her hand and leading her out of the room.

"So..." Emily starts, a smirk lifting her lips, "you haven't run out the door to another meeting... Is this now a work or personal visit, Mr. Langford?"

"Hmmmm..." I pull her to me and bend down to kiss her. "A little bit of work and a whole lot of personal," I growl as her arms curl around my neck and kiss her gently. Pulling back, I look at her. "Are you sure you are okay, Em?" Searching her face again, my finger traces the small red cut above her eye. It looks sore, a little angry, and like she really hit something hard.

"Yes, I'm sure. Thank you for making sure, though," she says sweetly, but then she's stepping back, letting her hair fall across her face again. I bite my back molars, still not liking this distance she puts between us whenever I broach the subject.

"So, work, tell me what you came to say." Her arms cross in front of her chest, protective mode and sass in full effect.

"Beasley is still keen to buy the school. He is not going to stop, Em, and as his law firm, I need to help him in his business dealings," I tell her regretfully, swallowing roughly.

"And?" she prods, her hip jutting out, starting to get defensive.

"And we will be calling meetings after meetings and throwing everything at it. I want you to know in advance that it is not personal. Michael is the lead on this, but I have to be present. You need to know that anything you say or do while I am around, I will use. I just want to make it clear. Draw a line." My mind flicks to the file that Michael put on my desk this morning. A file of information he has found on Emily. I sat looking at it all morning. He went through his police sources and found out a lot of details about her history, but I left it unopened. I'm not sure I want to delve into her life as thoroughly without her knowledge anymore.

"Okay," she says with a sigh, staring up at me. She doesn't seem to be closing me out, so I take the opportunity.

"But anything not case related..." I say as I walk toward her, my arms grabbing her hips and pulling her close. "I am totally up for." I kiss her again, moving gently, not wanting to hurt her face. She kisses me back, her stance softening as her hands move up to grab my suit jacket and we deepen the kiss.

Pulling away, our lips now only inches apart, I look her in the eyes. "I want you to stay with me next weekend, in the city. I have a charity function that my mother is organizing, and I want you to come with me." I'm not sure what her response will be, what to expect. She remains quiet as her eyebrows pull together. She looks concerned, but hasn't said anything, so I continue. "Michael and my brothers will be there. Plus, a few other business associates. It is a fundraising gala, so it should be fun." Honestly, it will only be fun if she's on my arm.

She still doesn't say anything, but I see her mind ticking over, thinking about it. "I will look after you, Em. I know you don't come to the city much, so we won't stay long, and then we can go back to my place. I will bring you home first thing Sunday if you want me to, so you don't have to be away from home. Oh, and George said he will take Rosie..." I add, trying to get her over the line.

"I don't have anything to wear..." she says in a considered whisper. I exhale a breath, relieved that's the only thing holding her back.

"I will organize it all, so don't worry about that. I will come over and swim with you and Rosie Saturday morning, and then I will bring you to my place and have hair, makeup, and an outfit ready for you." I want to make this as seamless as possible because I also know she hates being away from Rosie.

"Well, it is part of our agreement."

"It is, but how about we do this just for us? I want you to meet my brothers. I want you on my arm," I say before

I swallow, laying out my cards. She has to know this has nothing to do with our arrangement, right?

Her shoulders soften, and she gives me a small smile. One I'll keep with me all day.

"Okay," she agrees as her big eyes gaze up at me. "Just for us."

"Okay," I reply, leaning in, taking her lips with mine and feeling like I have just hit the jackpot.

24

EMILY

I watch my daughter as she sits up straight, ready to try again.

"Siri, call George," she says in a loud, clear voice. My phone is right in front of her on the coffee table as we both sit on the floor in front of it.

Calling George now, the automated voice repeats, and we hear it ringing. She giggles a little at her success. We are usually both tired after a big day at school, but we have been sitting here since we got home, me teaching her how to use the phone, even though it is just past five and I need to start getting dinner ready.

"Hello?" George answers, like it isn't the tenth time we have done this in the last fifteen minutes.

"George, it's me!" Rosie sings, ecstatic that she now has a new skill, her independence growing.

I have been saving for months to buy this phone, my old phone no longer suitable and one Rosie couldn't use. I needed something that she could operate with her voice, and Siri is our latest addition. I tell myself it is in case of emergencies, and it is. But I know Jeremy is our most likely emergency. I should really move back in with George. It is the smart and safer choice. But I don't want to. Losing my independence, losing my sense of self, my identity... No longer Emily Carr, but the woman who constantly needs a protector or someone to hide behind, it makes me feel pathetic. But as frustrating as this is, I'm grateful to have the option all the same.

"Okay, girls, I need to work, and you need to call someone else," George huffs, pretending to be grumpy, when deep down, I know he loves it. But we say goodbye, knowing he is doing the monthly financials for the school.

He is stressed, though. The fire department arrived at the school this morning, because apparently, they received a tip that we were operating without everything up to code. As soon as they arrived, George and I knew what had happened. Beasley is no doubt starting to exert his control, but aside from a few minor defects, we were fine.

"Okay, bye!" Rosie sings into the phone, and George hangs up.

"Who else can we call, Mommy?" Rosie asks, still keen to keep playing. I think about Sarah, but she is having a parent-teacher meeting, and I know Allie is just starting night school for her teaching diploma.

"Oh, I know! Siri, call Ben!" Rosie says, bouncing in her seat.

Calling Ben, the automated voice says.

"No, Rosie. Stop, Siri," I panic because I am sure he is working or busy with something more important.

"Hey, baby," he answers, his swoony voice piercing through the fabric of uncertainty that I was cloaked in moments ago, now leaving me flushed.

"Hi, Ben!" Rosie almost screams in delight, and I hear him laughing through the line.

"Hey, Rosie! What are you up to?" Ben asks, and I imagine him in his office, taking a break from his paperwork.

"Mom is teaching me how to call people on her new phone!" she says in delight.

"Is she now? Well, you can call me anytime you want, okay?"

"Ahhh, you might regret saying that. She has already called George ten times in the last half hour." I slide into their conversation as a smile graces my lips that the two of them get along so well without me.

"Well, I could use the distraction. I'm at my mother's."

"Oh, does she let you use her Siri, Ben?" Rosie asks innocently.

"No, Rosie, she doesn't." He sighs, but then catches himself. He really must have a strained relationship with her. It is sad because I can't imagine not being close to my child.

"How was school today?" he asks, and I can hear people talking in the background.

"Oh, we went to the library today. We met the mayor! And someday, I want to meet the president!" Rosie says with a big smile. She loved learning all about the government today. Mayor Simplot is obviously making time for us in his busy schedule now that he has some serious sucking up to do to George.

"Really? What about the governor?" Ben asks, and I hear the voices behind him getting louder.

"Who is our governor, Ben?" Rosie asks, and I wonder where he is going with this.

"Well, he is right here. Hang on, I will put it on speaker." If I wasn't sitting down, I would fall over.

"Governor Langford, say hello to Emily and Rosie," Ben says, and as Rosie sucks in a breath, my eyes nearly bug out of my head.

"Hello, Emily and Rosie!" Ben's brother says through the phone, and I am lost for words. Good thing Rosie isn't and carries the conversation for both of us.

"Governor! Ben, how do you know the *governor*!" Rosie almost screams in excitement.

"Rosie, Ben's brother is the governor. His name is Governor Langford," I say, trying to get her to calm down, while also smiling at the pure joy on her face.

"I hear you have been spending time with my brother, Rosie. He has told me all about you," Harrison says, and my heart beats faster at the thought.

"He has?" Rosie asks the very question playing on my lips.

"He has. He told me you like reading and painting," Harrison says in what I would imagine is his professional governor voice, and I wonder what is going on.

"Boys! Who are you talking to! Get in here!" I hear a woman shriek from the background, and it is enough to have both Rosie and I rearing back.

"Sorry, Rosie, I need to go. My mom is yelling at me," I hear Ben's voice lower in a mix of jest and anger as he takes us off speaker.

"Wow. She sounds really mad. Do you want to come over here for dinner instead?" Rosie whispers.

"Rosie, I am sure Ben has lots to do tonight," I interject.

"I would love to, if that's alright with you, Em?" he asks, and even though he can't see me, I am smiling.

"Of course! See you soon," I offer, now mentally thinking about what I have here to cook.

"Great, see you in a bit," Ben says quickly before ending the call, and I look down at Rosie.

"Wow. I just met the governor..." Rosie whispers, the events of the last five minutes rendering her silent.

"He sounded nice." I have no other words. Why would Ben introduce his fake fiancée and her daughter to his brother? Never mind the fact that he's told him all about us? And what kind of woman screams at her grown children like that?

I AM JUST TURNING off the stove, having found the ingredients for a large Bolognese and whipped it together with the fresh herbs that my neighbor offered me yesterday. The whole apartment smells delicious.

There is a knock at the door. My heart jumps and I stand still, my body unmoving, until I hear a knock again.

"Is that Ben?" Rosie asks tentatively from where she is in the living room.

"Rosie," I hiss quietly. "Go hide." I help her into her room. The sane part of my brain tells me it is Ben, but my flight-or-fight is flaring. I need to take every precaution. I can't be flippant with my safety like I was before.

"Be careful, Mommy," she whispers as I hand her my phone, and she hides in her spot under her bed. We practiced this, talked about what we should do. It is part of the reason I got the phone and have been teaching her how to use it.

I hate this. Fear consumes us both. Our cortisol levels peak so much that I am a jittering mess all the time. The fact that my daughter has a hiding spot is soul-crushing. Another knock sounds, and I close her bedroom door to walk toward the entrance.

"Who is it?" I yell as I grab a chair, ready to put it in front of the door. I installed an extra lock and two more chains after Jeremy's visit, but I didn't get a chance to putty the small hole in the wall. That is something that I need to fix this weekend.

"It's Ben." I hear his voice, and my shoulders immediately lower as I clutch my chest in relief.

"Rosie, it is Ben; you can come out," I yell to her as I go to the door and start unlocking it.

I hear Rosie come out of her bedroom just as I open the front door.

"Hi!" I say, my hands still shaky as I wipe them awkwardly down my thighs, trying to get myself under control as relief sweeps through my body at seeing him. I smile easily, already feeling better.

"Hey... sorry. I'm later than I hoped," Ben murmurs, looking stressed, running his hands through his hair before he looks at me. His face relaxes when he does, and he walks straight to me, his hand curling around my waist and pulling me to him.

"It's okay. I just finished dinner, so you're right on time." Smiling up at him, he hums, holding me tighter.

"It's so good to see you, baby," he murmurs quietly, putting his lips on mine, and I sink into his hold, never wanting to leave. We pull apart slowly, the promise of food probably the only real motivation we have to move. And I step back to let him inside, and as soon as the door closes behind us, he exhales heavily, like the weight of the world is on his shoulders.

"Are you alright?" I ask, because he still looks super stressed.

"It's been a long day, but I'm glad I am here. I needed to see my fake fiancée tonight," he offers with a cheeky grin, wrapping his hands around my middle again now that we are safely inside. I melt into his body, leaning on him, feeling protected. As he takes a deep breath, I feel the stress of the day leave him in an instant. Likewise, I relax into him, comforted by the fact that he is here.

"Oh, I almost forgot I brought you these," he says, pulling a small packet from his pocket.

"What is it?" I ask, confused.

"Earplugs for when you do music with the kids next." He winks, and I snort a laugh.

"Thanks, although I don't think they will block out much," I say, laughing, looking at the tiny foam earplugs that squish in my hands before forming again. It is sweet he buys me these little gifts like this, many not more than a few dollars, something that is small change to a man like Ben, yet they always have meaning. Something I don't miss.

"Hi, Ben!" Rosie says from where she is standing in the living room. We pull apart, and Ben walks over to her, grabbing her hand.

"Ben, is your brother really the governor?" Rosie asks him, and I am relieved that her mind has already moved on from what we just practiced. Mine, on the other hand, will take me a little longer.

I leave them chatting while I get dinner organized and set the table. I don't often cook large meals because Rosie and I generally don't eat a lot. Aside from George, I haven't cooked for another man in a long time, and I am a bit nervous for Ben to enjoy it.

As I get everything ready, I observe him and Rosie for a beat. The two of them are sitting on the sofa as Rosie shows him how she uses the new phone. They call George two more times together as Ben watches her intently, concern etched into his brow before he breaks into a huge grin from seeing her so happy.

"Dinner is ready!" I call out to them, and Rosie is quick to stand, grabbing her small cane and making her way to the table. That is the other thing I am currently saving for. Her cane is great, but it's getting a little small as she grows, and it got damaged a few months ago in the door of the bus, the bottom half of it now encased in thick tape to keep it together.

"Smells delicious," Ben says, coming to stand in front of me, his hands resting on my hips.

"I hope you are hungry," I offer, looking over the spread I have made. Fresh bread, cheeses, and the Bolognese, something you would probably see in a small Italian town—although I am sure not quite as tasty.

"When it comes to you, baby, I am always hungry," he murmurs before leaning down and kissing me quickly, a small smirk playing on his lips. It feels natural. Like this is my life. I welcome it, even though I know I shouldn't. The lines of our agreement are now so blurred, I am not sure what is real and what is fake.

"Ben, come and sit next to me!" Rosie says from the table, and I help get her settled, Ben taking up the seat at the end, us two girls on either side of him.

"The firemen came to school today!" she says enthusiastically as we all eat our meals.

Ben's eyes flick to me in question.

"Firemen? Was there a fire today?" he asks, his forehead creasing.

"No. Apparently, they received a tip that we were operating facilities that didn't meet the code," I explain, my eyebrows raising in a sarcastic manner, and I watch his face as the penny drops.

"Beasley?" he mutters in question.

"No doubt," is all I say, before I move the topic to safer waters. We haven't received any more meeting demands yet, and for that, I am thankful. But I am not stupid, and Ben has already made it clear how this will go. I know Beasley has something up his sleeve; I am just waiting for him to show his cards.

"What happened to your wall?" Ben asks, again with concern etched into his face, looking at the door handle-sized hole in the plaster.

"Oh, I just threw the door open a little too quickly the

other day." I smile, taking a sip of my drink at the same time, shielding my face from his eyes. I hate lying to him. Weeks ago, the lies flew off my tongue no problem, but now things are different. They leave a bad taste in my mouth, one that is hard to remove.

Rosie remains quiet as she twirls her pasta, finishing her bowl. I didn't tell her what happened, but I am sure she knows. She may not have her sight, but her hearing is impeccable, and George and I have been speaking about it all at length this past week as he tried to get me to move back into his place, rather than be here on my own.

"Finished, Mom!" Rosie says, just as Ben and I both finish too.

"Rosie, why don't you go and get ready for bed," I suggest since it's getting late, and Rosie stands, grabbing her cane and walking to her room. Ben sits for a moment, watching her before standing to help me clear the table.

"She is incredible. You are such a great mom," he states softly, and I pause as I rinse the dishes. It has been a long time since anyone has said those words to me. Glenda was the last person, saying the same to me on her death bed. It was the last time we spoke.

"She is the best daughter a mom could ask for." Rosie is as resilient as they come. "Nothing is too hard for her. Just like the phone this afternoon, she keeps trying and trying until she gets it. She works harder than any other kids her own age. Although I may be biased," I add, smiling. When I look at him, he's frowning, seemingly lost in his thoughts. And I think I know why.

"Have you ever gotten along with your mother?" I ask, trying not to pry, but I can't help it.

"She is just all about appearances. She has us four boys, but she is not concerned with our happiness or welfare, just how we look to the outside world," he says, taking a deep breath.

"I have learned a lot through Rosie. When you don't have vision, there is so much more to be grateful for. What other people think is really not what is important." He nods, leaning over and pressing a kiss to my cheek.

"How did she lose her sight?" Ben asks as he wipes down the counter while I finish the last two dishes. Bile rises in my throat as I think back to that night in Jeremy's office. I remember it vividly. Me at seven months pregnant. I was slow to show, so my belly had only bloomed a few weeks before. I remember waddling into Jeremy's office that night, thinking I would surprise him. When I opened the door and saw him having sex with a woman who wasn't me on his desk, the only thing I could think to do was run. My heart starts racing as I recall that night like I am living it again. Jeremy chasing me, me running to the stairwell, not wanting to wait for the elevator. Him pushing through the door after me, yelling at me for being fat and stupid or some other cruel words to that effect before I felt his hand on my shoulder. I even remember freezing, waiting for the pain that usually happens when he grabs me, but this time, there was nothing. He pushed instead, and I flew down the flight of stairs, landing directly on my belly. The vivid pain I felt before I fell unconscious is not something I will ever forget.

"She was born blind. She has never had sight," I say quietly, deep in thought, scrubbing the dish in hand harder, even though it's already clean. Ben's arms circle around me, pulling me to his body. I lean on him, comforted by his warm touch. The heavy feeling outweighs any ability I have of keeping a straight spine, and I take a few deep breaths and pull myself together.

"You are amazing," he whispers, kissing my neck, then my jaw, before his hand grips my chin and he turns my head to face him. "The most amazing woman I have ever met." I want to cry, but with happiness this time. I know he means what he says, I can tell by the look in his eyes. I am falling for him harder and harder every time we are together.

"Ben! Can you read me a bedtime story?" Rosie yells from her room where she stands in her pajamas at the door.

I smile then, and Ben laughs. "Go, there's only one dish left, and she will be asleep before the first chapter ends." Rosie has had enough activity tonight to have her sleeping for days.

"I won't be long," he says, kissing me on the lips quickly and stepping away, then walking to my daughter as I watch from the kitchen. She slips into bed, the small night-light on, and Ben sits next to her, perched on a small pink chair, looking like a giant in comparison as he begins to read her the story of *Beauty and the Beast*.

As predicted, Rosie is fast asleep before the first chapter is over, and I sneak in, kissing her good night, then switch off the lights and turn on her sleep music.

As I close her door, I notice Ben watching me intently from the living room.

"She sleeps with music on?" Ben asks as I make my way to the sofa and sit next to him.

"Because she was born blind, her circadian rhythm is a bit off, meaning she doesn't sleep as well as we do, often waking at all hours of the night. The music is on a timer and stays on all night until she is due to wake up. So when she wakes in the middle of the night, if she can hear the music, she knows it is still dark and sleep time. It also helps her to have a deeper sleep, keeping her mind from wandering."

Ben nods, again the crumple in his eyebrows telling me he has more questions.

"The first day I came into the classroom, I helped Rosie with some painting. She painted her family. Just you and her," he says, and I nod, not sure where he is going with this.

"It's just us, Ben. It has been for a long time." I answer as best I can without the whole horrid story coming out.

"She mentioned her father was abusive," Ben continues, and my world starts spinning. I sit stunned for a moment before I swallow and try to find the words. I had no idea Rosie spoke like that. As Ben looks at me, I see his jaw clenching, and his hands grip each other in front of him.

"Like I said. It is just us, and it has been that way for a long time," I say again, the response rolling off my tongue automatically. My heart is racing, and I feel the tears starting to well. I want to tell him. I want to tell him everything. I think about George's advice, about maybe getting Ben's help with it all, but I need to take care of this situation myself. I can't drag him into it. I just want to enjoy him, enjoy us, for however long it will last. He nods, but I can tell it bothers him that I'm not being more open.

"Come here," he says, his demanding nature coming out, and I raise an eyebrow.

"Get your sweet ass over here, baby. I want you on my lap." His frown turns into a smirk, and my body moves over the sofa all on its own. Hands landing on my waist, he pulls me up like I weigh nothing and plants me on his lap. Facing him, my legs fall on either side, the skirt I am wearing sliding up my thighs a little.

"It has been too long since I had my hands on you," he murmurs, his large hands grabbing and molding to my ass, pulling me to him so I can feel him hard underneath me. My body reacts instantly, my shoulders lowering from my ears as I let out a breath I had no idea I had been holding. I feel feminine, flirty, and sexy in his embrace. No longer the tired single mom, but a woman.

"Does everyone always do as you ask?" I quiz him, knowing that he is a man who always gets exactly what he wants.

"Always. Want to test that theory? Because there is something I want right now..." His eyebrow quirks in a challenge.

"Sure. What do you want?" I ask playfully as one of his hands moves from my hips up my waist, sliding up my side, following my curves until he finds my breast, and he brushes his thumb across my nipple, before moving his hand farther up to cup my chin. Even fully dressed, his light touch makes me shiver.

"I want my lips on yours," he groans, his eyes full of lust, while his other hand grips my ass even tighter.

"You do, huh?" I bite my lip to tease him, leaning just out of reach.

"Come here," he whispers, pulling my face toward him and encasing my waist until there's no space between us. I moan at the feel of him beneath me, my lips meeting his like they're magnetized.

His mouth moves against mine slowly, like he is taking his time, discovering me all over again. The agreement we have in place and the situation we find ourselves in outside of these four walls is now nonexistent. We are just two people finding each other, getting to know each other, devouring each other.

I open to him, white-knuckling his shirt as his tongue meshes with mine, his grip on me remaining strong. Feeling secure, my body leans on him, then he pulls back slightly, leaning back into the sofa. With his head relaxed, his eyes fixate on mine, hands moving up and down my bare thighs. My skin tingles with every pass as anticipation builds between us. I feel heat at my core, along with his throbbing length beneath his zipper, pushing against me.

"You're so beautiful," he moans, his hands coming farther and farther up to my skirt, until he pushes it all the way up, bunching it around my waist. I should feel exposed, my red thong not really hiding anything, but his hands roam all over my ass and down my thighs and back again. He moves a little underneath me, his pants now fully tenting, my underwear doing little to hide my arousal.

"Ben..." I whisper in warning, my eyes flicking to Rosie's door.

"Can you be quiet? Because I really need to touch you right now," he grits out, and I bite my bottom lip and give him a nod. Rosie's door is closed, her music is on, and she is already out cold. But this is the first time I have had a man in my home like this while Rosie is home.

Before my mind can continue down that rabbit hole, I feel Ben. His hands glide up my inner thigh, his thumb brushing against the pitiful amount of lace covering me. He moans when he feels how turned on I am already.

"You are so wet for me, Em, so perfect." I whimper when he rubs lightly, and at the sounds, his other hand delves into my hair at the nape of my neck to pull me back to him. Our tongues tangle then, the slow and sultry now over, and diving straight into the deep end as we devour each other.

My lips part with a sharp inhale as his hand slides under the lace, his finger circling my clit in tender strokes. It only takes a moment for me to be writhing on top of him, our shared breaths becoming more like pants.

"God, I want you so bad, baby," he whispers against my lips as his finger pushes inside before pulling out again, then swirling around my clit over and over, spreading the wetness before repeating the action with a mastered stroke.

"That feels... so good..." I moan, my voice shaky as I grind down on his touch. Our foreheads meet as we come up for air, pausing our kiss for a moment to look at each other instead. It is like we are the only people in the world. It always feels like that with him.

"I wish you could see yourself right now. So goddamn sexy, out of breath, and taking your pleasure from my hand. You're soaking me, baby." I move faster from just the sound of his voice, never mind his words. He moans, jolting a little underneath me; he is extremely hard, his length digging into my leg from beneath his pants. I can't wait to have him inside me again.

"Faster, Ben. I need more... I want you... Please, please, give me more," I almost beg, not even finishing a full thought, as my hips move at a wanton pace against his hand.

His other hand moves down my spine, then he splays it on my lower back, guiding my hips for me and pulling me closer.

"I'll give you more when you come for me," he whispers, looking right into my eyes.

"Ben... Ben..." I pant out, so close to the edge. I have never felt this needy in my entire life.

"That's it, baby, take what you need. Come for me." My head falls back as tingles rush up my spine and down my legs as my body listens to his command.

"Ben!" I whisper-shout, as his free hand races up and cups my face. I whimper, sucking on his thumb as it brushes over my lips, the move stifling my moans as I bite him a little before falling against his chest.

And with one curl of his fingers inside me, my whole body starts to shudder, almost convulsing as my hips barely continue to move on their own. My orgasm is so powerful, I am almost seeing black dots, my hearing just a hum as I catch my breath and tremble back down to earth. I don't even adjust myself when he slowly removes his hand from my center; I just let out a little whine from the new emptiness.

I hear him chuckle then, as he runs his hand up and down my back, and I sit back up, feeling extremely relaxed. Almost drunk on what he just did to me.

"You okay there?" he asks, pushing my hair back from my face.

"So good," I say with a smile, one that I know I am going to find very hard to remove.

"So now you know it's true..." he says, his hands still roaming over my body. It is like he can't get enough, not that I'm complaining.

"What's true?" I ask, tilting my head as I look down at his smirk.

"That I always get what I want." The look on his handsome face is devilish. He knows he is pushing my buttons, that I am not one to back away from a challenge.

"It seems that you do." I laugh, smoothing my hands up his chest as his move up and down my bare thighs.

"You know what else I want?" he murmurs as his thumb skirts up the inside of my thigh and brushes against my center again, making me twitch.

"What else?" I say, altogether too breathily, not able to help the fact that my body feels like liquid around him. My hands move down his chest, feeling every chiseled muscle beneath my palms, only stopping when they reach his belt buckle.

"I want you on your knees, with your mouth open wide, showing me exactly what that smart, sassy mouth of yours can do." I bite my bottom lip so I don't drool at his demand. He watches me carefully, no doubt wondering if I will comply or slap him. He knows I don't take orders from anyone, yet for him, I'm ready to slide down onto my knees easily without any hesitation. The thought of tasting him is now the only thing on my mind. I almost crave it. I want to watch him come undone at my touch.

I want to see him unravel.

25

BEN

There is a lot about Em I like. Whether she is a dowdy schoolteacher making kids smile, a spitfire sass in the boardroom, or a whimpering mess underneath me, I'll take any version in stride. But right here, right now, this flushed, panting, moaning woman is by far my favorite.

"Are you sure you can handle me?" she asks with a quirked brow as I watch her sink down onto the floor. My heart rate increases, seeing her on her knees in front of me, her blue eyes staring up into mine. I want to grab her, maul her, maneuver her in any which way I can have her. My desire for this woman is insatiable. But I refrain, sitting still and letting her lead, my hands clenching beside me to stop me from taking over.

"That's the smart, sassy mouth I was talking about," I grit out, her hands making quick work of my belt before opening my suit pants and pulling out my cock.

I hiss a little as she touches me. I'm already so turned on from watching her come, my length throbs in her grip.

She leans forward then, a vision of sensuality, flattening her tongue and licking me from the base to the tip. Swiping up a drop of arousal, she rolls her tongue around, then sucks me into her mouth.

"Shit... that feels too good," I groan, my hands shooting up to my thighs, itching to touch her.

"Hands back by your sides, Ben. You had your fun, now let me have mine," she says smoothly, smirking as she presses a kiss to my tip with her eyes glued to mine. Reluctantly, I let my hands slip back to my sides, and she lowers her head again, our eyes not leaving each other's as she puts my tip back into her mouth. Swirling her tongue, she releases me with a pop, then goes back to dragging her tongue up and down again and again. Her light, wet caresses have my cock twitching.

"You're teasing me," I grit out, my eyes glued to her mouth and her bright blues. They shine with mischief, right before she takes me all the way to the back of her throat.

"Mmmmm," is all she replies, as I'm left groaning like I've never had a blow job before. I keep my voice down, just barely, as her delicate hand wrapped around me moves in tandem with her mouth.

"Fuck," I breathe out, trying with every ounce of my restraint to stay quiet, my hands now gripping into the sofa. I watch as she works me over, hypnotized, wondering how the hell I found her and what I need to do to keep her.

The vibrations from her response run down my cock and up my spine.

"Baby, you are so good at that. So goddamn good. You

look so pretty with my cock down your throat." I'm barely hanging on to my sanity, my need to hold her, grab her, thrust up into her, is all-encompassing. I am needy as fuck, and it scares me, because I have never given up control like this.

She takes me impossibly deeper then, sucking me down with more swirls of that vicious tongue. My body feels hot all over as I suppress a curse, my grip on the sofa now white-knuckled. If I wasn't already sitting, I am sure I would have fallen over.

"*Fuck*. You like making me crazy, hmm? You're gonna make me come if you keep that up." I feel her moan around my length in response, her teary eyes flicking up to mine again. When her lips try to smile, stuffed full of me, my balls tighten, ready to explode. My eyes remain glued to the best fucking show in town as my dream woman treats me to pleasure like no other.

"Baby, I'm coming…" I warn her, almost ripping the material from the sofa as she teases me and changes her pace in a way that sends me straight into heaven. I bite my bottom lip to prevent myself from yelling the apartment building down as I let go, deep in her throat, a growl, low and animalistic, rumbling from my chest as she wrings me dry. Her mouth is still an instrument of magic as she pulls back and swallows, tenderly licking me again as I slowly find my bearings.

"God, where have you been all my life?" I ask in awe, looking at her as she sits back with a cheeky smile lighting up her face. I don't hesitate to grab her hand and bring her up onto my lap.

She chuckles as she relaxes into my hold, and I tilt her lips to mine.

"You want to stay tonight?" she asks me quietly, our faces only an inch apart. My eyes roam hers, and my smile is immediate.

"I can't think of anywhere else I want to be."

Before she gets too comfortable, I stand, keeping her against me.

"Whoa, I can walk," she says, her hands gripping on to my neck, scared to fall, but what she doesn't seem to realize yet is that I will never let her go. I will always catch her.

"Let's take a shower, and then we can watch a movie. I brought snacks," I say, smiling at the range of candy I have stuffed in my briefcase.

"Snacks?" she questions as I walk through her bedroom door, closing it softly behind us.

"Yes, snacks, although I prefer to eat you, but I figured I can do that later tonight..." I murmur, placing her on her feet in the bathroom. She laughs lightly, a flush taking over her cheeks, but no denial in sight. Grabbing her top I pull it over her head, then I lower her skirt to the floor.

She reaches forward and pulls my pants down, and I make quick work of my shirt as she turns on her shower. I forgot how small it is compared to mine, but we both fit with ease. My hands are magnetized to her body as they roam her curves, grabbing the soap and lathering it over her skin.

"Oh, your hands are magic," she says on a sigh, leaning her head back under the water. It flows down her hair as I massage her breasts and then lower my hands down her body.

"My hands like feeling every inch of you. Turn around," I say, taking every opportunity to do exactly that. I want nothing undiscovered.

She gives me her back, and I grab her hair, putting it over one shoulder and lathering her smooth skin, giving her shoulders a massage at the same time. I've never been one to share showers before. I don't find showering particularly relaxing, preferring to be in and out quickly, but I do not want to move from this spot. Between the hot water, the steam, and her beautiful body, I already feel my cock twitch again. So, I have no intention of leaving anytime soon.

"My turn." She faces me, grabbing the soap from my hands and starting with my chest before wandering down my torso. I watch the water drip off her breasts, and as her hands lower farther down my body, I feel her grab my cock. Leaning down, I suck her nipple into my mouth.

"Ben…" Her breathy plea is meant to be a warning, but she continues to run her hand up and down my cock, which is growing harder by the second, so I don't stop either.

"If you want to pump my cock, baby, then I'm going to need to feel you too. You had your way with me on the sofa, and now I am itching to taste and touch you everywhere I can reach." I'm lost in the delicate skin of her breasts, not bothering to come up for air.

Her fist tightens around me, and my hand wraps around her waist, keeping her close. I step her backward until her back hits the wall, caged in by my body. The tiles are cold and her nipple peaks even more between my lips. I bite it a little, hearing her gasp at the contact, before I suck it fully into my mouth, and she moans.

"I want to fuck you against this wall," I murmur against her, my cock ramrod straight in her hand.

"Yes, please," she moans sweetly as my lips travel up her neck, causing her head to lean back, exposing her neck to me.

"I don't have a condom," I whisper in her ear, annoyed with myself for not putting one in my suit pocket.

"I'm on the pill. And I'm clean." I pull away and look down at her. Is she serious?

"Me too. I get checked regularly. Are you sure?" I ask again, my heart racing at the thought. Going bare with Em will be my undoing. I just know it.

"Yes, I'm sure. I need you inside me," she begs a little as I press kisses to her neck, making my way back to her lips. My hands drift to her backside, and I lift her up effortlessly, positioning her onto me as her legs circle my waist. I slowly ease inside her, and my eyes almost roll to the back of my head at the feeling. If I knew showers could be this good, I would have spent way more time in them.

"Holy shit, Ben. You feel..." Em moans, her voice lost as I thrust deep, holding there for a second for her to adjust. "God, you feel so good."

She's right; I fill her up perfectly. I've never felt anything like this before—also never not used protection before. And with this new sensation, feeling her as I'm meant to, no condom in our way, I'm a goner.

"So fucking sweet. You're gonna make me an addict for this pussy, baby." Pulling back, I begin thrusting and grinding into her, deeper and harder, feeling all of her. Her breasts bounce in front of me with every pounding movement, and I lower my head again, sucking on her nipple as her hands wrap around my head, hanging on tight.

"You look so good at the mercy of my cock. I want to do this in the morning too. Can we do this every fucking day, baby?" I groan. I don't know whether it is the water running down her body, the fact that I am bare, or if Emily has some magic hold on me, but I never want this to end.

"Every day. I vote for every day," she pants out, and I feel my balls tighten just as her body starts to squirm and she arches her back.

"Oh, Ben... Don't stop," she commands on a moan, biting her lip so she's as quiet as possible.

Just the look of her succumbing to pleasure pushes me over the edge, and I come right along with her, my hands gripping her ass so tight, her flesh molds against my palms. I grind my teeth, wanting to shout the roof off this bathroom, but refrain as I sink deep inside of her one last time, giving her my everything.

It is then I know. This woman has ruined me for all others.

26

BEN

After my second trip on a bus in a matter of weeks, I now find myself in the darkened aquarium, illuminated water and fish swimming overhead. It would be serene any other time, but at the moment, all I can hear are kids laughing and yelling over the top of each other, amazed at the large shark circling us. But my eyes are not on the shark, but rather they are glued to Rosie, who is standing close to her mother, who leans over and whispers to her constantly.

I tune my ears, trying to hear them, and realize that Em is describing everything she sees. From the colors, each fish, coral, bubbles, and even what some of the other kids are doing. Rosie is still as she listens intently; she looks happy, but she isn't herself. Her posture is not as straight, her smile not as wide.

"You okay, Gavin?" I look beside me to see him slumped in a wheelchair, looking like he would rather be anywhere else.

"I just want to get out of this thing," he bites out,

clearly not happy that he needs to be wheeled around. Given the distance around this place, there was no way he could maneuver it all with just his walking stick. My eyes wander over the chair, one that the aquarium provided. It looks uncomfortable, takes up a lot of room, and I have no doubt that it is decades old. I grit my teeth. *I wonder what these things cost...*

Then I notice Michael, the deaf boy, tapping Em's shoulder, grabbing her attention, before signing something to her. Em turns toward him a little and signs back, speaking the words she signs at the same time, Rosie nodding along on her other side at whatever they are saying.

Meanwhile, my cell phone continues to vibrate in my pocket. Work, my brothers, Sasha, all calling me as it is a regular workday, although my environment couldn't be further from my office if I tried.

I ignore the vibrations as I watch over the group, feeling unsettled. I have a million other places to be today, but I promised Em that I would support the school excursion as part of our agreement. The thought leaves a bad taste in my mouth; the agreement now so blurred, I don't even know what is real and what is fake anymore.

My eyes flick to a shark swimming overhead, next to it a smaller version, a baby, the two gliding through the water close together, looking lonely yet having each other. They swim an entire loop of the large tank before starting over again, never wavering from each other's sides.

A flash to my left grabs my attention, and I groan to myself when I see a photog. I have no idea how he knew I was here or how he got inside. But luckily, a staff member also sees him and tells him to delete the photo and leave or they'll confiscate his camera at the front desk. He slinks off begrudgingly, but it has me on edge. They have been following me more and more, our engagement now nearly top gossip news. Thank God they haven't found Em yet, but I have had to increase the security around my penthouse and estate, and I have had to take a few different ways to Em's house to lose a tail. I also have a security team already organized to drop on Em if I need to. I don't want her life disrupted, not because of me. I need her and Rosie safe and not worried or stressed about fucking paparazzi chasing them home from school.

I make my way to the other side of the group to where my girls are, needing to be beside them.

"Rosie, let me help you," I say, just as my hand encases her small waist, and I pick her up, placing her on my hip. Her small body is so light, it is as if I am holding a doll. Taking over from Em, she presses a chaste kiss to my cheek before attending to another student beside her. I tell Rosie all about the sharks and then comically describe the human diver who just appeared to feed them, explaining what they are eating and how it all occurs.

"Ben, won't the shark eat the diver?" Rosie asks innocently, yet it is a good question.

"No, the food he is holding is much tastier. The shark knows what he wants to eat, and it isn't a human. He prefers a different diet," I tell her, my eyes watching for anything else I might not have detailed yet. I am now looking at everything with fresh eyes, not wanting to miss even the smallest thing. The colors are vibrant, the world shining with a new glow as I take in every inch of our surroundings that I would usually take for granted.

Glancing over at Em, I watch her for a beat as she maneuvers Gavin's chair to get a better view while signing something to Michael at the same time. Her multitasking skills are above anyone else's.

"Your mom works too hard," I mumble to Rosie, who is now comfortable in my arms and leaning her head against my shoulder.

"I know." Rosie sighs. "Grandpa George tells her all the time. Is her sore eye better now, Ben?" Rosie asks in her soft voice, and my jaw clenches as I think about that small bruise still lingering near Em's temple.

"She looks amazing as always, Rosie. How did she get it anyway?" Em has brushed me off each and every time I have asked, so maybe Rosie will give me more information.

"When I stayed at Grandpa George's, she got it. I heard him on the phone to Mommy that night when he thought I was asleep. He wanted to take her to the hospital, but she wouldn't let him." My body stiffens.

"I'm glad Grandpa George is looking after her." I try to keep my tone light, not wanting Rosie to think anything is wrong.

"Do you think Mommy is beautiful, Ben?" Well, I guess our conversation is taking a slight turn.

"Very beautiful. The most beautiful woman I have ever met," I say, smiling as my gaze finds Em again.

"I think she likes you too." Rosie giggles, almost like she can sense I'm staring at her mother.

"Really? What makes you say that?" I ask, amused as a little smirk pulls on her lips.

"She laughs more. Her cooking is better, and she sprays a lot more perfume before you visit." I huff out a laugh at that.

"Well, I'm glad I can help with the better cooking, and your mom always smells amazing, Rosie." Lavender will never be the same again. "Do you like me spending time with you and your mom?" I decide to ask, curious to know if I have her approval. And a bit nervous I might not for some reason.

"Yes! And don't tell Mommy, but you are way better at reading *Cinderella* than her. Plus, I have more fun swimming with you too," Rosie says in an excited tone, and my pulse rate slows back to normal, relief settling over me. As I hold her in my arms, I start to think whether this could be my life. Kids, excursions, work in the city, Em and Rosie to come home to. I have never given a relationship much thought before, especially after Sasha, but I can see it. And I like what I see.

"Time to move, class. This way," George says in his *I mean business* voice and all the kids turn their attention from the tanks. I put Rosie down, but keep hold of her hand, and she grips her cane in the other. The cane looks old, held together by tape, and almost too small for her. It's upsetting to me. Where the hell is her father, and why doesn't he contribute to her needs?

Em pushes Gavin in his chair, and I can tell it is hard for her as she's using her whole body to do it. Gavin's not a small boy by any stretch of the imagination.

"Here, let me," I offer, passing Rosie over to Em. As I

give it a push, it's definitely not as easy as it looks, so I'm glad Em doesn't argue. Instead, she smiles my way, mouthing, "Thank you." I give her a smirk and a wink, watching her face soften even more, before Michael pulls on her sleeve and they start signing again.

"Right, we are going to head up to level one to see the starfish pond," George says, pulling my attention, and a few of the kids giggle and gasp. Clearly, the starfish pond is a highlight. "Gavin, Rosie, and Michael, you go with Miss Carr and Mr. Langford in the elevator, the rest, please follow me." He takes them up a flight of stairs with a few other parent helpers, and I hear Gavin huff from where he is sitting in front of me.

"How are you doing there, Gavin?" I ask as I look down at him, wishing I could help him somehow.

"Fine." He waves me off, and I let him be. There's got to be a better way for him to get around. Being wheel-chair bound must be frustrating, especially when he's still able to move around a bit without one.

My eyes flick to Rosie, and I watch her take a few tentative steps forward with her cane, touching the braille panel next to the lifts. The confident child I have seen previously is no longer there, and in her place is a shy, scared young girl.

"What are you reading, Rosie?"

"It's telling me that we are on ground level, and that on level one is where the fish are," she whispers.

"I can't believe it tells you all that with those dots," I say, mesmerized by the situation. I look at the dots on the silver panel, noticing it's scratched and dented, with no care taken for something so important. I swallow the tension rising in my body as I think about my own building... I'm not even sure we have braille panels. That needs to change, along with accessibility. I am sure we have the minimum requirements, but that doesn't mean the minimum is what we should have. I make a mental note to talk to my brothers about some changes.

The elevator arrives, and we all pile in. Gavin's chair is hard to maneuver, so much so, we end up facing the back wall, with Em, Rosie, and Michael all standing to the side next to us. The kids chat happily as the elevator moves at a snail's pace up to the next floor.

"So how many work calls have you ignored already this morning?" Em asks, a small smile on her face as she looks up at me.

"About a hundred," I joke, even though it feels like it. My leg is permanently vibrating due to my phone.

"Thank you for coming. We would have had to cancel the trip if you couldn't make it," she says, and I see the first signs of exhaustion on her face.

Understanding washes over me at exactly how difficult it is for parents to bring their kids out to simple places like this when they have impairments, whether it's their vision, hearing, or something else. George is here, as are a few parents and caretakers, yet I have been run off my feet, helping kids walk, eat, and find their way around. I even took Gavin to the bathroom in this chair, which was a full job unto itself.

My need to touch her overrides my sensibilities at the moment, so I grab her hand, pulling her to me.

"Ben..." She gives me a warning, her eyes flicking to the kids, who are all too enthralled in talking about whether they are going to touch a starfish or not to bother noticing us.

"Get used to it, Em. It has been at least thirty minutes since I've had my hands on you. That is way too long in my book," I say, bringing my lips to her forehead and kissing her quickly.

She huffs out a small laugh as her arms curl around my waist and she tucks into my side.

"You make me laugh." Shaking her head with a smile, the elevator comes to a stop at our floor.

"The sound of your laugh is almost as good as hearing you moan," I whisper with a wicked grin. That has her eyes snapping up to mine as she slaps my chest playfully, her cheeks pinkening.

If I get the chance to make her laugh a little every day, then all would be okay in my world.

27

EMILY

I stalk to the classroom like I am on fire and stop so suddenly, I almost slip and fall to the floor. Sadness sweeps through me as George and I take in the damage.

"It is all gone. Everything is now worthless." He pushes a chair out of the way, resigned as we look at the destruction left behind. George got a call early this morning from our volunteer cleaner. She arrived on-site at six a.m. to clean the bathrooms and walked into my classroom to see it flooded, water knee-deep after a broken water pipe. The front offices are the only rooms that escaped damage.

I worked hard to make my classroom a welcoming space, where the kids could come and not only learn and be with each other, but to find solace in their life when they can't find it anywhere else. It was where I worked with Glenda. The room was hers before she died and I took over entirely. All memories of her are now washed down the hall, and that makes my chest ache.

"I don't understand…" I say in a whisper, my eyes glassy to the point it is hard to see. It is eerily quiet as we stand here alone and defeated. We canceled school today, and Rosie is spending the day with Allie while I help George with the mess.

I stroll around the wet classroom, looking over the disaster zone. The fire department just left, having been here for the past few hours, fixing the pipe and cleaning the water away. Now all that is left are the mushy books, lifting cheap linoleum flooring, walls blackened by water marks, and my drenched files. Mud, slush, and debris is everywhere we look.

None of that matters in comparison to seeing all of Rosie's braille books and art paper damaged. Ruined, no longer usable. The kids' workbooks, special art supplies, the phonics and decodable readers for my dyslexic children, and the custom signing chart I had made for the entire class to start learning more about how to support Michael… all of it is gone.

"They want the land. They will stop at nothing," George spits out. He is angry, and I don't blame him. The fire department was pretty clear that the pipe had been tampered with and it doesn't take a genius to figure out who would be responsible. But with no proof, we just have to live with the damage, not able to recoup a thing or hold anyone responsible.

"But look at Rosie's books!" Tears run over onto my cheeks, as I can't hold them back. These things cost money. A lot of money. Many took me hours to source, create, and develop. Not to mention, the time and stress to apply for grants and funding. I feel at a total loss.

I look down, seeing Rosie's new braille pen on the floor, now broken. It took me forever to save for it. Something I really wanted her to have and start using. While she has some books and things at home, we kept most of her collection here.

And now most of it is gone.

My phone rings, and grabbing it, I see that it is Ben. I decline his call. My heart is shattered. He is the last person I want to speak to right now, but also the only one. The need I have to melt into his embrace is startling. Yet he is the enemy. Not that any of this is his fault. He would never condone this, I know that. But as my sadness gives way to fury, and he and his clients are where I am directing my rath.

Neanderthal: Pick you up at 7, Em?

His text comes through, and I stare at it through my tears. We have a date night planned for tonight. No doubt dinner somewhere swanky, so he can parade me around in front of all the people in his network. I have enjoyed our dates, getting to know each other more and more, but as my eyes flick around the room again, I know there is no way I can make it tonight. This mess will take all day to get cleaned up.

Doubtfire: Something has come up. I can't make it. Sorry.

I rush my reply before I give it another thought. George and I need to try to take care of this mess, and then we have a meeting with the parents at the local community center down the road. Everyone is calling and asking questions, stressed and worried about where their kids will now go to get their basic educational requirements met.

When I hear another text come through, I ignore it. Pushing Ben to the back of my mind, my stomach sinks again from the pain of losing everything. I thought I was past this pain. I thought that I had hit rock bottom with the only way being up. I was sure that the heaviness of what life could throw at me would ease. Not so, it appears.

"We will be alright, Em. But I really want you to reconsider moving in with me. Between this and Jeremy, it is a lot. I know you and Rosie will be more settled back in your bunker," George offers, looking at me as though I am about to break.

"I do miss that bunker..." I murmur to him, referring to his basement, where Rosie and I lived for a while, the space as large as the entire house footprint. Our independence and safety assured, it was our own little private oasis. Just what we needed as we recovered back then. Perhaps just what I need now.

"It is all yours. Just say the word." I give him a small nod. While I love the bunker, I feel like going back there would be admitting defeat. I am not ready for that yet. This is not over. The school is still ours. I still have a job. Rosie still has me.

"We need to work out our next steps, George. This is no doubt the work of Beasley, and you and I both know this is only the tip of the iceberg. What will we do?" I almost plead to George, and his lips thin. He is not happy.

"Let get this placed cleaned up first and then think about what we need to do." He gives nothing away in terms of what he is thinking. He could still take the money. There is no way we can bounce back from this.

"I guess we better get to work," I say quietly, the fight I had nearly all but gone. The mop and bucket at my side look comically redundant in the vast mess of the room.

"I guess we better."

Grabbing the mops and cleaning products, we try to fix the mess a billionaire left.

28

BEN

I have been feeling off all day. Em canceled our date tonight, and I can't say I'm not disappointed. I want to see her. I want to see her every damn day.

A knock at my office door breaks through my thoughts as Sandra walks in.

"Beasley is here in the conference room, ready for your two p.m.," Sandra says, walking in and putting some files on my desk, the small mass now gathering into an insurmountable mountain.

"Is he alone?" I ask. He has been quiet, and I am on edge, knowing that he has something brewing. He always has something brewing.

"He's alone. But his smile is a mile wide," Sandra offers, and my brow furrows. My eyes flick to my cell again, as I look for any news from Em, yet my screen is blank.

"That can't be good. What do I have this afternoon?" I look at her, my own plan building.

"After Beasley, a meeting with the acquisitions team

at three p.m., then a meeting with the financial auditors at four p.m. At five thirty p.m. is the conference call with the construction team with Tennyson, before your dinner arrangement." Sandra rattles off my schedule, and I clench my jaw. I don't even have a fucking minute to myself. Something I used to love is now something I loathe.

"Cancel it," I say to her as I grab the files for Beasley.

"Which one?" she asks, starting to tap at the tablet in her hand, ready to adjust my schedule.

"All of it. After Beasley, I am out for the day," I say, standing, my body now itching to be with Em. My curiosity has piqued at where she is, of whom she might be with.

"Oh. Sure. Shall I move everything to next week?" she offers, her eyebrows high in question.

"Yes. Great." I already feel lighter as I walk past her and out of my office, strutting down the hall to get this meeting over with.

I push through the door to the conference room and see that Michael is already here and looking uncomfortable.

"Johnathan," I say by way of greeting, extending my hand for us to shake. Sandra was right. He looks too happy.

"Why the hell are you engaged to our opposition?" He jumps right in as I take my seat.

"I disclosed it to your team in writing as soon as it happened. I can assure you that Michael is managing this case; I am merely here as support." I run my hand down my tie and take a seat at the board table, feeling on edge.

"Well, it doesn't matter now anyway," he quips, taking a sip of his expresso that we offered him, in a pristine Hermes porcelain cup.

"Why, what has been happening?" Michael asks, clearly just as out of the loop as I am.

"Oh, I just have a feeling they will let go of that school sooner rather than later." I know by the look on his face he has done something.

"What did you do?" I ask, my stomach feeling heavy.

Beasley merely shrugs at me. Michael starts talking, going through a few things with Beasley, so I grab my cell and shoot off another text to Em, asking her if everything is alright at the school. Even though I know deep down, it's not. I wait, seeing my message has been read, but I get no reply.

Something is going on, and I am going to find out what it is.

As soon as Beasley left my office, I was gone. Sandra had Ralph waiting at the curb outside the office, and we were out of the city in record time. As we pull up outside the school, I can already see that things are not how they are meant to be. There is not a spare space in the parking lot, something that I have never had to combat before. There are people everywhere. Some I recognize as parents, who are standing around the entrance as Ralph double-parks to let me jump out before he circles to find an alternative lot.

I pull at my collar as I push through the door and see Margaret battling parents at the front desk.

"She's in her room, Ben," Margaret says to me before quickly picking back up her conversation with a parent. Her eyes flick to me quickly, already knowing who I am here to see. Although I see her lips purse like they haven't before. Clearly, she is stressed.

I push through the doors and stop short in the hallway. It is a mess. Water damage, chairs, desks, flooring, all stacked on top of each other in the hallway. People are walking around with garbage bags, mops, all of them eyeing me warily... like I am not meant to be here.

I pace to Em's room, dodging the people crowding the halls, my shoes slipping on the slush that remains, as I wonder what the hell is going on.

"Em!" I rush out as I push through the door and see her mopping up the floor. Her head flicks up quickly, surprise written on her face, but her shoulders look weighted down.

"You have some nerve," George seethes, stalking toward me. I've yet to see him so angry.

"George!" Em admonishes softly, dropping her mop and walking over to me.

"What happened?" I ask, but the sinking feeling in my stomach tells me I know exactly what happened.

George huffs and turns his back to me, too angry to engage.

"We had a broken pipe. The room flooded. We lost everything," she tells me, and I search her face, seeing reddened eyes. She has been crying.

"Em lost everything," George reiterates as he picks up his broom and walks out the door, leaving us alone.

"*Everything* is gone?" I ask, my eyes sweeping across the room, and the small pile of damp rumble in the corner tells me the answer is yes. I spot a small book on the floor, and homing in on it, the cover looks familiar. I step toward it and bend to pick it up, water dripping from the pages. It is Rosie's special copy of *Cinderella*, the one she read to me the first time I met her.

"Everything..." Em says, and I can hear her voice break.

"But you have insurance, right?" I ask tentatively, standing back up and walking over to her. The look on her face has me stopping short, though. Her big blue eyes are glassy, and she slowly shakes her head.

"What caused the water pipe to break?" I press, nausea building.

"What do you think?" Em smarts, as she straightens her back, rolling her shoulders, her eyes piercing mine.

"Beasley," I breathe out, and her nostrils flare at his name.

"All Rosie's books and supplies, all Michael's signing books and charts, all the decodable books... everything is gone. Everything." I grab her then. Pulling her body to me, she sinks into my chest as I wrap both arms around her. She doesn't weep, but she holds me tight, and I can feel her taking deep breaths, trying not to let her tears fall.

"Em, I had no idea. I never would have advised him to do this. I don't condone this, I don't..." She steps back from me and puts her hand up in a silent request for me to stop.

"There are spare mops in the corridor. Might as well make yourself useful while you are here, Mr. Langford," she says, exhaling heavily and grabbing her mop. I survey the room again. My shoulders tense as I take it all in.

"Give me a minute," I say to her before I step out of the room into the corridor and pull out my phone. I call everyone I know and then more. I have Sandra calling a professional cleanup crew and paying them double to get here within twenty minutes. I have called Beth and asked about replacement school supplies and books. Eddie is getting a professional crew in tomorrow to assess and provide new furnishings, and I spoke with Tennyson about increased security.

I step back into the room just as the cleanup crew has arrived.

"I thought you had left?" Em says, her shoulders slumped, looking exhausted. I hate that she thinks I'd do that.

"Of course not. I made some calls." As I pocket my phone, she looks up at me in confusion.

"Who did you call?" she asks, just as George walks into the room with the cleanup crew following.

"Ben?" he interrupts, coming to stand in front of me.

"I arranged for the crew here to clean up the school today. I have arranged a fit-out crew to be here tomorrow to assess and provide whatever you need to get the school furnished and ready to use. I called Harrison's office, and they are going to arrange all new supplies, books, art, you name it. That will all be delivered once the school is ready to receive it. And my brother Tennyson is looking into security, so that this can't happen again." They're both silent for a moment, mouths agape.

"Thank you. Thank you so much," George says in a rush, taking my hand and shaking it, relief and disbelief in his face.

"Where do you want us?" the cleanup crew asks, and George goes to meet with them to discuss workload, while Em continues to stand still, staring at me with glassy eyes and trembling breaths.

"Why?" she whispers. "Why did you do that?"

"For you. For Rosie," I say honestly. I really want to give this woman the world. "If I could grab every star, every planet, I would give them all to you. I mean it."

"Ben... I..." she whispers, shaking her head as a lone tear rolls out from her eye. I walk to her then, crushing her to my chest. "Thank you," she says as her hands wrap around my waist and I feel my shirt become wet. Her tears are silent, but they fall freely, and I have never felt more helpless in my life. I've done what I can to make this better, but I hate that she has to carry any of this burden in the first place.

Slowly, she pulls away from me, and I lean over and peck her lips. "We better get to work."

This might not be the date I had in mind, but I need to be here. I need to help her with this so she can see me as someone she can lean on. Have the faith in me that I want to prove I deserve. So I shed my jacket and roll up my sleeves, getting to work cleaning up the mess my client made.

29

EMILY

I take a nervous breath as I sit in Ben's car next to him, getting closer to his apartment. We had a great morning. As he promised, Ben turned up early again this morning with coffee for me, and a muffin for Rosie, and we all went swimming together. The school is closed, the cleanup all done, and now we just need to wait for the furniture and fit-out to start. We are continuing with our weekly swimming classes, as it is a great way for all the kids to see each other and play together, even if they are all at different educational institutions now.

George still hasn't discussed what he is going to do with the school. Ben has taken some of the pain away with his generosity, but it will still take time to get it back on track and fully up and running. With all the kids now expected to spend a month or maybe two at different schools in the meantime, it may be in their best interest now to stay there rather than moving back. Especially because we can't be assured that this won't happen again, and Ben can't come to the rescue every time.

My eyes flick to watch Ben in the driver's seat next to me. I know he is a good man, and he proves it more every day; otherwise, I wouldn't have him around Rosie. Not for the first time, though, I wonder what I'm doing. Our engagement may be fake, but our feelings are starting to feel very, very real. But other than our feelings, nothing else has changed. The school is still being pursued, and Sasha is chasing him more than ever. I'm not sure where it leaves us.

"Rosie did well this morning?" Ben says, and I watch as a small smile comes to his face at the mention of my daughter.

"She did. She loves the pool."

I think about Rosie and Ben this morning, and my stomach flutters at the memory of them playing together. I never would have thought this man would be so good around children. He is a highflyer, city slicker, suit-wearing, billionaire lawyer. Something my history tells me I should stay right away from, yet here we are, driving to his apartment, where I will stay with him after the fundraising gala tonight and have the most amazing sex of my entire life.

I'm nervous. I'm nervous to go to the gala and meet his family. I'm nervous being in the city again. I'm nervous about leaving Rosie. She has stayed at George's a lot, but I have always been in the neighborhood. This time, I am going to be hours away and staying the night in the city, not able to get to her quickly if I need to, so it is a new kind of anxiety setting my nerves on edge. Like he can read my mind, Ben squeezes my hand again, letting it rest in his grip on his strong thigh.

My other hand rests on his luxurious black soft leather seat. Looking around his car, I see a child's car seat in the back. It is brand new, top of the line, and safely secured, and I smile, thinking about how generous and caring he is to purchase such an item, obviously thinking he would need it. The car slows as he drives into a parking garage at the side street of a high-rise, and we go into another gated area, which looks reserved for fancy rich people. I say that because all I can see are sports cars, Bentleys, and a few fancy-looking Escalades parked side by side.

"This is my private entrance," he says as he parks. "My brothers and I all live in this high-rise, and we have the top four floors." Quickly jumping out of the car, he comes around to open my door. Stepping out, I take a deep breath as he grabs my bag from the back seat and we walk to the elevator, which opens immediately at our presence.

The elevator is pristine, just like the garage, and I feel embarrassed about my tiny apartment and the building that it is in, knowing it is nothing like this. There is not one scratch, no peeling paint, no graffiti, no stained carpets, and certainly no smell. As we step in, he presses the button that says PH2, and I swallow. *Of course he lives in the penthouse.* I look at the buttons on the elevator, and I can see there are four penthouses—*one for him and each of his brothers.*

As the elevator makes its way up the forty floors, I take a breath to steady my racing heart. The clean lemon-fresh aroma is a far cry from the dampness I normally smell in my apartment block, and again I internally cringe at the distinct differences between us.

He squeezes my hand, and I look up at him. His gaze resting on my face, he asks, "You okay, baby?" I nod, not sure I can use my voice. I give him a small smile, and he bends down and kisses me, which helps calm my nerves a little.

We break away from each other as the elevator stops at his floor. The doors open right into his living room space, so I don't have time to prepare myself for the onslaught of luxury that slaps me in the face.

I stop a few steps in and look around. The floors are polished gunmetal-gray marble, his furniture black leather, glass and chrome features heavily decorating the space, and there is a large luxurious rug covering the main living area. Floor-to-ceiling windows show the city skyline overlooking the large park across the street, the view of the sunset tonight no doubt a highlight every day. It is very masculine, and nothing at all like the dainty apartment Rosie and I call home.

He has an oversized plasma screen on one wall and some decor peppered around the room. Along one side, the room opens up to a massive kitchen, which is black, glossy, and full of high-end appliances. I see a formal dining area just beyond it and a breakfast bar with comfortable-looking stools in front.

"Baby?" he says, and I whip my head around to look at him, now acutely aware that I am gaping at his residence. I bring my lips together and smile, feeling extremely overwhelmed. You would think that I would be somewhat used to seeing places like this, having lived in a similar place with Jeremy for a while, but this place is next level, and nothing like I have seen before.

"You have a beautiful home, Ben," I say on a breath, and he walks to me.

"You are beautiful, Em. This is just stuff," he says, sweeping his arm out around the room, then he takes my lips again, his arms grabbing me around the waist and pulling me to him tightly.

A loud buzzer noise sounds, and I pull away and look around, not sure what it is or what to expect. Ben walks over to the wall and picks up the intercom.

"Come up," he says, before returning his attention to me. "I will let in the team, and then I'll show you around." I wonder what team he is referring to. The elevator doors open again, and three women walk out, two pulling a suitcase each and another pushing a clothing rack full of garments in zippered bags.

"Where would you like us, Ben?" one of the women asks.

"Down the hall, second room on the left," he says, nodding in the same direction.

They nod and walk down the hallway, clearly familiar with the place.

When I look up at him, his eyes are already on me. "I told you I would organize your dress, hair, and make-up." My eyebrows rise in surprise. He did say that, but I thought I would be doing my own hair and makeup and perhaps there would be a suitable dress that he picked up midweek. Like a rental or something. But by the looks of the women and the amount they are carrying, this is going to be an onslaught I am not prepared for.

"Come on, let me show you around so you can shower and get ready," he says, taking me by the hand and guiding me down the hallway.

The tour takes us to three spare bedrooms, each with their own bathroom. An office, another living room, what looks like a gym, a room with a bar and billiard table, and then his master suite. He drops my bag in his wardrobe, which is bigger than my entire bedroom at home, and lets me take it in. I walk around slowly, my eyes glued to everything. His bed is huge, so big, I am sure at least five adults could fit with ease. The plush carpet feels soft under my feet and floor-to-ceiling drapes frame the large windows, with French doors-style panes that open to a massive private terrace, with outdoor furniture and an amazing view.

"Let me turn on the shower for you and you can freshen up." I feel like I am sleepwalking as I follow him into his bathroom and am immediately gobsmacked. Again, marble on the floor and walls, a double-sink vanity unit, one wall entirely mirrored, and a two-person shower. On the other side is a soaking tub, big enough for a party, with low windows next to it, which allow you to soak with a view of the city as well.

"Perhaps I can help you undress..." Ben says, walking up behind me, dropping his mouth to my neck, his hands exploring under my top. I lean my head back against his shoulder and close my eyes. He is solid, protective. I feel safe and adored by this man, and although I feel completely out of my comfort zone here, I concentrate on his touch.

His phone vibrates in his pocket, and he groans. Stopping his kisses, he grabs his phone and looks at the screen.

"Sorry, baby, I have to take this. It's my brother," he says, showing me the screen. The name *Harrison* flashes on it, a stark reminder that I am with the governor's brother.

"Here," he says, leaning into the shower and fixing the temperature. "Relax in here, and when you are done, put on a robe and head to the spare room to the team when you are ready. I will be in the den if you need me." He kisses me again as steam fills the bathroom, and he walks out, smirking at me, making me smile in return.

I do as he says, and strip naked to enjoy his hot shower, lathering my body in his soap, smelling him all around me. Once clean and dry, I put on a robe, which looks new and unused, and the perfect size for me. I grin, knowing he must have purchased this just recently, and I tiptoe down the hall. Opening the spare room door slowly, the team of people Ben has assembled are all ready and waiting.

"She's here!" one woman coos, while another hands me a glass of champagne.

"Ohhh." I take it with surprise as I am ushered into the room, the door closing swiftly behind me.

"Come sit, darling. Let's get you ready for the ball!" she singsongs, encouraging me to sit in a seat they have set up in front of a mirror. I don't drink a lot, but maybe this glass of bubbles will steady my racing heart. Taking a sip, I sit down, spotting the rack of clothing. One woman gets busy with the hairdryer and the other two talk with me about the clothing and what I like to wear, so we can confirm a dress and colors. Once decided, I exhale any jitters, relaxing into getting pampered as I let them get to work.

30

BEN

As I pull on my suit jacket and look in the mirror, I am happy with the result. I have a million suits, but I bought a new one this week, with the assistance of the same stylist helping Emily down the hall. I wanted tonight to be perfect. It is crisp, all black, and perfectly tailored, and I hope in conjunction with the formal dress Emily wears, we are a stunning couple. It has been a few hours since Emily has been in the room with the team, and I look at my Rolex, knowing that we need to leave soon.

The car is waiting for us downstairs, and I hate being late. My shiny black dress shoes click on the polished marble as I walk to the kitchen to wait for her. Grabbing a glass, I pour myself a whiskey, and as I lift it to my mouth, I stop midway, my eyes taking in the woman who leaves me breathless.

She is fucking gorgeous. Her floor-length dress hugs her curves, blood red, with embroidered sparkles that glisten in the light when she moves. It is strapless, and her breasts look immaculate as her complexion glows against the vibrant color. Her long hair is styled in glossy waves without a hair out of place as it drapes around her neck and down one side, showing off her diamond and ruby earrings. I subtly adjust myself because just the look of this woman makes me stand at attention.

My eyes devour her, my hand gripping onto the kitchen counter as I drink her in. She is glamorous, absolutely otherworldly. Entirely out of my league.

I put my glass down without taking a sip and stalk over to her. She is taller with heels on, but she still looks up at me like I am her everything.

"Mr. Langford, you look very dapper this evening," she says on a breath to me, smiling as my hand reaches for her waist and rests on her curvy ass. I stand in front of her, taking her in.

"You are breathtaking, and I am not letting you out of my sight." I peck her on the lips, not wanting to ruin her makeup before the night has started. Her eyes widen so slightly, I would have missed it if I blinked. I have no idea what is happening here. It is a contract, an agreement, an arrangement... whatever we're calling it. But I stepped over that line weeks ago, and now she just feels like mine. My doorbell buzzes, startling us apart, and I thread my fingers through hers.

"Ready to go?" I ask, just as the team of women walk out and discreetly leave. She nods, and I grab my phone, ensuring I have my wallet, no doubt about to spend too much money on an auction prize I don't need to support the charity.

The drive is short, the function being held at a nearby

six-star hotel, which has the largest ballroom in all of the city. Within seconds of our car stopping at the front, the hotel doorman opens our car door, the luxurious efficiency almost startling. Instinctively, I reach out, grabbing Em's hand, and together we step out and walk through the dazzling glass doors into the large marble foyer.

There are people everywhere, as tonight's event is one of the most prominent charity events of the year, and I don't miss all the eyes on us as we make our way through the crowd. A few flashes go off around us, and where usually I would stop in front of the media wall and have more photos taken, I feel Em's body stiffen. So I keep us walking, bypassing any media, and we make our way straight inside into the already very full ballroom. I scour the room and spot Eddie and Tennyson over in the far corner, so I beeline right to them.

"Boys," I say with a sly grin, shaking their hands in greeting, knowing I am, without a doubt, with the most beautiful woman in this entire room tonight.

"Eddie, Tennyson, this is Emily Carr," I say, putting my arm around her back, bringing her closer. She smiles and nods, extending her hand, and they shake.

"Nice to meet you," Eddie offers before introducing her to his date, Natalie.

"Pleasure is mine," Tennyson murmurs to her, and I elbow him in the ribs. He cackles at me then, before introducing his date, who looks entirely too young for him and already seems bored even though the night hasn't even begun.

The women make small talk, and I am pleased to see Em already hitting it off and looking more comfortable.

She is good like that. She can walk into any room and genuinely talk and listen to whomever is with her. She isn't clinging to me and can hold her own. It feels good to have her here with me.

"Fuck me, please tell me she has a friend," Tennyson says to me quietly as he sips his whiskey, and I smile, like the cat who got the canary.

"Keep your eyes on her face, asshole," I say to him in jest, nudging him in the side as I see his eyes roam over my woman.

"Punching above your weight with her, brother." Ribbing me again, I can't help but smile wider. Fake or real, I'm fucking happy, so sue me.

"How is everything with the school?" Harrison asks as he steps into our conversation.

"The school is cleaned, but there is still a lot of work to do. Beasley is still interested and will probably pull the same shit again," I reply, and he sighs in frustration, before being pulled away immediately. Such is the life of the governor. He is trusting me that I know what I am doing, which is bad, because I have no fucking idea how I am going to keep the woman and the client. I'm not particularly wanting to deal with the latter, but knowing I need to be really sure about him before I make any rash decisions. I need to have a formal meeting with my brothers to discuss it further, as Eddie and Tennyson need to agree on all family business arrangements such as this. Millions of dollars will be wiped from our bottom line if we let him go. It will hurt.

"And I thought this night was going to be delightful,

but here comes our dark cloud to spoil it all. As per usual," Tennyson murmurs.

"Boys!" my mother says as she sashays up to us, giving us the once-over. "Nice to see you all made it." The smile plastered on her face is as fake as the wrinkle-free skin on her forehead.

"Hi, Mom," Eddie murmurs.

Tennyson ignores her completely, turning and walking away, back to his date, who looks to be taking selfies near the bar.

"Benjamin. Who is your date this evening? Is this the supposed fiancée I have heard so much about, but have never met?" Her words knife me a little as she looks over my shoulder. I feel Em come up beside me, her fingers intertwining with mine at our sides.

"Mom, this is Emily. Em, this is my mother, Diane." I make the introductions and internally cringe that I didn't prepare Em for this at all.

"Ohh, how lovely to meet you. I would like to say that I have heard so much about you, but Benjamin has told me nothing." My mother speaks pointedly, and I feel her words like barbs on my skin.

My eyes flick to Eddie's over her shoulder, and I see him roll his eyes. Tennyson is already at the bar, getting another drink, so there's no chance of him coming back over now. He and my mother are hardly on speaking terms and haven't been for years. Harrison and Beth are chatting with some people across the room, constant attention following them wherever they go, which means he's also no use to me at this instant.

"Likewise, Diane," Emily says politely with a smile, and I squeeze her hand in mine.

"I haven't seen you around before, Emily. Tell me, what is it that you do?" my mother prods, taking a smaller step forward to the point that I feel suffocated. My shoulders rise higher and higher toward my ears. The stress builds in my neck as my mother very obviously looks her up and down.

"Oh, I don't live in the city. I am a special needs teacher in William Heights." I like the way Em is proud of what she does and where she is from. She doesn't hide away from it, and her voice doesn't waver. She isn't trying to cover it up because people here think it is beneath them. My mother, on the other hand, clearly doesn't like the answer. Her whole demeanor changes, and I even see her take a small step back like she will catch a disease if she gets any closer.

"Oh, well. Benjamin. Really?" She looks at me accusingly, ignoring Em completely now. Like I purposely dragged a girl from the wrong side of town here with me tonight just to toy with her. My teeth are grinding, and the anger swirls deep in my gut.

"Really what, Mother?" I challenge her, squaring my shoulders with her like I am getting ready for a fight. I saw what Harrison had to endure. It is not something that she will get a chance to pull on me.

"A teacher? William Heights?" she questions, shocked. "I swear, you boys do this on purpose. Where is Sasha? She is who you need on your arm, not..." she says as her hand waves up and down toward Emily, and I feel my hand gripping hers so tightly that I might break her bones.

"Mother, I—" I start, but Eddie saves us all.

"Mom, I see Lilly over at the front of the room. She looks like she is looking for you," Eddie pipes up, pointing out our old family friend, who is now Mom's sidekick. Mom never had a daughter, and now she is turning Lilly into a mini-me. Lilly is picking up all Mom's bad traits and none of her good ones—although I am not sure there are any good ones left.

"Oh, of course," she says, walking away without another word. Her work as a socialite tonight is more important. It is always more important.

The drink waiter comes past, so I grab us drinks and pass a champagne to Emily. She is already a little buzzed from the one glass at home. I don't say anything but gulp the whiskey immediately before placing the glass back on the tray, now empty.

"I know you don't really drink, but you might need that," I say, nodding toward the glass in her hand.

Emily leans over and whispers in my ear, her soft voice skirting my collar, immediately relaxing me. "I now understand why she won't teach you how to use Siri." I smirk at her, huffing a laugh as I lean down to her ear.

"You are the only person I ever want to talk to anyway." I get a genuine smile in return, and I peck her on the lips. Our gazes hold each other's for a beat. The whole world around us pauses, and my heart feels like it stops in my chest.

"Excuse me, we need to steal this one for a moment," Eddie says, pulling on my arm.

"Eddie, I want to stay with Em," I say sternly, really not wanting her on her own.

"She is fine; the other girls are here." Eddie gestures to his date." Why don't you girls go over to our table, number two at the front?" he says to Em and his date as he pulls me away.

"It's fine. Go. I'll be at the table when you come back." She smiles, and I grin at her like a stupid teenager. Shaking her head at the probably goofy look on my face, she laughs and waves me off.

I am so fucked.

31

EMILY

I watch Ben as his brother drags him over to the far side of the room, and I melt from the way he just looked at me. I am not sure when it happened, but I have fallen for him. Hard. He is everything I want in a man. Everything I want for Rosie. I feel almost whimsical and terrified at the same time, because I have no idea what is going to happen. Yet, for the first time in years, I really want to try.

Taking another sip of champagne, I try to steady my thoughts. It's my second and last glass, because I already feel light-headed. My body has enough nervous energy strumming through it, my flight-or-fight one hundred percent turned on now that Ben is not near me. Eddie's date slinks off to talk to someone she knows over near the bar, and I stand solo, watching the crowd. An event such as this is exactly Jeremy's thing, and I wouldn't be surprised if I see him tonight. That thought has me almost dry heaving. But I am here with Ben, his brothers, and about five hundred other people, so I feel safety in numbers is on my side tonight.

"Hi, Emily?" a female says from next to me, and I turn to face her.

"Yes, hi?" I offer her a smile.

"I'm Beth, Harrison's partner. I wanted to come and say hello," she says, and I smile wide. I knew she looked familiar, her face one that was plastered on many TVs during the elections a little while ago. She's just as young and beautiful in real life.

"Oh, so nice to meet you!"

"Likewise. We are sitting at the same table, but I saw you being introduced to Mrs. Langford, so I wanted to ensure you are okay..." I laugh at first, thinking she is joking, but I realize that she is dead serious.

"Oh, yeah, I'm okay. She seems... nice?" Even though she was a little rude to me, I figured it was just the stress of meeting me, her son's fiancée, for the first time.

"She really isn't. But don't worry, she is like that with everyone. So you and Ben?" Her brow raises, and she takes a drink of her water.

"Yes, well, he is a really nice guy," I say simply, not really sure if she knows we are fake, thinks we are real, or if she even knows what is going on.

"He is. He looks totally smitten by you too," she offers with a grin.

"Oh?" I ask, my eyes flicking over to where Ben is, and I see him looking right at me. He raises his class and gives me a wink, one that makes me smile.

"Looks like you both are," Beth murmurs, and we both laugh.

"Listen, I need to go and mingle, but I will see you at the table after," she says, her smile now beaming, and I watch her float away, dodging people, being stopped by a few. I look around the room, taking in all the guests. There is no one here I know except for one person. Mr. Beasley is over on the far side of the room and is currently in a very animated discussion with Ben's mom. I watch them for a beat, until they both look right at me, and I swallow roughly. There is no doubt they are talking about me now, so I decide to make my way to the bathrooms to freshen up before we all need to take our seats.

I maneuver through the crowd, feeling jittery again. With my steps measured, I find my way, thanking my lucky stars that there is no line and keeping my head low, not wanting to draw attention to myself. Being with Ben means I have a big target on my back, and I know people are watching me and trying to figure out who I am since I am not from their world. I pray that I can enjoy the evening unscathed, but even I know I am not that lucky.

"Well, look what the cat dragged in," a female voice says as I push my way into the bathroom and stop mid-stride.

Sasha. Looking an equal mix of stunning and yet not wearing enough clothes. Her dress is long, tight, and black, with a myriad of cut-outs showing her glowing tanned skin, her amazing breasts, and her legs that seem to travel longer than is humanly possible. It leaves very little to the imagination.

"Hi, Sasha," I say, keeping things simple and polite, not needing any trouble.

"What games are you playing at?" she hisses, and I look around the small bathroom, finding it empty.

"What do you mean?" I'm starting to realize that she may not be that easy to get along with.

"Everyone in this city knows that Ben is mine. Yet you showed up from God knows where, and you're now wearing a diamond on your hand, pretending you belong, when we both know you don't." She's basically growling by the end of her rant, and I start to question if she could know the engagement is fake.

"Sasha, I have no idea what you are talking about." Shrugging her off, I act as if I'm bored of her and head toward the open stall.

"You are never at these events, and then all of a sudden you show up! So unless Ben has been keeping you hidden somewhere, I am going to assume you are hired." She throws out the accusation of me being an escort, and my shoulders tense. I am many things, but getting paid for sex is not one of them.

"Oh, well, since you're so concerned about my where-abouts, I spend most of my time at the estate. Ben and I prefer it out of the city. We like our privacy," I offer with a sweet smile as her jaw drops. Ben told me he never took anyone to his estate so I knew that would shock her.

"Besides, from what I hear, you are the only gold digger in this bathroom." I shoot her a smile before locking myself in the stall and holding my breath. I hear Sasha about to say something, but then two other women walk in, so I take the opportunity to do my business, freshen up, and when I walk back out, she is gone.

I take some deep breaths and try to pull myself

together. I don't particularly like arguing like that. I prefer not to have conflict of any kind. But I need to hold up my end of the agreement, even when Ben is not with me.

The women smile at me as they look me up and down. I straighten my dress, put on some fresh gloss, and walk out, mingling back in with the crowd to make my way to our table. As I stride across the hall, confident in my heels, I feel a hand grip around my upper arm, to the point of pain.

"Why am I not surprised to see you here. Are you with your *fiancé*?" he spits out quietly, close to my ear, his breath hot and smelling like strong liquor. My body shivers. I knew it was too good to be true. First Ben's mom makes me feel less than welcome. Then Sasha confronts me in the bathroom. Now Jeremy is cutting off my blood supply to my arm as he drags me inconspicuously to the side of the hall and around the corner. I believe that in life you get signs, and if tonight is not the biggest sign that I need to never come into the city again, I am not sure what is.

"Let go of me," I hiss, pulling my arm from his grip. It throbs as I look down, spotting angry red hand marks.

"You need to fucking end this charade, prancing around with a fucking Langford," he growls low, his jealous tone sweeping over my body and making me tremble, then he plasters on a big smile at a few businessmen who walk past.

"I suggest you leave me alone and get on with your own pathetic life." I might be terrified, but I am also angry. He can't keep doing this to me. I won't let him.

I turn quickly and strut out of the hallway before he

can grab me again, so close that I see the crowd within reach. But I am not that lucky.

I feel his hand grip my arm again, searing the same spot, causing me to curl my body a little as harsher pain shoots up to my shoulder. I see people a few feet in front of me, none of them looking this way, all in their own conversations.

"What the fuck did you just say to me?" he seethes, his tone low and deep. As I glance around, I spot Sasha down the other end of the hallway, watching our interaction with interest, and my stomach drops at being seen like this.

"You need to let me go. Do not cause a scene." I'm almost pleading now, because I don't want this to blow up and embarrass Ben at his family's gala. My body is hot, my palms sweaty, my heart racing. He needs to let us go. Let any notion he has in his mind that thinks I am his fade away. It has been going on for far too long and showing no signs of stopping.

"A scene? I will fucking cause a scene. You are mine, Emily. No one else will have you, especially not a fucking Langford." I knew it. I knew this new ferocity from him was solely due to Ben and me being together. I watch him as he looks me up and down, his lip curling and his nostrils flaring.

"Maybe I should have a word with my new brother-in-law, the governor. I can discuss the harassment policies and new laws around partner violence. Maybe his new government needs a firsthand account of what that is like. Maybe someone they can put in front of the media to tell her story," I say to him, my tone firm. I never used to have the courage to stand up to him before. In fact, I would do anything to either avoid or appease him. Even though I don't want to cause a scene, I don't want to totally back down either.

He looks down at me, his jaw clenching. I have no intention of putting my experience up for media fodder, but he doesn't know that.

"You are fucking delusional. As if anyone would believe a poor woman from William Heights." He looks unsure as he says it, and I know I have hit a nerve.

"Maybe the governor will want to know all the details. Not just the abuse I have endured, but how I was left without money to care for my baby, a single mother who had to climb out of poverty and start over all on her own with no support system," I continue, and I see a fire burning in his darkening eyes.

"Don't you say a fucking word. You can walk out there tonight and pretend like they care, but I want you to end this fucking engagement. He can't have you. No one can." I rip my arm from his for a second time, and together we stand there, staring at each other. He is massive; there is no outrunning him. I glare up at him, trying to see if I can find at least a sliver of the man I first met, the one who doted on me, cherished me, gave me everything. But his expression is vacant, if not enraged. He is no longer the same man, and I am no longer the same woman.

"Just leave me alone," I say quietly as I step back, and he lets me this time, the vein in his throat throbbing. This is bad. I turn quickly and walk away, trying to gasp for the air I can't seem to capture. Keeping one foot in front of the other, I don't stop until I'm mingling in the crowd, finding solace at the sight of Ben across the room.

32

BEN

I stand with Eddie and a business contact of his, where we have been discussing a potential new deal for the past twenty minutes. It is a large client who we are trying to win at the moment. While I am engrossed in the conversation, my eyes flick around the room.

Every five minutes, my eyes have been wandering, looking for Emily. The last I saw, she was laughing and chatting with Beth, but the joy at seeing them getting along was short-lived because I haven't seen her since.

"So, Ben, I will have my office call you this week to arrange a time?" the client says to me, bringing my attention back to the present.

"Yes, of course, it will be great to chat further. I am sure we can help you out," I reply with a smile, giving his hand a firm shake to seal the deal. He currently works with our biggest competitor, so it is an important meeting to get.

As he shakes hands with Eddie, I spot her. Over his

shoulder, I watch as Emily comes from the hallway, not looking like herself. She is still stunning, breathtakingly so, but her posture has changed, her smile not as bright, and she is rubbing her arm like she is cold.

"Excuse me," I say to Eddie and the other men as I go toward her, feeling something's amiss. As I get closer, she pulls her shoulders back and blows out a big breath, and it isn't until I am a few feet away that I see her arm is red and marked, and not at all how I left her.

"Em?" She whips her head around, almost jumping ten feet into the air.

"Oh, you startled me," she says with a light laugh, clutching her chest.

"What happened?" I ask her as I lift her arm, and I don't miss her sharp intake of breath when I touch it.

"It's nothing. I just fell into a wall in the bathroom. Was a little wobbly on my heels," she says, brushing it off, giving me another big smile. One that doesn't reach her eyes.

"Em?" I growl, not wanting to push her, but knowing she is not okay.

"Can we talk about it later?" she whispers, her eyes looking up into mine. I can see clear as day that something is very wrong, but I nod, grateful at least she is going to open up to me later. I will make sure we leave as soon as we can after formalities.

"Shall we go and sit down?" she suggests, and I look around then, noticing people taking their seats. I know she is brushing it off, as it is something she does a lot. It doesn't sit well with me, but I grip her hand, strumming her palm with my thumb and leading her to our table.

Pulling the chair out for her, I put my hand on her back, caressing her a little. I make sure she is seated and settled with Eddie on her other side before I join her, keeping my chair closer to her, with Harrison on my other side, him sliding a whiskey in my direction.

As the event kicks off, my eyes wander to her. Her hand is back on her arm, and I know without any question it isn't from slipping in the bathroom. I just don't know why she wouldn't tell me the truth.

My eyes wander the room, looking over everyone here tonight. I spot my mom at the head table with Lilly and a few others. As I continue my perusal, my eyes land on Jeremy Lucas, who is looking directly at me. Or us, as his eyes seem to be pinning Emily, although she is not looking his way, too engrossed in conversation with Eddie. My body stiffens as I remember him from weeks ago, how he grabbed Em on our first date. I don't like the way he looks at her. The jealousy coiling in my stomach is new, and I lift my arm up, draping it around the back of Emily's chair. The movement causes him to flick his eyes to me before he catches himself and gives me a small smile before looking away. He is sitting next to Beasley, of all people. I had no idea the two of them knew each other, but I watch them both chat like they have known each other for years.

The emcee comes on and gets things underway by introducing my mother. She walks up to the stage elegantly and gives a speech about the importance of health checks. Even though my eyes are looking at her, I am acutely aware of Emily, my hand lazily strumming her bare shoulder as I feel her tense body slowly relax under my fingers.

"You okay, baby?" I ask her quietly, my gaze lowering to hers.

"It was just a slip. But thank you," she says, keeping up her little lie, and while her small smile is genuine, my mind is racing, wanting to know what happened. I grab my drink and take a sip, the whiskey burning but making me feel a little more centered. I try to think of all possibilities, thinking of scenarios until the room applauds. Snapping out of my thoughts, I watch my mother as she drinks it in like the air we breathe, and it is then I realize that I didn't hear a word she said.

"Now, ladies and gentlemen, we are at that point in the night for the auction!" the emcee announces, keeping everyone's attention on the front of the room.

I sit back along with the rest of the crowd to watch the auction, all proceeds going to the charity, the auctioneer one of the city's best. Tennyson bids and wins a lunch with our governor, which the crowd eats up with raucous laughter. Eddie bids on a weekend in Vegas, but is outbid at the last moment. Harrison remains quiet, watching with a smile, his political career ensuring he no longer takes part in bidding or gambling of any kind.

"Next up is our final item tonight, a pink diamond necklace donated by our esteemed City Jeweler. This piece is meant for someone special. It's cluster of rare diamonds in a variety of shapes and sizes that has been carefully crafted into what can only be described as a breathtaking work of art the jeweler calls 'The Emily.' Valued at over one hundred and fifty thousand, we are starting the bids at one hundred thousand." And at that, I immediately put up my paddle.

Emily and my brothers all look at me. Her eyes are wide and her mouth agape. Tennyson laughs, and Eddie and Harrison both shake their heads with small grins.

"The bid is at one hundred thousand here at the front. Do I see a bid for one twenty-five?" Immediately, Jeremy Lucas puts up his hand. I clench my jaw as he gives me a smirk, and my eyes flick back to the auctioneer.

"Do I have one thirty?" he shouts, and I raise my paddle.

"One forty," Jeremy yells, clearly wanting everyone in the room to see him bidding such a high amount, and a few gasps come from the crowd. Everyone here likes a good auction battle, and they are about to see one.

"Do I have one fifty?" The auctioneer looks to me, and I nod, raising my paddle quietly. When I glance at Emily again, I don't think she's moved a muscle, her face one of complete bewilderment.

"Fuck. Go, Benny Boy," Tennyson murmurs to me as he leans back in his chair with a whiskey, watching the show. I spot my mother eyeing me from the other table, her lips pursed, clearly preferring I don't win this auction piece, but I have absolutely no intention of letting it go. The Emily is mine.

"One sixty!" Jeremy yells and sits back, like he has already won, not expecting me to continue.

I narrow my eyes, looking back to the auctioneer. "One seventy?" he asks, and I nod, holding up my paddle once more.

"We are at one seventy, folks. This is a beautiful neck-lace, one that is sure to be treasured. The Emily's pink diamonds come from the Kimberly in Australia, the last of their kind now that the Pink Argyle Diamond Mine has closed. The potential for this piece to increase in value over time is significant. This is not just a necklace; this is an investment that can be handed down for gener-ations. Do I have an advance of one seventy?" The auctioneer looks directly at Jeremy, who I can tell is seething, where he sits in his chair. But he remains silent, shaking his head.

He is out. I have won.

"Going once... Going twice... Sold! To Mr. Benjamin Langford at table two." Cheers ring out in the room. Before I can address what I know is going to be pushback from Emily, the auctioneer's assistant strides over to me a moment later, taps her tablet with my details, and they move on to wrap up the event. With the formalities of the night now over, the music's back on, and the dance floor comes alive.

Harrison gives me a backslap as he stands, no doubt going to work the room with Beth by his side. Tennyson slides a glass of whiskey in my direction, knowing that I probably need it. I have money. A lot of it. But I have never spent so much on jewelry as I have these past few weeks. My eyes flick to the large diamond shimmering on Emily's hand before I look back up at her, taking in her expression.

Her face is pale, her eyes slowly blinking, and as she goes to grab her glass of water, it nearly spills due to her shaking hands. She drinks it almost all at once before she places her glass back on the table and meets my gaze.

"That was a lot of money, Ben..." she whispers, her voice quivering.

"It's a good investment. And it goes to a good cause," I say, and I give her a small smile. My fingers are still absentmindedly strumming her bare shoulder. I know she feels uneasy, so I move closer to her, pulling her to me.

"It will look stunning around your neck," I whisper into her ear as I run my nose down her neck, and I hear her intake of breath as she shivers against me.

"Give me your lips, baby." I feel everyone's eyes on us, the crowd looking right at me after the arrogant display of wealth. They're curious about the woman sitting by my side who inspired me to spend an obscene amount of money. And I want them all to know that she's mine, to have no doubts of where I stand.

She tilts her head up and looks at me, her large eyes shining with emotion, and I tenderly grab her chin. Suddenly, nobody else is around. She's my only focus.

"I didn't mean to make you uncomfortable, Em. Pretend it's just us. If the money bothers you, think of who it's helping." Her eyes are hard to read as she searches mine, but then she nods in my grip, a tear ready to spill down her cheek as it clings to her lashes. "It's okay, baby, I got you. It's just us here," I whisper to her over her mouth, and she relaxes at my words before I press my lips to hers gently. I want more, much more, but in this room, in front of these people, a quick kiss will have to do.

I hear a throat clearing behind me and turn to see the auctioneer.

"Mr. Langford, if you would like to accompany us to the back room, we will process your winnings," he says with a large smile, one I match.

"I'll be back in a minute, and then we can go," I whisper to Em, who still looks like she is in a state of shock as I follow the auctioneer to get things sorted.

I am halfway to the back room when Sasha runs right into me.

"Sasha," I grit out, not stopping.

"Congratulations, Ben, what a beautiful piece," she says, her steps quickening as they try to keep up with my stride. I don't want to talk with her. I don't want to leave Em at the table without me for any longer than necessary.

"Ben, please, I need to talk to you," she says, almost out of breath.

"No," is all I say, as a few people stop me to shake my hand, and I weave my way through the crowd. Only, she's still right on my heels.

"I just want to tell you what I saw in the bathroom earlier, with your fiancée." Stopping dead in my tracks, I turn to look at her. She smiles brightly as I stare down at her. It used to make me feel like a king, but now annoys me more than anything.

"What?" I bark.

"Well, you didn't hear it from me..." she whispers as her eyes dart around, brushing hair over her shoulder.

"What, Sasha?" I growl, ready to walk away.

"I saw Emily with Jeremy Lucas, and they looked

rather chummy. I would say that your new fiancée may be an even bigger gold digger than me!" she says, almost in glee, and I snarl. Fucking Jeremy Lucas. He's a disgruntled ex who needs to stay in his lane. No wonder she was not herself when she came back from the bathrooms. If he had his fucking hands on her to cause that mark on her arm, he is seriously going to regret it. My blood boils at the thought, my heart pounding harder. Whatever chance he thinks he has with Em, he is mistaken, because just like the necklace, she is mine.

"I think you will hold that title for a very long time, Sasha. Excuse me." I push past her without another word, continuing to the back room to get back to Emily as fast as possible. This night started out perfectly, yet my pleasant mood is now spoiled. Emily is not like Sasha, not at all. I know it deep in my gut. She hasn't asked for a cent. She won't even let me pay for lunch. As I look over the auction paperwork and sign the required forms, Harrison's words ring in my ear.

You have given her a quarter of a million worth of diamonds on her finger...

When my last signature has been scribbled, making the transfer of funds, I can now round that number up, closer to half a million. But it doesn't even make me flinch. She's worth it all and more.

I may feel a little unsettled, but we're going to turn this night around. And we're going to do that with her wearing nothing but that pink diamond necklace around her neck.

33

EMILY

As Ben leaves, I take some deep breaths.

"More water?" his brother Tennyson asks from next to me, having just moved into Ben's seat. Eddie sits on my other side, watching me carefully.

"Does he normally do that?" I ask, still stunned, yet comforted that his two brothers are looking after me. After that display of wealth, I don't feel like myself. You would think I would be somewhat understanding of it, given the ring on my finger and the amount he has helped with the school. Not to mention, he lives in both a magnificent penthouse and a stunning estate with uninterrupted views of the city. But hundreds of thousands of dollars for a necklace is insane. I'm not sure if I should be disgusted or honored. It is an exquisite piece, of that there's no question; even I can appreciate the craftsmanship. It's just... I have no idea whether it will look priceless or choke me as he places it around my neck.

"Sometimes. He will be quiet for a while, then bam, out of nowhere, he meets a woman he can't stop talking about, buys her a diamond ring, brings her to our family charity dinner, and bids an astronomical amount at a public auction in a declaration of love." My eyes widen at his statement, and he grins over the top of his whiskey glass. By my count, he is up to five since I have been here. He holds his liquor well.

"I'm just teasing. Ben is a little arrogant when it comes to money, but not in a bad way. He is purposeful, deliberate, and so I can only assume he has a need for a diamond necklace called The Emily," Tennyson quips, and my body feels heavier at the mention of love. He thinks Ben loves me? Clearing my throat, I push my shoulders back to compose myself.

"He is not giving that necklace to me. He can't..." I feel like I am about to break out from my skin, and I take some more deep breaths. My hand automatically comes to my arm, rubbing it lightly, wanting the remaining throbbing to go away because it is clouding my judgment.

"What happened to your arm?" Eddie asks, as his eyes home in on my red skin. I didn't miss Jeremy's look at me when he stood up from the table after his bidding loss and stalked out of the room. He doesn't like to lose. Not one bit. My anxiety is peaking, and I need to try to relax before I totally lose myself tonight.

"Oh, I get hives when I'm nervous," I mumble, the lie falling from my lips altogether too easily. Eddie's lips thin, much like Ben's, so I can tell he doesn't believe me.

"Well, I just had a very interesting conversation with my dear friend, Jonathan Beasley!" Ben's mother, Diane, struts up to the table, her hands on her hips, hissing the words at me like I have done something wrong.

"Excuse me?" I say, sitting up and pushing my chair back a little to look at her. Just the mention of his name puts me on edge.

"I am told that you are the one stopping him from purchasing the slum of a school he wants to redevelop." She's seething in anger, but trying to contain it in this public setting. My eyes blink up at her. I feel like I am having an out-of-body experience right now.

"I'm sorry, but William Heights is not a slum—" I start to explain before I get interrupted.

"Mother," Eddie pipes up from my other side, looking pained. My eyes flick to Tennyson, whose back is now ramrod straight, his teeth clenched, and his jaw ticking. He throws back his entire glass of whiskey, then pushes his seat back and stalks off, away from the table without saying a word.

"Oh, you know perfectly well. You are playing my son. You put on an expensive dress that Benjamin has obviously paid for, all because you are a conniving piece of work, trying to mess with what is men's business. How typical. My stupid son sees a tight body and falls over backward for you and right into your lower-class arms. He has lost his mind buying you a diamond necklace not worthy of your neck. I can't believe he doesn't see through you for the piece of trash you are!" My eyes widen at her cruel words spoken quietly, and I hold my breath. *Did she just call me trash?*

"Mother, that is enough," Eddie says again, now standing. I am confused for a beat, as Mrs. Langford meets my eyes with what can only be described as pure venom before a familiar face walks up beside her.

"Diane, let's get a drink," Sasha says with a wicked smile on her face, before she curls her arm inside Ben's mother's like they are best friends. Both women look down on me like I am nothing before turning and walking away.

That was the weirdest interaction I have ever had. Having never met Jeremy's family, I have no experience with parents-in-law, yet I am pretty sure that is not supposed to happen. My heart is racing, and I feel totally out of place.

"Sorry for my mother, she can be a handful at times," Eddie mutters, and I give him a small smile, even though I'm now shaking. I swallow and try again to calm my racing heart, my eyes pinging to the back hall where I saw Ben walk to, yet I can't see him returning. As I sweep my gaze back to Eddie, I am pleasantly surprised to see someone I know over his shoulder.

Ian is an old friend of George's and is the main funder for our school. Without him, our school couldn't even operate. He spots me and gives me a beaming smile, and I don't wait as I stand and move away from this table, the need to bolt from this event strumming through my body.

"Excuse me for a moment," I say, giving Eddie a tight smile, but my anxiety is starting to dissipate now that I see a friendly familiar face. Eddie nods, then he sits back in his chair, giving his date, who sits on his other side, some attention.

I fix my dress as I make my way over to Ian, who upon seeing me, opens his arms wide.

"Emily, I thought that was you!" he says, looking extremely dapper for a man in his seventies.

"Hello, Ian, what a pleasant surprise!" I give him a small hug in greeting. I don't know too much about Ian Shaw other than the fact that he is filthy rich, like most of the men in this room. He made his money in real estate, I think, and has been good friends with George since they were kids. While they don't spend a lot of time together these days, they still get along well, and it has been a while since I have seen him.

"I didn't know you came to these things." His eyes quiz me, clearly confused as to why a suburban mom like me would even be in this room tonight.

"Oh, I don't usually. Something a bit different for me tonight," I offer, not sure how much I should say.

"How is Rosie?" Ian asks, his eyes lighting up, and so do mine.

"She is great, thank you for asking. She is in love with Cinderella and all the fairy tales at the moment," I say with a giggle as I think about my beautiful daughter.

"I heard about the flooding. I wish I could give more, but I just don't think I can support the refurbishment right now," Ian says quietly. Who is he kidding? He could probably build an entirely new classroom, but where he invests his money is not a decision for me to make.

"Thanks for considering it, though. George mentioned he had called you," I say, not wanting to tell him that Ben has stepped in anyway. If he knew we had other funding, he might pull his, and I don't want that to happen. If he doesn't fund us, the school is as good as gone.

"I will always honor my ongoing financial commitment, so once you get it back up and running, be assured that you will always have the funds to continue," he reiterates.

"Thanks for everything you do for us, really. George and I are extremely grateful."

"Is George with you? Who are you here with?" he asks, stepping a little closer to me. The move is an odd one, but I assume it is because he can't hear me over the music.

"She is with me. Her *fiancé*," I hear Ben's voice almost growl from beside me, his hand wrapping around my waist as he kisses me on the cheek, making it obvious to Ian that I am spoken for. I smile to smooth any tension I feel now swirling around us, but Ben doesn't match it.

"Ben, this is my friend Ian Shaw," I say warily, but I don't let my concern show, keeping my smile bright as I look between them.

"So how do you know each other?" Ben asks, staring right at Ian, his grip on my waist firm. I wonder where his manners have gone. I am quiet for a beat, not sure what is going on.

"I support William Heights Elementary. Emily here was just telling me all about Rosie's new fascination with Cinderella, that's all," he says proudly, like a grandfather would about his granddaughter. My smile falters. *This is work talk*. Him finding out that Ian funds us in any way is information Ben could use against us to get Beasley the school. I don't think he would do something like that, not with how things have changed between us, but... how can I be sure?

"Well, we need to get going. Shall we?" Ben looks to me, and I quickly say goodbye to Ian before we walk out the door, hand in hand. He is walking fast, clearly just as eager to get out of here as I am. We don't say goodbye to his brothers, his mother, or anyone else, and we are both in the car in record time, where his grip remains on me for the entire trip home.

34

BEN

I am fuming. My body feels like it is about to explode. How can a simple charity gala turn into such a shit show? I was going to punch him. Sure, Ian Shaw is over seventy, but after seeing Sasha jump up and down on his cock six months ago, I know he is still fit enough to keep up with younger women. When I saw him step closer to Em, I almost lost it. My strides quickened as I walked to her from across the room, and I was next to her in a flash. There is no way he is ever going to touch her.

The car ride home was silent. My eyes kept flicking between her face and her red arm, my anger with Ian Shaw and Jeremy Lucas escalating more by the second. My only saving grace was her hand in mine on my thigh, which I held tightly and really didn't want to let go. Even now, as we make our way up in the elevator to my penthouse, my grip remains.

"Ben..." she whispers, looking up to me. "We need to talk about tonight." I can see her nerves plain as day. She looks unsure, and I hate that. I have so many things running around in my brain from tonight that I haven't had time to digest or even think about. I don't want to lose Em. I want to do right by her with the school; I want Jeremy Lucas out of the picture and Sasha to leave me alone. I want my mother to be pleasant to my fiancée and for Em to feel comfortable on my arm. But mostly, I want to have her all to myself tonight, without any of our potential problems in the way.

Now that I know where the school gets their money, I hold important information. Information that could help me get the property for Beasley and information that would no doubt hurt my relationship with Emily. All it would take is one call from Beasley to Ian, offering him a deal he couldn't refuse to stop funding the school, giving the school no choice but to cease operation. No funds equals no school, making the sale a given. But I don't want him to take the school. Not anymore.

"Just tell me one thing, and then the rest can wait," I say, knowing that this is a heavy conversation better had when we are both rested and not feeling as on edge.

"Anything." I know she means it. She is going to open up to me, tell me whatever I want to know.

"Did Jeremy Lucas do that to your arm?" I watch her sharp intake of breath, but her gaze doesn't falter from mine.

"Yes. Yes, he did," she whispers, her body almost deflating at the admission, her eyes getting glassy. "He is..." she starts to say, and I put my finger to her lips. I want to know. I want to know everything, but I already know I am not going to like it, and with the mood I am in,

I am likely to do some serious damage to him if she tells me anything further.

"No. Not now. Tomorrow, or later in the week, but not now. Now, I just want you and me. Just the two of us. Everything and everyone outside of these walls can wait." I don't want our reality to seep in yet. I want one more night. One more night with this woman, when we only have eyes for each other. Because I know the heavy stuff is coming. I need to get my client sorted. I need to get the school fixed. I need to talk to Em about what she is hiding from me. There is so much I need to do. But I just need to feel her, be with her. She makes everything better. She makes *me* better.

She purses her lips, not looking convinced. I pull her to me, my hands wrapping around her waist, my head coming to her jaw, where I kiss her delicately before I move my lips down to her ear.

"Tonight I just want you, Em. Just me and you," I whisper against her skin, breathing her in, needing this time. I have to center myself, and just the feel of her does that for me. I feel her body relax into mine just the same, and I exhale in relief.

"Okay. Just you and me," she says, her hands running up my body and curving around my shoulders. Her fingers massage my scalp as I bite and kiss her neck, Em giving me more access as I do. I pull her even tighter, never wanting to let her go.

I squeeze her hip, ensuring she is real, reminding me that she is here. With me. In my mind, our agreement is no longer. It was a stupid decision that had led me to a very real conclusion. I want the girl. I really fucking want this girl. She is everything I have always wanted—kind, caring, smart, beautiful. Sure, Rosie was an unexpected surprise, but not an unwelcome one. As Emily gives me a small smile, her eyes glisten, watching me as I push all other thoughts aside, only focusing on her.

The elevator makes it to my place, and she steps out with a click of her heels, bringing more color and life to my penthouse than all the expensive artwork and decor combined. I follow her slowly, captivated by her.

She kicks off her shoes and immediately loses a few inches, then she pads across the marble tiles to my floor-to-ceiling windows, looking out at the sparkling city lights. Watching her in the reflection, I walk up behind her, my hands itching to touch her. I rest them on her bare shoulders, sliding them down her arms, and lowering my lips to her neck. I hear her exhale, her shoulders lowering, so I pepper kisses over her skin, my hands traveling over her dips and curves to her waist.

"You look so beautiful tonight," I whisper as my lips move up her neck and drag along her jaw, her head now resting back on my chest. I spin her then and pull her close. My hands encasing her waist, she lifts up her arms, her fingers caressing my face longingly as she looks up at me. This is exactly where she needs to be.

"I can assure you, that by morning, I will look nothing like this at all," she murmurs as her hands travel to my shirt, and she begins to unbutton it. I shrug off my jacket once she reaches the last one, both hitting the floor in a pile at our feet.

"By morning, you will look completely and thoroughly fucked if I have anything to do with it." She hums in agreement, her plush lips curving into a sexy smile.

"Turn around, baby," My voice is all gravel, and as she turns, I reach to her back and slowly lower the zipper on her gown, letting it fall graciously to the floor and holding her hand as she steps out of it.

Now only in her matching red strapless bra and underwear, I stand back, admiring the view. Feeling parched, my tongue sweeps across my lower lip, ready to taste every inch. I let my gaze wander over her body, from her dainty painted toes to her long, luscious hair, my cock straining against my pants.

I squint my eyes a little at her in question.

"What?" she asks, her head tilting. "What's wrong?"

"Something is missing..." I murmur, my hand rubbing my cheek, devouring her openly.

"That would be my dress?" she says sassily, and I grin.

"No, this." Pulling my hand out of my pocket, The Emily necklace dangles from my fingers. I watch her mouth drop open a little as she stares at the diamonds glistening in front of her.

"Turn around," I demand of her.

"Ben, I don't think—" she starts, but I cut her off.

"Em, turn around," I say a little softer and watch her swallow. I wait for a beat, and then she turns slowly back around to face the windows and I drape the piece around her neck.

"You are the most beautiful woman I have ever met. Gorgeous, both inside and out," I say, fastening it closed.

"Ben..." She whispers my name, and I place a small kiss at the back of her neck where the necklace clasps.

"It's too much..." Her fingers reach up to touch it gently, like she's scared of its worth.

"Show me." She listens, turning back around to face me, and my eyes lower to take in the scattering of diamonds around her neck. Her breaths are rapid, her breasts heaving with each one. The necklace moves with them, and the diamonds illuminate her already glowing skin, like art in motion. It's a vision I'll never forget. "You were born to wear my diamonds. I want to fucking bathe you in them."

Our eyes meet then, pulled together and locked in a trance of something more than lust.

She steps toward me, light on her feet, her hands running up my arms and back down, and I watch her slowly lower onto her knees in front of me. I raise my eyebrow in question, my body tensing and all too ready to feel her in any way she'll let me. She gives me a cheeky smile in return before her hands move up to my waist and unbuckle my black leather belt.

My heart is thumping, my dick is aching, but I stand still, watching her, letting her lead, already knowing having her like this is what every single man in that room tonight desired.

"You are phenomenal, you know that?" I say, watching her closely, never wanting this moment to end.

"I suppose diamonds do that to a woman," she quips as her hand wraps around my already rock-hard dick.

I grit my teeth at the feeling. "I'll remember you said that when you get mad at me for buying you matching earrings." Her eyes send me a warning glare right before she pumps my length, drawing a deep growl from my chest.

I grow impossibly harder in her palm, the look in her eyes turning me on even more than her touch. Her gaze doesn't waver from mine as she leans forward, wrapping her warm, wet lips around me. She tastes my length thoroughly, sucking and licking like she's enjoying this just as much as I am. I can't help bringing my hand to rest on her head, hissing slightly as my fingers grab her hair and she takes me deeper into her mouth.

"Baby, fuck... that feels so good. You look perfect on your knees for me. So beautiful and perfect," I grit out as her pace speeds up a little. She gains more confidence, taking me deeper and sucking harder with every movement. My grip on her hair tightens, and I pull her head back, opening up her throat a little wider and watching as she continues lapping me up with her diamonds glistening below.

"I have the best view in all of the city tonight," I groan to her, and she moans, the vibration hitting me in the balls.

"Fuuuuck yes. Moan like that again, so I know how much you love this." And she does, moaning and pushing me to the back of her throat. My hand shoots out, slapping the window behind her so I can steady myself before I lose my footing.

"God, I want you, Em. I want you so goddamn much." I'm basically panting, close to the point of seeing stars from her warm, wet mouth.

She mewls, shuddering below me, her chest moving

quicker than before. Then I notice one of her hands has traveled down her body, touching herself.

"Good girl. Touch that needy pussy, baby. You look fucking amazing," I murmur as my hips begin to move of their own accord. Glancing up at the window, I see the mirror image of us, reflecting back her fantastic round ass, her long hair flowing in waves down her back, and behind her, the city lights that flicker in the distance, reminding me of her perfect blues. When my eyes land back on her again, squirming as she circles her clit, I can't hold back any longer.

"Em, baby, I am going to come," I say in a rush, waiting for her to move, but she doesn't. Staying exactly where she is, she looks up at me as my hips shudder and so do hers. She moans around my length again, her movements shaky as she edges closer. "Yesssss. Fuck. Come with me, just like that." My hand tightens on her hair when she sucks hard, swirling her tongue one last time as I push to the back of her throat.

I shout my release into the living room, panting and moaning as her throat drinks down my orgasm. Leaning into my hand, which is still against the window to keep me upright, the stresses of tonight leave my body with a flush.

She pulls away quickly and rests back on her legs, staring into my eyes as she cries out my name, wringing a gorgeous orgasm from her body. I'm speechless as I watch her, unable to look away even if the world was ending right outside this window. She's shuddering as she comes down from the high, catching her breath, but I don't miss a sly, almost proud smile as it spreads across her face.

I don't wait. Bending down, I scoop her up, throwing her over my shoulder. She squeals at the sudden Tarzan-like act, so I slap her ass for good measure as I stomp down the hall to my bedroom.

Because tomorrow is never promised, and all we have is tonight.

35

EMILY

I barely have time to catch my breath and register what is happening before my body is tossed onto his bed. It is so big, I land in the middle and bounce a little before he is on top of me, his mouth on me, taking me, owning me, and completely devouring me, just like his eyes have promised all night.

We are both frantic, grabbing, touching, pulling closer. I have no idea what he will say once he knows the truth about my life. It is a lot to take on, and I wouldn't blame him if he ran far away from me, so if tonight is all we have, then I want to embrace every second. I don't ever want to let him go.

My body is buzzing after tasting him and seeing him come undone, the diamonds around my neck forgotten as the desire swirls deep within me. It's all-encompassing. His lips are everywhere, hands molding to my curves, his body hot and heavy on mine, and I still want more.

"You are all mine tonight, Em. I plan on tasting every inch of your beautiful body before making you come, with my hands, my tongue, and my cock, over and over and over, until you're begging me to stop," he says as his lips travel across my skin.

"Promise, promises," I tease breathlessly as his lips finally touch mine. His hands cup my face as he holds me to him, his need for me evident in his claiming touch. I grab on to him then too, feeling his strong arms flex beneath my touch, his broad shoulders as they support me, before I rest them at the back of his neck. Our bodies mesh together so fluidly, like they were always meant to be.

There are a million things we need to discuss, but being here together like this makes everything fade into the distance. Nothing else matters when I am with Ben. He takes care of me. He takes care of Rosie. He takes care of us.

"God, I want to kiss you forever," he murmurs against my mouth, breathing his admission into me and bringing new life to my lungs.

His hands roam down my body as his tongue tangles with mine, reaching behind my back and unclipping my bra in one smooth motion. Throwing it across the room, his worshipping mouth lowers to my chest. I rest my head back on the soft pillow as he lowers me to the bed, his tongue swirling and lips sucking my nipples, his carnal desire for me growing more and more with each touch. He bites my nipple slightly, the pained pleasure making me arch into him, whimpering for more.

"Ben, this is not enough. I don't think it'll ever be enough." I want his hands on my body, his lips on me, his attention, his focus, his yearning. I want it all. I was young when I first met Jeremy and I had no idea what sex was meant to be like, my experience limited. But now, after being with Ben, I can clearly see the difference, and I know that Jeremy didn't ever truly respect me, not even from the first moment we met. Ben and his desire for me is explosive yet tender, and like nothing I have ever had before.

His mouth travels farther south across my stomach as his hands reach my hips, and he pulls off the small amount of lace material I have left covering my body. But his mouth doesn't stop. Lifting my leg, he kisses my ankle, slowly traveling up my leg. He promised to kiss every inch of my body, and so far, he is sticking to that promise. When he reaches my inner thigh, he leans down toward my center with his eyes on mine.

"I wanted to get you naked before we even left tonight," he says, giving me another kiss closer to where I'm growing desperate for him. "I can't keep my hands to myself around you." He kisses my inner thigh again, this time dragging his lips across the sensitive skin there. "I can't stop thinking about you, in the morning, at work, at night." Dropping another kiss, he teases me with a few more in quick succession, making me squirm. "I want to be with you all the fucking time. I want you more than I have ever wanted anybody." And with that, I'm trembling with need, just as his hands spread up my inner thighs, pushing my legs wider, and his eyes trail down to my wet center before coming back to me.

"I'm all yours, Ben," I whisper, our eyes locked on each other.

"You're mine," he confirms, lowering his mouth to my

body, where he gives me exactly what I've been aching for. As he begins licking and sucking, slipping his tongue inside me, my head falls back on a moan.

I whip one hand up and grab the headboard as the other reaches forward and threads into his hair. I am panting as my body arches and grinds for more. I've never been like this before, his skill leaving me breathless and eager to come again. It's needy and completely out of control, the way my body moves for him. My legs spread wider, stretching, giving him full access to anything he wants to do to me.

"Oh, God, right there..." I bite my lip lower as my hand holds him closer, my arousal heightening with every satisfied groan he rumbles against me. Little moans and whimpers break through my throat as I become a shaky, writhing mess beneath him. And he doesn't let up, his rhythm unrelenting no matter how many times I buck my hips.

"Ben... Ooooooh... You're so... good," I pant out as I feel the rush of my orgasm washing over me. He continues lapping at me as my body squirms, muscles tightening as I scream out his name again and again before I'm completely limp and melting into the mattress. He presses one more kiss to my clit, making me twitch as his hands roam up my torso, following my curves, over my breasts and back down again. My breathing slows as I come down from my high with his touch working to soothe me.

"This body is mine," he says as he peppers kisses up my torso. "These fucking amazing tits are mine," he says as his tongue swirls around my nipple. "These gorgeous lips are mine," he says, his mouth closing in on mine, our tongues connecting for only a moment before he pulls back slightly. Looking down at me, he cups my jaw, his thumb brushing over my cheek tenderly. "I want you, Em. Not just now, but forever. None of that was lust talking. I want you to be mine," he says as his eyes search mine.

I stare at him for a beat, my heart almost stopping in my chest. I am left speechless for a moment.

"I know we have a lot to work out, but I am officially ceasing our agreement. I want the diamond to stay on your hand permanently. I want to spend all my days with you from now on." Touching his forehead to mine, I breathe him in. *Is this a dream?*

"And Rosie?"

"That little Cinderella is embedded in my heart just as deep as you are, Em. But the question for you is, am I in yours?" I swallow to try to bring moisture to my mouth, nodding before any words leave my lips.

"Ben, you pushed your way into my heart the minute we met," I say honestly, and like he was holding his breath, he exhales heavily before a wide smile takes over his face.

"Then I am all yours, baby. You, me, and little Rosie, we will make a perfect team."

36

BEN

It's Monday morning, and I'm buzzed as I walk into my office. I had a great weekend with Emily. I can't stop thinking about it. When we finally woke from our slumber on Sunday, we talked about the school and what may happen, about our situation and dissolving the agreement, and then Jeremy. She opened up a little about how he is persistent and violent at times, even now that they're apart. I still don't know the full extent, but I know much more than I did. I grind my teeth just thinking about it, but I have plans this morning to arrange some security starting tomorrow.

When I dropped her off at home yesterday, I felt hollow. My chest hurt as I drove back to the city solo, so much so, I didn't end up at my apartment, but rather I went to my estate. I watched the twinkling lights, letting my mind run wild with thoughts of our future, imagining how much better my life will be having her in it permanently.

Rosie is adorable, and while I have never thought I

was the type of man who would have kids, surprisingly, the idea of being a father figure to her has settled within me without any hesitation. I had to force myself to put my phone down last night after I started searching online for the best schools nearby for kids with vision impairments, and then getting excited because I found one within a short drive of my estate.

Strutting through the office, I can't help but smile at Sandra as I walk up to her desk.

"Good morning, Sandra!" I chirp, and she smiles at me in surprise. I am not a total asshole of a boss, but this happiness level from me isn't the norm.

"Good morning, Ben. Happy Monday," she says, handing me my morning coffee as I walk through my office door.

"Did you have a good weekend?" I ask. Again, this small talk is not totally unusual, but definitely not part of our usual scope.

"Yes, although not as good as yours, it appears?" She eyes me in question, and I smirk at her, grabbing the morning papers from my desk. I nod to her, and she walks out of my office, closing the door behind her.

I sigh as I take a seat at my desk and flick through the newspapers to see the gossip pages. Photo after photo from the fundraising gala. People have always been interested in who I date. It is just part of the territory of being one of the Langford boys, and as I turn the page, it's filled with image after image of all the major players from Saturday night, including Emily and me. It takes me back to how beautiful she looked, and I close the newspaper on the image and sit in contentment, leaning back in my chair.

My thoughts are consumed by the beauty naked and wrapped in my sheets all weekend, when my phone buzzes, yanking me out of my thoughts.

"Yes, Sandra?"

"Your mother is here to see you—" Sandra barely finishes before my office door flies open and my mother walks straight in.

"Thanks, Sandra," I grit out before placing the phone down and sitting back, my good mood now disappearing.

"Good morning, Mother, to what do I owe the pleasure?" I ask sarcastically, and her lips thin.

"I come in peace," she says, taking a seat in the armchair in front of me, and I smell the bullshit from here.

"Glad to hear it." Looking at her stoically, I wait for her to continue.

"I spent yesterday thinking about you and your new fiancée." I don't miss the way she tries not to sneer at the mere mention of Emily.

"And what did you think about?" I push, not giving her an inch.

She sighs then and gives me a rare smile.

"Benjamin, I know I am not the easiest person, especially to you boys..." She smiles sweetly as the understatement of the year leaves her.

"But I can see how much Emily means to you, so I am going to make an effort." Her hands clasp on her knees in front of her as she sits straighter, her smile locked in place.

"Come again?" I ask, sitting forward, wondering if I heard her right.

"Well, I guess you could say I learned a few things when Harrison met Beth and, well, while Emily is not my first choice for you, if you want her in your life, then maybe that is something I just need to get used to and not make it so difficult. Lord knows that Beth and I still don't see eye to eye on things, and so I want to have a better start with Emily."

She looks like she means what she says, but I search her face nonetheless.

"I don't expect you to believe me. I know I have a lot of ground to make up for. But I would like to invite Emily to lunch and get to know her. Perhaps I can even tell her all your childhood embarrassing moments... isn't that what mothers-in-law usually do?" My mind is spinning at the change in her demeanor.

"Well, I think lunch would be okay. Where should I book?" I ask her as I look at my schedule for this week.

"Oh, don't you worry, I will take care of it. But it is girls only. I don't want you there messing it up. I will take her to the Four Seasons. Their restaurant is delightful for lunch," my mother says as she stands. "I will get her number from Sandra on my way out." And before I can reply, she's already sashaying out the door.

"Bye, darling!" she hollers as I sit dumbstruck. My mother is many things, and nice is not one of them. But I believe her when she said she wants to do better with Emily than she did with Beth. That was horrifying, and I am glad she can see the error of her ways.

I get busy calling Em to ensure she is ready to hear

from my mother, then organize Ralph to pick her up and take her. Em was hesitant at first. But I assured her it would be at least tolerable, and that Ralph will be only a call away, should she need to leave early. I don't particularly need my mother to like Em, but with her and Rosie being a part of my life, it would be easier. And more pleasant for everyone around. Maybe Em will be the glue that holds the Langford family together?

37

EMILY

T o say my nerves are getting the better of me is an understatement.

"You will be fine," George mutters, the two of us in my living room, Rosie playing in her room.

"I have never met in-laws before. I am not even sure what I am supposed to talk about," I say, wondering where my confidence has gone. Between the school shutting down last week because of the flooding, Ben and I successfully talking through the issue of Beasley and cementing our feelings for each other, as well as starting to tell him a little about my history with Jeremy, his mother reaching out with an olive branch has almost tipped me over the edge.

"You listen to me. Any parent would be damn honored to have you as a daughter-in-law. Now grab your bag and get out of here," George says, acting grumpy when, really, his true feelings are shining through.

"Thanks, George," I say, rushing to him and wrapping my arms around him.

"Go on. Shoo. I've got some new library books for Rosie as a surprise, so she won't even know you are gone." He rubs my back, and I pull away. Giving me a nod, I grab my bag and walk out the door, leaving my apartment and William Heights for yet another trip into the city.

RALPH PICKS me up in Ben's Bentley and takes me straight to the Four Seasons. I tried to at least look the part in some tailored black trousers with a soft cream blouse. And my hair is pinned neatly, with a light coating of makeup. He drops me at the door, telling me he will wait around the corner in the VIP parking lot, which eases my nerves somewhat. I keep my head high as I walk in and greet the hostess of the restaurant, who must recognize me immediately because with just a simple nod, she takes me toward the back to where Mrs. Langford must be sitting. My nerves start dancing in my stomach again as I glance around the room, even though I keep my head high and my stride strong.

As we veer around the back corner, we enter a private room. *Of course she would have a private room*, I think to myself. The woman practically bleeds money; she probably has someone to follow her around to wipe her mouth after she eats too.

"Emily, so glad you could come." The way she greets me is in complete contrast to what she sounded like on Saturday. There is no venom, no anger, and my eyes widen as I see her with her arms open, welcoming me like a perfect host.

"Mrs. Langford. Good to see you," I say, taking a few steps toward her before I stop dead in my tracks. I barely register that the hostess has left and closed the door to the room behind her as my blood turns cold. Sitting at the table with Mrs. Langford is Mr. Beasley, looking like a pig in mud, and next to him is Jeremy. His eyes are molten as he glares up at me, not doing anything to hide the fact that they run up and down my body.

"Wh—what is going on?" I am now stuck halfway between the door and the table, Mrs. Langford looking at me with a changing expression of ill intentions.

"Well, dear, I am very close friends with both Mr. Beasley and Mr. Lucas, and we all had a rather interesting conversation at the gala on the weekend. Imagine my surprise when both these prominent businessmen seemed to know a lot more about you than I did, even though you are prancing around the city on my son's arm. So I invited them along today as well. It appears that all three of us have a need to chat with you." Her smile doesn't waver, but I can now see the evil in it. How could a woman be so horrible? Sure, she may not know about my history with Jeremy, but she knows who Mr. Beasley is and how we are connected. She has set me up.

If Ben knew about this, he wouldn't be happy.

"I don't think this is a good idea. Let me call Ben, and..." I start to pull at my bag to grab my cell.

"Stop!" Jeremy barks, and my body jolts, listening to him immediately. His voice vibrates around my body, our history enough to make me stand at attention. I am too scared to move as my eyes flick between them all.

"You see, my dear, Benjamin is not destined to be married to someone so..." Mrs. Langford says, looking at me up and down before she continues. "*Suburban.*" She purses her lips, seemingly happy that she found the right description.

"Sasha is someone who is much more his speed, don't you think so, darling?" I am about to answer when I hear another voice.

"Of course, Diane. I am much more aligned to Ben's needs," Sasha's voice purrs from behind me, and I watch her strut in from the side of the room like she is walking a catwalk, until she is standing right next to me on the left. Her eyes run down my body and fixate on the diamond sitting on my finger. She reaches out and grabs my hand, her grip so hard, I feel like my bones will break as she pries the diamond off my finger, quickly slipping it on her own. This woman is deranged.

"Well then. I guess that is settled. You, Miss Carr, are no longer Benjamin's fiancée; that role is for Sasha to fill. Mr. Beasley, you had something you wanted to say?" Mrs. Langford says, turning to the fat man who is sitting and looking at his watch like he has to be somewhere else.

"I am taking the school, Miss Carr. If I don't get the school, I will no longer be a client of the Langford Law Firm, and I will move all my business directly to their competitor. I know I don't need to tell you that a move such as that will have a massive hit to Ben's bottom line, not to mention it will severely impact his reputation, having lost a major account within months of his brother's departure as CEO," Beasley says, standing, and I feel like I am going to faint.

"What?" I am struggling to keep up. If I want Ben to succeed in his position, I need to give him the school? That is blackmail. Of course I want Ben to succeed in his role as CEO. But even though the school may be flooded, it is not entirely out of the woods yet.

"I don't understand..." I say, looking at them all for more answers. I feel so small right now, so helpless. I'm not a woman who cowers, but right now, I don't even know who I am.

"Of course you don't, you stupid girl," Mrs. Langford mutters like I am frustrating her.

"Emily. It's time we went home. Your little parade in the city is now over. You are mine, will always be mine, and won't ever be coming into the city again," Jeremy says, standing and buttoning up his business jacket like he is finishing a meeting.

"I am not going anywhere with you." Taking a step back, my eyes stay firmly on him.

"I need to run. I will have Ben call a meeting, and Jeremy here has promised to get George to sign those forms this afternoon. Jeremy, I trust that you have this in hand," Beasley says, and Jeremy nods. What the hell are they talking about?

"Good to see you, Diane. I hope lunch next time is over more pleasant business dealings," he says, giving me a filthy look, followed by a smirk before he walks out the door, closing it behind him.

"She is all yours, Jeremy. I have organized those photos to be sent to Ben now. My friend did an excellent job of photoshopping them," Sasha says as she strides over to Jeremy and places a kiss to his cheek, giving me a wink. I feel my body wanting to lurch forward and empty the contents of my breakfast.

"What photos?" I ask tentatively, taking the bait.

"Oh, Jeremy and I got a little busy yesterday. While you and I don't look the same, my friend can manipulate photos extremely well. Ben will get a nice set of Polaroids this afternoon, of whom he thinks is you having unbelievable sex with Jeremy here," Sasha says, smiling. At that, I'm completely at a loss. What have they done?

"Come along, dear, we need to get wedding planning." Mrs. Langford grins at Sasha as they both follow Beasley through the door, it again closing solidly behind them.

I am left watching Jeremy like he is about to pounce. He stands tall, too confident, his hands in his pockets like he is in full control. My heart is thumping in my chest as I wonder how I can get out of this situation. A cloak of confusion drapes over me, my mind racing to try to sort out what exactly is going on.

I glance at the door behind me. I could make it out to the restaurant. He can't do anything to me out there. I would just need to run and scream and I could probably reach Ralph... But then Beasley will take his business from the law firm and Ben will take a hit. A very public hit. Everyone out in that restaurant now knows exactly who I am, and while I don't care if I come off crazy, I know the reputational damage to Ben will be more significant. I can't do that to him. He loves his work, and he loves his family.

But I need to think of Rosie, and I need to get to safety.

My hands grip my handbag, and I make a run for the door, but Jeremy is just as quick. I open the door at the same time his palm slams it shut, and he pushes me against it.

"Now, now, Emily, that is no way to treat me. After all I have done for you. We are going home via the private back door. I have my car waiting, and then I am going to take you to your god-awful apartment to get George, because he needs to sign these fucking papers. Then I need to ensure you know exactly who you belong to, and I want your little disabled offspring to hear it too," he says, making an appalling reference to Rosie before he pushes his hips into my back, and I feel him already hard. I vomit a little in my mouth as he licks up my neck.

"You are such a vile fucking asshole. You make me sick," I grit out. I want to end him. If that's the only way to stop this, then that's what I want.

"You have no idea..." he says before spinning me around and slapping me hard across the face. The last thing I remember is seeing my old cell phone fly out of my bag and across the room, out of reach, having left my new one with Rosie in case she needed to call me.

Even though I am now the one in danger.

38

BEN

My leg is bouncing with nerves as I think about Em, who is currently meeting my mother at the Four Seasons. I am starting to doubt the idea, but it is too late. Ralph already picked her up, so I just hope my mom is on her best behavior.

The knock at my office door startles me.

"Hey, Ben, express courier just arrived for you," Sandra says, walking in, handing me a brown envelope before retreating just as quickly and closing the door again.

I wasn't expecting anything, so I rip open the envelope and upturn it, and about five Polaroids fall out. It is unusual, but I am careful enough not to touch them with my bare hands. I am a lawyer, after all. I flick them over with my pen, and the blood leaves my body at what I see before me. My eyes home in on one of Emily with a man who isn't me. My teeth grind as I look at the next one and I see clearly Jeremy Lucas as his lips meet Em's bare neck, the two of them fully naked, Em straddling him. My anger rises as I look at the next one, and the next one, each growing progressively worse. Every photo has the date and time of last night printed at the bottom. Em's hair looks the exact same color and length as it is now.

"What the fuck?" I seethe, pushing my chair back as I stand angrily, shoving all the files off my desk so all I can see are these Polaroids.

"How the fuck did this happen?" I start pacing the office, trying to get a handle on things, wondering what the hell is happening. Pulling at my hair, I lean over my desk and look at the photos again. I know these are fake, manipulated or something. They can't be real. This can't be happening. This is not Em, it just can't be.

But who would do this? Who would send me these? I look for any sign they are fake, but each Polaroid shows Emily with her long hair, her eyes closed in most of them, her face half-hidden. Her body looks the same. Jeremy's lips close in on her nipple in one image, and I want to stab his eyes out.

I grab my cell and bring up the group text I have with my brothers, typing in 911 before I start pacing again. Our 911 call is something that we do in times of need. The four of us drop everything to get to each other, and in this case I have called them all to my office. I need my brothers. Right the fuck now.

"You okay, Benny Boy?" Tennyson asks as he and Eddie walk through my office door. It has taken them mere minutes to get here, both already downstairs in their offices.

"I don't know," I huff out as I continue to pace, my hand raking through my hair on a continuous loop.

"What's going on?" Harrison asks, barging into the office and closing the door. Our governor is looking a little disheveled, and all three of us turn to look at him.

"What? I had the morning off. I was upstairs with Beth," he says, patting his hair into place as he sits on the edge of my desk, the other two sitting on my sofa. All three of them survey the mess of files on my floor and look at me with concern.

"What's going on?" Eddie presses, the quiet tension in my office palpable.

"Emily," I state, not knowing where to go with this.

"Emily? What happened with Emily?" Harrison starts to stand up, already knowing that he isn't going to like what he is about to hear.

"Well, we talked on the weekend and decided to give us a real go. Be together, for real." I take a deep breath, that all now seeming like a distant memory.

"But..." Tennyson says, waiting for the bomb to drop.

"I just got these delivered," I say, pointing to the Polaroids on the coffee table, each of my brothers grabbing one to take a look. I feel sick, sick that my brothers are seeing Emily like this, but equally pissed off that someone is going to the trouble of sending these to me.

"What the fuck?" Harrison barks, his eyes dark and stormy as they look back at me.

"Where did they come from?" Eddie asks, throwing

the Polaroid he had back on the coffee table, not wanting to look at any others.

"Express delivery just now. No sender details," I state, the whole thing feeling really off.

"Are they real? Not doctored or anything?" Tennyson asks me, eyes narrowed.

"It's not her. It can't be her, can it?" I ask them, almost pleadingly. I watch their faces for a tell, but only see deep concern etched into each of them.

"Does it look like her?" Harrison asks, stepping forward to look at me and not the photos.

"Yes. I guess?" I feel panicked, my chest heavy.

"No. Ben," he almost yells. "Does it look like her?" His harsher tone has me taking another centering breath before I force myself to look at the photos again.

"It can't be her. Deep down, I know it can't be her," I say, shaking my head. But there's still that whisper of doubt that needs confirmation from my brothers, to know I'm not crazy for trusting her. I've been burned before, and this is triggering every insecurity I thought I had moved past.

"It isn't her," Tennyson states strongly, stepping forward next to Harrison. "I don't know her well, but she doesn't seem like the cheating kind. She has a job, is a single mom, and looks at you like you are her everything. I mean, she wouldn't even have the fucking time to be with someone else anyway." His words penetrate, and I agree with every one of them.

"Is there anything in these photos that make you think that this is or isn't her?" Harrison asks, his legal hat on tight, looking at the evidence.

"They used to date. He was violent. I haven't deep dived yet, but she just started opening up to me about him. He grabbed her at the gala," I say, my words tumbling out so fast, I am not sure they make any sense.

"I saw her arm... it was red and angry," Eddie pipes up, coming toward me now too.

"Yeah, she said they broke up years ago," I tell them, and Harrison nods.

"I fucking hate Jeremy Lucas," Tennyson growls as he rubs his chin, looking back down at the photos.

"So what? He is sending you fake photos to make you break up?" Eddie asks, his eyebrows furrowed.

"It doesn't make sense," Harrison butts in, still trying to pull pieces together.

"I had a feeling she knew him right from the beginning. She hid from him the first time she was here in my office because he walked past. I knew then something wasn't right." I'm shaking my head at myself for not telling him to back off sooner, for not catching on right away.

"So if she hid from him then, that clearly says she doesn't want to see him. Then he bid against you at the auction on the weekend. He saw the two of you together. Do you think he is the one that sent these to you? That makes the most sense, right?" Tennyson asks, and for the first time, none of us can connect the dots. What would be his motivation? Is Eddie onto something... he is trying to get us to break up?

"Have you called her?" Harrison asks, and I shake my head. My eyes look at her naked body on Jeremy's, and I feel sick. I hate him.

"Maybe you should call her. Tell her about them and see what she has to say," Tennyson says, looking at me tentatively. Like I am a bomb about to explode.

"She is the one for me. She is it. She is... everything." They all finally understand, I can see it in their eyes. Emily is mine. Will always be mine.

"Ben, Beas... Shit, sorry, I didn't know you were busy," Michael says, looking flustered as he barges into my office.

"It's fine, what is it?" I wave my hand at him to continue as I sigh. My mind is racing in a hundred different directions, but knowing that the show here at work must go on.

"Um, Beasley has called a meeting. Urgent. He is on his way in, and so is George," Michael says, smoothing his suit. He looks like he just ran a mile to get here, he's so flustered.

I raise my eyebrows in surprise.

"Apparently, they have struck a deal. They are coming in to sign the paperwork. They will be here in ten minutes."

I stand still in shock, my stomach sinking. "Agreement?" I ask him.

"They will meet us in the conference room," he says with a nod before he closes the door, leaving my mind whirling.

What the hell is going on today?

"Sounds like Beasley got his way, then." Harrison looks at me in question, but there's suspicion in his eyes.

"Looks like it," I murmur, feeling a migraine coming on.

"What can we do for you?" Tennyson asks, looking down at the photos, then reaching over and flipping them over. It's a move that shows the respect he already has for Emily, even if he doesn't believe it's her captured in these moments. And with that, I decide it's time to get my shit together. This isn't the time to break down.

"Just let me get this meeting out of the way to find out what the hell is going on, and then I will be back. We need to figure out where to go from here. Because someone is sending me these photos, and I'm not stopping until I know who."

39

EMILY

My head is pounding as rough hands drag me from the car and pull me up the walkway. My eyes squint in the sunlight, before we bash through the glass doors.

We are at my apartment.

I look at the hard grip on my arm and my eyes travel up to see Jeremy looking disheveled as he rushes us both up the stairs. He is too quick, and I trip, but he yanks my arm hard, pulling me to standing as I wince in pain.

"Stop..." I say weakly. My head is spinning, and I try to grab on to any memory I have of what is happening. I look down at my clothes and remember I was having lunch with Ben's mother...

"Get inside," Jeremy seethes, opening the door to my apartment and shoving me in. We startle George and Rosie who are sitting on the sofa. George immediately says something to Rosie, and I watch, heartbroken, as my daughter walks swiftly with her cane into her room, shutting the door. I hear her lock it, something I only installed last week, and I now thank God that I did. I know she is safely under her bed, no doubt her racing heart pounding in her ears.

"What the hell are you doing?" George demands as he stalks over to where Jeremy has me pinned against him. My eyes widen, because I have never heard George so angry. He reaches out to grab me and pull me away from Jeremy, but stops at the last moment, his eyes going wide.

"Not so fast, old man," Jeremy says as I feel something cold and metal against my temple. My body moves in slow motion at the terror freezing my veins, the sounds of them yelling now muffled in my brain. All I can think of is Rosie, knowing that no one is coming to save us.

"So right now, you are going to get into my car, and go into the city to sign those fucking papers, or else, when you get home, she won't be breathing," I hear Jeremy grit out, and George's face pales.

"This has gone too far, son," George says, the words barely registering, the thumping inside my head almost overtaking every other sense.

"You better leave... Tick... Tock..." Jeremy sneers. George looks at me with deep concern etched into his brow before he runs out the door.

The door slam shuts, and I swallow. I am alone. With Jeremy. My biggest nightmare.

"Now, my darling Emily, all we need to do is wait. I wonder what the hell we can do to pass the time?" Jeremy stares down at me like the devil, his eyes wandering over me slowly.

"You know we were so good together. You are so perfect for me. Always were. Why can't we just go back to the way we were?" Jeremy says, almost sweetly, letting go of my arm finally. The pain sears through it as the blood pulses back into my muscles.

"You ruined it. It was all fine until you ruined us," I growl out. If I am leaving this earth today, then I am not leaving without a fight.

"It is your fault for getting pregnant in the first place. We were fine until you decided to keep that fucking baby!" he yells, and I jump a little, my heart heavy knowing that Rosie can hear him.

"You just need to leave. Find someone new. There must be a million women who would love the chance to date a man like you." The words taste terrible on my tongue as I say them. Not wanting any other woman to go through what I have, but I need him to leave. I need him to walk out, close the door, and get in his car and drive away.

"Oh, I fuck plenty. There are lots of women. But there is only one Emily... and she is all mine." When he licks his lips, I feel the salty tears as they fall silently down my cheeks.

40

BEN

I feel on edge as I make my way to the conference room. If George is here to sign off on the paperwork, I wonder what changed his mind. I should be much happier about it all than I am.

But I feel like shit.

Walking into the conference room, I see everyone seated. Everyone except Emily. I stop, my eyes grazing over everyone. Michael nods at me to take a seat, Beasley sitting like the Cheshire cat beside him. But George is alone. And he is not looking at me, not even giving me an acknowledgement.

Heading around the table, I take a seat on the other side of Beasley.

"Good afternoon, George," I say confidently, but he gives me nothing in return. He looks straight ahead to Michael. He is on edge. Not happy.

"Where do I sign?" he asks, appearing keen to get it all over with. Michael clears his throat and pushes across the contract and a pen.

"George, if you can sign on page three, nine, and twelve, that would be great. Although I would advise that Emily or your lawyer of choice look over the contracts before—"

"No need," George interrupts him and grabs the pen, starting to sign without even reading a single line. We are all quiet as we watch George sign the school over without any pushback, and I grip the table. He shoves the paperwork back to Michael, then goes to stand.

"Is that all? I need to go," he says, appearing in a rush to leave.

"Just one more, George. I need you to fill in this form in relation to who you want the check made out to," Michael says, pushing another piece of paper over to George. I look at Beasley, and I don't know how I know, but I know he has done something. The way he is sitting is too confident. Like he knew it'd be this easy as he looks down his nose at George who is twice the man he is. The feeling in the room is totally off.

Michael flicks his eyes to me, deep concern etched into his brow. He feels it too. I look around the table, and everything else is as it should be. Sandra has a glass jug of water and a small bowl of chocolate Milk Duds because they are Harrison's favorite. They make me think of Em and her little birthmark.

I watch as George rushes to pick up the pen and gets busy filling in the details. The silence is deafening and the urge to say something, to acknowledge the entire fucked-up situation, springs through me, but I remain silent. My jaw clenched.

"There. Is that all?" George asks Michael, who nods and stands, reaching out his hand.

"Congratulations, George. I know the school meant a lot, but hopefully the ten million will soften the blow," Michael says, but George stands and walks out, not shaking his hand, not saying another word. He just leaves and actually runs out the door.

I watch as the conference room door closes behind him, and Michael clears his throat.

"Good work, boys. It took a few weeks, but we got it in the end. Ben, please thank your mother for me," Beasley says to me with a glint in his eye.

"Sure. Wait, for what?" I ask, confused, as I lean over and grab the file of paperwork to give to Sandra.

"Oh, without her and her connections, I couldn't have made this a done deal. Your mother is a smart woman. Evil, but smart." Grinning, he follows Michael out the door, and my stomach feels like I swallowed lead.

Once Michael and Beasley leave the room, I sit for a moment, my head in my hands, deep-rooted pain throbbing in my chest as I think about all the kids, Rosie, and Emily. Then with a sigh, I sit back and look at the paperwork, cross-checking that George signed where he was meant to, and the air leaves my lungs when I see the final page. It is the payment details page, where he wanted the money sent to. But it isn't his bank account details on the form, rather stating that five million dollars needs to be given to the Vision Impaired Center and the other five million dollars needs to be given to the Women's Domestic Violence Center.

I'm utterly gobsmacked. He didn't even take the

money. He was offered ten million dollars, and he gave it away. I am in awe of this man whose beliefs are so strong that he turns down that amount of money. Still, I try to connect the dots, realizing that it was never about the money for George and Emily and always about the school.

I feel sick that my own firm benefits by a few million, when George just gave away ten. He gave it away because of Rosie and wanting to help other kids like her. Looking back at the paperwork, I am trying to work out the domestic violence connection, and then it slaps me in the face.

Rosie telling me about her father being a bad man.

Emily with bruises on her face from her "fall."

George's extreme caution around me and always looking out for them both.

My eyes home in on the small bowl of Milk Duds Sandra left on the table, and I jump up, running back to my office where my brothers are waiting, hoping that I am very, very wrong.

41

BEN

"Where are the photos!" I pant as soon as I push through the door.

"Over there, but, Ben, you need to—" Eddie says, lifting a file from his lap that must have fallen from my desk earlier.

I scurry to the Polaroids, staring at them intently.

"What is it?" Harrison asks me as he comes closer.

"Em has a birthmark on her left hip..." I say, the mark now so vivid in my mind as my eyes run over each and every photo. Damn, why didn't I think of this earlier?

"What? What are you talking about?" Harrison quizzes.

"Em has a birthmark the size of a Milk Dud on her left hip. None of these photos show it. None of them show it!" I shout, looking over them again, my heart lightening, knowing for sure this isn't her. I don't know who they are or why someone would do this, but I knew they were off. It isn't her. The relief pouring through my body is instant. I knew it couldn't be; I just couldn't see the truth behind the photos.

"Here, let me look." Harrison grabs them from me, looking over them more thoroughly.

"Ben, you need to see this," Eddie says again, standing, and I look up at him, renewed hope fluttering in my chest.

"Have you seen this file on Emily?" Eddie asks again, his eyebrows raised.

"I haven't looked at it. Michael got it weeks ago when we first met her. I was going to look through her history and see what I could find out about her to help with Beasley's case, but then I got to know her and thought it might be a bit creepy," I say with a shrug.

"You need to see this," Eddie pushes, his tone serious, and all us boys look at him.

Tennyson looks over his shoulder first.

"What the fuck!" He stands up ramrod straight and rips the file from Eddie's grasp.

"What?" Harrison questions, his tone demanding. In his new position as governor, he needs complete transparency.

For the first time in his entire life, Ten is speechless. With the file open wide in his hands, he just looks at me. "I'm sorry, bro..." he says, handing me the file.

I grab it and pull it open to see pages and pages of reports, pictures, and victim statements. Pictures of Em's body, bruised, bashed, distorted. I flick through them all, looking at the dates, six months ago, a year ago, going all the way back to years earlier, when as a pregnant woman, she was pushed down the stairs in a building not far from here.

My eyes scan quickly, looking at details, names, police departments, and one name consistently comes into my vision: Jeremy Lucas.

"What is this, Harrison? Tell me what I am fucking looking at here," I grit out, my blood starting to boil as Harrison looks over my shoulder.

"Domestic violence. Partner violence. Abuse, broken bones, verbal altercations..." he murmurs, as he grabs the file, looking through each page, his forehead creasing with concern. My heart hurts, my head hurts. I am pulling my hair as I start to pace again, the nervous energy I felt before now replaced by the anger swirling in my body at someone having their hands on her.

"I knew it. She told me Jeremy was violent, but I didn't know it went on for years! That he is Rosie's father!" I almost scream, angry at myself. Murderous when I think about the situation.

"Where is she now?" Tennyson asks, and I stop pacing.

"Having lunch with our mother," I state, and all three of them look at me as though I am mad.

"I have so many questions about that, starting with *why*?" Tennyson asks, basically shouting.

"She came here talking about wanting to make amends, meeting Em properly, not wanting to make the same mistakes as she did with Beth," I say, my eyes flicking to Harrison, and I see his jaw clench.

"She seemed to genuinely want to talk with Em, so I spoke to Em and she agreed, given that we are now moving forward and being together for real." It made sense at the time, now I am doubting everything.

"For a smart guy, you are so fucking stupid some-times," Tennyson bites out before slumping back onto the sofa, his head in his hands.

"Where did they go?" Eddie asks, looking at me with concern. The dread I felt about them being together earlier is now mixing in with what Beasley said about my mother before he left and the new information I found out on Em's history. I feel like I might vomit.

"Four Seasons. Ralph is waiting outside for her and said he would call as soon as he had her," I offer them, and all three of them look at their watches.

"It is four thirty in the afternoon," Harrison states, and I look at him in disbelief. I have been so preoccupied with everything that I totally forgot about the lunch. It is odd, since Mother is always quick to eat, and I am sure she would have been quicker than usual with Em.

My cell phone rings then, and I pull it from my pocket.

"It's her," I say, showing the boys the screen, Em's name appearing.

"Well, fucking answer it," Tennyson grits out to me, and I do.

"Em, hey. Is everything okay?" I say, my breath coming out in a big rush.

"Ben?" Rosie's little voice comes through. "Ben?" she says again quickly, and I can hear her crying.

"Rosie? What's wrong?" I ask, now on high alert. With my brothers beside me, I put her on speaker.

"Ben, the bad man is here. He is hurting Mommy. You

need to come help us," she says, her voice panicked and distraught.

I look at my brothers, and Tennyson has already sprinted out the door, Harrison on the phone.

"I am coming, Rosie. Where are you? Are you in danger?" I ask her as we all follow Tennyson, running down the hallway to the elevator.

"I'm hiding under my bed, and I've locked my bedroom door, just like Mommy told me to," she says, sniffling, her voice wavering. The poor thing is scared out of her mind.

"That's good, Rosie, you stay there. Tell me what you can hear. Tell me everything." My brothers and I reach the basement, Tennyson organizing our ride.

It is then I hear it. A gunshot, and my whole world crumbles.

42

EMILY

I have no idea what time it is, or even what day.

My head is swollen, bruised, my body sore and damaged. My clothes ripped. I lie on the hard linoleum floor next to my dining table as my ex sits across from me, eating what appears to be ramen noodles. My eyes flick to Rosie's door, and I see it still shut, and I wonder how long she has been in there.

She knows not to come out. She knows to remain in there until I get her.

I lick my dry lips and hiss a little, a cut at my mouth tasting metallic. I slowly and quietly take some breaths, centering myself, trying to figure out what has happened. I look over my body, and from what I can see, I am intact. Purple welts run up one arm, and my legs have bruises and marks. My head is throbbing, but I can wiggle my fingers and toes, and my underwear is all exactly where it should be.

Looking up at Jeremy, I see him watching me. His eyes remain on mine as he slurps another forkful of noodles.

He is playing with me. Drawing this out, waiting for something.

My body jumps when I hear a noise at the door, and George pushes through it, panting like he has run a marathon. His eyes land on me, where I am curled up on the floor, and he is by my side in an instant.

"I did what you asked. I signed the damn papers. Now you need to leave," George says as he tries to pull me up by my arm, and I whimper at the pain that radiates up to my shoulders.

"Good, now transfer that ten million dollars to me," Jeremy says as he takes another bite like he's at a work meeting. He is cool, calm, and now I know what he was waiting for. He was waiting for the money.

"What?" George asks, his eyes bugging out of his head. "You didn't say that before I left. You just told me to sign the papers." I can hear panic in George's voice as it rises an octave.

"I don't fucking have to explain myself, *Dad*. Give me the fucking money," Jeremy yells as he stands, pushing back the chair in the process, which slams hard onto the floor.

Dad? Did he just say Dad?

"I owe you nothing. I signed the school away, and that money is now gone to charity. I don't want it, not one penny. Now you need to go and leave us all alone," George says, but my head is scrambled.

Did George just say he left ten million dollars to charity?

"I am not fucking leaving without that ten million dollars," Jeremy seethes, his temper now escalating. His shoulders draw back, his hands clenching into fists by his sides. He is winding up like a toy, the pull cord getting tighter and tighter, waiting to let loose and explode.

"You don't deserve it. Not after all that you have done," George spits, holding me closer.

"I am your fucking son!" Jeremy screams as saliva flies from his mouth. My head whips to George in fear and question, and he looks at me. His lips thin, and I see sorrow clear on his face.

"You are no son of mine. You hurt people; you steal; you left your mother and me years ago with nothing. You took our whole life savings!" George says, and my stomach sinks.

"You ignored me. You and Mom put all your time and energy into that fucking school. So what if I stole your money? It was money I was owed." Jeremy heaves out his words. I have never seen him so angry, even when he was taking it out on me.

"You were never interested in the school, in the community. You have only ever been interested in yourself, not what you can do for others," George says subtly, now pushing me behind him.

"Others? *Others*? What about me?" I feel like the windows are going to rattle with Jeremy's voice getting louder and louder. He is a bomb ticking. I can feel it.

"Your mother and I gave you a stable home, a loving home. We put you through college, and then you trashed our home, took all our money, and left. I never saw you again until you turned up in Emily's life," George says, his voice almost pleading now. I am light-headed, feeling fuzzy, most likely from a concussion, but my hearing is working perfectly. *Jeremy is George's son?*

"What... What is going on?" I ask, looking between the two of them.

"Didn't he tell you that? Didn't he tell you that he is my poor excuse for a father?" Jeremy bites out, their dislike for each other obvious.

"I thought I raised you better. For years, we looked for you. And then while your mother and I were searching every shelter in the city for you, upset that our son left and we had no idea where he was, whether he was alive or dead, imagine our surprise when we met Emily and slowly connected the dots. You are now living like a millionaire, all the while, your girlfriend catches you fucking your secretary in your office and runs from you. So you chase her and push her down the stairs!" George roars. "That little girl in there is blind because of you and your actions. And even now, you can't let them go. Even now, all you want is money." George is vibrating with rage, and I am struggling to remain upright. My head is filled with a mix of disbelief combined with waves of nausea that thrum through my body.

"It is too late for you. I have given the money away. I have given it to foundations that can try and make amends for your poor behavior. Money is evil, it makes you evil, and you need to leave before I call the police," George says, pulling his cell phone out from his pocket and beginning to dial.

"Don't do that, *Dad*," Jeremy sneers, and I hear the distinct sound of a gun clicking, aimed right at my head.

"You get that gun away from Emily, and you run out that door, son. That is the only way you are going to survive this," George warns, and my body shakes as I stare right at the barrel. *Is this the last thing I am going to see?*

"Her death will be on your conscience, old man. Not mine." Jeremy smiles, his eyes firmly on his father while the gun rests on me.

Suddenly, I am pushed to the side, my body slapping onto the hard floor, my head hitting it hard. I look up and see the two of them struggling against each other. There is yelling, flesh pounding, crashing. My chairs and table are now scattered as I scramble away from them and across the floor. George is old, but he is still fit; however, Jeremy is overpowering him. My eyes rest on George's cell phone, which flew over to the corner of the room, so I pull myself closer to it and out of the way, one arm not working as well as the other, my legs heavy and feeling like Jell-O. I reach George's cell phone and pick it up, dialing 9-1-1 immediately.

"9-1-1, what's your emergency?" the voice on the other end says.

"I need the police," I say, just before the gunshot rings out. I scream and drop the phone, as blood pools on the cheap flooring, circling my feet.

43

BEN

I am furious with myself as I pull up to her apartment block less than forty minutes later, after breaking every speed limit from the city to the suburbs.

Police swarm the streets. Harrison was straight onto the police chief the minute Rosie called, Tennyson already had the car waiting, and Eddie has been trying to contact our mother for information, to no avail.

I jump out of the car and run toward the apartments and am stopped by officers.

"Get the fuck out of my way." I push them aside and run up the stairs, taking them two at a time, ignoring the shouts and arms grabbing for me as I do.

Panic fills me as I make it to her door and step inside. It is a crime scene. Blood, broken furniture, police tape, officers photographing evidence.

"Shit," Tennyson says from right behind me. I hadn't even registered that he followed me.

"Harry and Eddie are downstairs dealing with the police," he says as we both take tentative steps inside.

"Where are they?" Tennyson asks as we both look around.

"Rosie?" I call out, my eyes searching. "Rosie!" I yell louder, my heart ready to fly out of my chest as I look over the place that was their home.

"Ben!" I hear her, and I run to her room where I see a few female officers with her.

"Sir." One stands up and gets in my face.

"That is my daughter, so I suggest you get the fuck out of my way," I grit out. My body feels feral, my anger is at an all-time high. I fucking hope Jeremy is dead, because if not, I am going to kill that motherfucker myself.

She nods and moves to the side, and I rush to sit next to Rosie on the edge of her bed.

"Rosie. I'm here, I am right here," I say softly as I grab her and pull her close to me, her little arms wrapping around my body as she crawls onto my lap and starts to shake and weep.

"Ben, you came!" She cries louder, her wails piercing through my chest cavity and opening it up like never before.

"I came, Rosie. I told you I would. I told you to call me anytime. You are such a good, brave girl. You know that, right? You are so, so brave," I whisper to her as I continue to hold her, rubbing her back to calm her breathing.

I look up and see the female officers talking to Tennyson, him giving them all our contact details as I hug Rosie tighter, ensuring she feels secure. My eyes trail outside of her room, where I see the dining table smashed onto the floor, dishes, and what looks like ramen coating the walls, along with more blood. Lots and lots of blood.

"Where's Mommy? I want Mommy," she says over and over, and I have never known heartbreak like this in my entire life.

"The ambulance took her. I want you to come with me, okay? We will go and see her," I say to her, not wanting to tell her that Em will be alright, because I don't fucking know if she will. I feel Rosie nod against my chest.

"Now I am going to stand, and I am going to keep you in my arms. We're going to walk out of the apartment and downstairs to my car, okay? I want you to curl into me and cover your ears." She has no sight, but her hearing is impeccable, so I don't want her to overhear anything that could traumatize her more. Again, she nods against my now wet shirt, and I stand, carrying her out of the apartment as quickly as I entered.

Because now, I need to get to my fiancée.

I PACE THE HOSPITAL HALLWAY, Rosie sitting close by with Beth, the two of them having a big conversation about the various books they both like, and I thank God for Beth at this moment.

I have already spoken with my brothers, and they support me in representing Emily in what will without a doubt be a hard legal battle to get Jeremy to stay away from her.

I currently have my team getting ready to talk with all of Emily's friends and associates, reporting on the dates and times they have seen her with bruises and marks, including a few weeks ago when I saw her.

How could I have missed this? I feel guilty for being so focused on work and the Beasley deal that I didn't put two and two together. I knew something wasn't right, and Em all but confirmed my suspicions, but I had no idea it was this bad. I should have pushed her for more information on the weekend. I should have asked more questions. I should have had security on her from the moment I met her.

My stomach churns as I think about what I walked into earlier today. Jeremy was apparently taken away in handcuffs before we arrived, the police finding him in shock at the scene. But he was soon released once he had his legal team on the phone. George, on the other hand, was not so lucky, currently in surgery with a gunshot wound to his abdomen.

"How is she?" Harrison asks, passing me a coffee.

"She's still out cold. Doctors say her body is exhausted and she underwent a lot of shock on top of her broken arm and bruises. But a few days in here, and then she can come home," I murmur as I rub my eyes and take a sip of the steamy hot coffee, which tastes like mud on my tongue.

"George is still in surgery, but they are positive he will be okay. Apparently, they just need to remove the bullet, which was lodged between his liver and his spleen," Eddie reports, he and Tennyson following up on George for me while I wait here for Em to wake up.

"You should go home and shower," Tennyson tells me, but I shake my head.

"I am not leaving here until she wakes and sees me and Rosie. Then I will take Rosie home and try to get some sleep. But I don't want Em to wake up and not see her," I say, confident that Rosie will be the first person she will want to see, hoping that I will be the second.

"Boys, I came as soon as I could! What is the emergency?" My mother waltzes into the hospital waiting room like she is walking into an event. Her chiffon scarf draped over her shoulder flows behind her in a whirl of red, followed closely by Sasha.

"Ben! What happened? Are you okay?" Sasha pants out like she has been stressed to get to me, yet her perfectly polished look ensures me that she took her time to get ready, and I wonder why she is here at all.

"I'm fine," is all I can grit out.

"Well, why are we here?" Mother asks, looking between us boys, and it is then I see the sparkle.

"What the fuck is on your hand?" I bark out, making Sasha jump.

"Oh. This... um... well..." Sasha is scrambling for words, having not seen me yell like this before.

"Oh, Benjamin. The lunch I had with that horrible Emily earlier today ended with her throwing this ring at Sasha. It was quite the spectacle, I can assure you. I am so glad she left you for another man," my mother says in a gossipy voice that I now know is laced with lies.

I shouldn't be shocked, yet I am. Tennyson has already walked away, and I finally understand why he does. Because the anger swirling in my body at the moment is all-encompassing.

"Mom, what did you do?" Eddie asks the question we are all thinking, as Mom's mask starts to slip.

"Whatever do you mean?" she asks, looking between Eddie, Harrison, and me nervously.

"Sasha, you have exactly ten seconds to get Emily's fucking diamond off your finger or I will be calling the police to charge you with robbery, in addition to the charges of accessory to assault and battery, perjury of photographic evidence, and conspiracy to attempted murder that I already will be speaking to the police about. Not to mention, I will be filing a protection order for you to keep over two hundred yards away from me and my fiancée," I spit out, not leaving out a detail. My blood is boiling, and if I don't keep a level head around these two, there is no telling what I will do.

"What? That is absurd..." she sputters, my mother shocked as she stands beside her.

"Ten... Nine..." I start, and I see Eddie stand nervously beside me, Harrison's eyes glued to our mother.

"Benjamin, stop being ridiculous. Sasha is the only one for you, can't you see that? She is tall, beautiful, comes from the right family, has the right connections," Mother spits out like I am the crazy one.

"...Eight... Seven... Six." Clenching and unclenching my fists, Sasha pulls the ring from her finger.

"What the hell is going on, and why did you boys call me down here anyway? We are miles out of town! Seriously, I don't have time for your antics today." Mom is now ramrod straight, not liking that things are not going as she planned.

"What happened today, Mom, when you were at the restaurant?" Harrison asks her, his eyes not leaving her for a second as I grab the diamond from Sasha, then set my attention firmly on our mother.

"I had lunch at the Four Seasons with Emily. She was late, terribly dressed, and upset at something or other. She put on quite a display, I'll have you know. That woman has no idea how to act in such settings, Benjamin. She is—" But I cut her off.

"*Enough!*" I yell, making everyone jump.

"Ben?" a little voice says, and I turn swiftly to see Rosie sitting on the edge of her seat.

"Fuck," I murmur, rubbing my head, forgetting about the little girl who is probably hearing some very adult conversations right now. Beth gives me a look to tell me I need to do better.

"I'm so sorry, Rosie," I mutter as I take a few steps to her and pick her up, her small frame clinging onto my hip, her dainty hands circling around my neck, and she rests her head on my shoulders. She is tired, we all are, but we are not leaving until we speak to Em.

"Benjamin!" My mother says my name like she is scolding me.

"That's your Mommy, isn't it?" Rosie whispers to me.

"Yes, Rosie, it is," I say with a sigh.

"Benjamin!" My mother's voice rises another octave.

"Don't worry, Ben, I will teach you how to use Siri. You don't need to ask her to do that. She doesn't seem very nice," Rosie says to me, worried for me. I huff out a small laugh and kiss the top of her head, keeping her securely in my arms.

"Benjamin, why are you cradling that little girl?" My mother's eyes pierce mine accusingly. "And why in the world did you call me to this hospital, Edward?" She turns to my brother, looking bewildered. I walk back over to her, taking in the look of disgust and mortification on her face as she registers Rosie's lack of sight. She doesn't even try to hide her reaction.

"I called you here because there was a terrible incident this afternoon, which left Emily here in the hospital, and we wanted to understand what happened to get her here. We are building a case, and we need as much evidence as we can get," Harrison says, keeping a calm tone, but I can sense his impatience right beneath the surface.

I watch my mother swallow roughly, and her face pales a little. My brothers and I all know that she is somehow mixed up in it all. Guilt is written all over her face.

"Fucking hell," Tennyson murmurs from a few feet away where he is sitting, putting his head down, not looking at anyone.

"Mom, I think you need to leave, and the police will come to visit you tomorrow to get your statement," Harrison warns in a controlled voice, even though I see his jaw clench.

It has happened again. Mother has stuck her nose in our relationships and caused a whole lot of pain and anger, when it just wasn't needed. She needs to pay this time. I can't protect her from this. I can't and I won't.

"Sasha, they will visit you as well, and I will submit that application for a protection order tonight. I don't want you near me, my fiancée, or my daughter ever again," I say, and I hear both her and my mother gasp quietly. It felt good to say the words. Em and Rosie are my forever, the women staring back at me in shock well pushed back into my past.

"Come along, Sasha," my mother says as she turns on her heel, her shoes clipping on the tiles out the door as Sasha follows suit.

"We have to do something about her," Harrison says, heaving out a sigh.

"If she is somehow involved, then the police will have my full support to charge her." I am done. It was horrible what Beth had to endure when she met Harrison, but now Mom lied to my face and put Em and her daughter in danger. I will not stand for it.

"She needs to learn a lesson, I agree, but a formal charge?" Eddie asks, none of us believing that it has come to this. Our younger brother is still giving her the benefit of the doubt.

"Well, we have to do something. Her insane meddling has to stop before something else happens. Something worse," Harrison says as his hand lands on my shoulder, giving me a supportive squeeze.

"I got a call earlier. My team found a property a few blocks away from the school in William Heights," Harrison says, and my eyebrows rise in question.

"I knew Beasley would get what he wanted, as he always does. So I had some interns on my team investigate any properties of a similar size that may be coming onto the market. As governor, we can't just let private businesses overtake community needs," he says with a smile, and I almost falter. My older brother continues to look out for me, and whatever that property costs, I already know I will be buying it. For Em. For Rosie, and for George.

Rosie feels heavier in my arms, and I look down to see her eyes closed. Her head rests on my shoulder, her mouth slightly open, and tuffs of air sneak out in almost a snore. Warmth runs through my body. Not only do I have her safe in my arms, but she feels safe enough with me to fall asleep, snuggling in tight. I hold her firm in the belief that nothing bad will happen to her or her mother ever again.

44

EMILY

I wake to the sounds of machines beeping, and I cringe as pain shoots through my head. I try to lift my hand to touch my head, but there are tubes and cables, and it is heavy. The bed is hard underneath me, and the sheets scratch my body from the starch. It is familiar yet not comfortable.

"Don't move too much," I hear a deep voice say next to me, and I slowly try to open my eyes, letting them adjust. The room is quiet, and the curtains are drawn, and as I take in the surroundings, I realize I am in the hospital. A flood of memories come back to me, making me groan.

"Rosie?" I mumble. My throat is dry, my tongue feels stuck to the roof of my mouth, and when I try to swallow, I feel nothing but sandpaper. My head throbs, and my lips seem a little swollen. I wonder how bad I look today.

"She is right here," Ben says, and I turn my head to his voice, looking at him for the first time.

Sitting in a chair pulled up right next to me at the side

of my bed, he sits. His hair is everywhere, like he has been pulling at it, and his suit jacket gone, his shirt rolled up to the elbows and crumpled. Curled up in his lap is my daughter. Sleeping peacefully, her little arms stay wrapped tight around his neck. My heart melts, and my eyes water.

"Is she alright?" My voice breaks as tears flow over my cheeks.

"She is. Tired, a little shaken, but she called me from her room. I heard the gunshot through the phone, and I got to her only a few minutes after the paramedics brought you and George here," he says, rubbing a hand down her back.

"And George?" I ask, now panicked, remembering George slumped on the floor at my feet, his blood coating my toes.

"He was in surgery for most of the afternoon. Bullet was lodged in his torso between his liver and his spleen, but it missed all main organs, and they removed it. He is stable and currently sleeping a few rooms down. They think he will wake up sore and tired tomorrow, but otherwise, he should heal well." The air leaves my lungs in one big breath. Tears fall freely now, the relief that we are all okay. The relief that Ben is here by my side, holding my baby. Looking after everything.

"Jeremy?" I mumble, closing my eyes again, wanting to know what happened. But also not.

"I am going to end him. I am going to absolutely annihilate him, Em," he grits out quietly, anger very evident in his tone. "The police took him in for questioning, but released him this evening. I gave a full statement, and it will go to court, and that is where I will bury him. I will make sure he is locked up for everything he has ever done to you. He will pay, Em, I will make sure of it." Ben says the words with such confidence; I know he will do it and stop at nothing to ensure it happens.

I open my eyes slowly then and fully take him in. He is not the polished man whom I first met. His disheveled appearance is all due to me. Embarrassment and guilt flood me for Ben having gotten caught up in my mess. The feeling is nearly unbearable as a sob crawls up my throat.

"I'm so sorry, Ben," I whisper, and I can't help the tears that fall steadily now.

"Don't you dare apologize. None of this is your fault. None of this is on you. You have *nothing* to apologize for. I just wish I could have stopped it all before it happened." Sitting forward, he grabs my hand, giving me a squeeze.

"But look at what has happened. Look at how I have brought you down. You are a successful lawyer, and now you are mixed up in my mess of a life," I say, trying to give him an out. An opening to leave should he want to. Because he should be running far, far away from me.

"My life was empty before I met you, Em, and now it is so full and colorful. I meant what I said. You are beautiful, amazing, smart, funny, and most of all, you are mine." I feel the ring as he slips it back onto my finger, not knowing what happened for him to get it back, but so grateful he was able to. He lifts my hand to his lips and kisses the inside of my wrist and then every finger, just like he did on our date.

"I want to marry you for real. I want you and Rosie to

move in with me. I want to give you both the world and never have another day apart." His voice doesn't waver, his eyes watching me closely. I bring my hands to my face and cover it, unable to control how hard I'm crying, and I hear him move and the bed dips next to me.

"It's okay, baby, I got you," he whispers, pulling my hands away from my face and kissing away my tears. "I got you both. Breathe with me, baby. Everything is going to be okay." He pulls me to his side and cuddles both me and my daughter.

"I never thought I would ever find my happiness. I was content. Rosie is everything to me. But then I met you and my world upended. And now... now I don't think I could ever live without you." I tilt my head to look up at him. "I love you, Ben. So, so much. I love you with everything I have."

Eyes alight, he leans in, kissing me softly, with tenderness, careful to not hurt my injured lip. Pulling back, he looks into my eyes, then back down at Rosie, before meeting my gaze again. "I love you, Em. I'm more in love with you than I thought was possible. And I love Rosie. You are both a part of me now, and I feel like the luckiest man alive."

"Mommy..." Rosie's little voice says as she wakes up, almost as if she's heard our declarations.

"Hey, honey," I whisper, leaning back to look at her, wiping my tear-stained cheeks in the process.

"Mommy!" she says, more jovial as I grab her and pull her to me. She crushes me with her weight, nearly jumping out of Ben's arms and into mine, and while my body groans, I don't mind. I need her more than the air I breathe. I lie back down with her in my arms, tucking her in tight, her body curling into my side.

"I'm here. We are going to be alright. Grandpa George too. We are all going to be alright."

George is Jeremy's dad; that realization comes back to me in a rush. I had no idea. Absolutely none. There was never any mention. No photos at George's house, and I didn't see anything when I helped him pack up Glenda's things when she passed. My chest feels heavy with the information, and I am not sure how I feel about it. But as I look down at my daughter, I slowly smile, knowing that all this time she has been spending time with who has turned out to be her true grandpa. And I know he loves us.

"We are going to be alright, Rosie," I whisper again into her hair, and for the first time in her short life, with us both wrapped in Ben's arms, I believe the words I say to her.

EPILOGUE - 12 MONTHS LATER - BEN

I rub my hands under the table, then take a drink of water. It's warm, having been sitting here with me all day, and doesn't give me the relief I need.

It has been a year since the incident with Jeremy, and while I know my two girls are tucked in safely at the estate we all call home, I am waiting for the final verdict.

"All rise," the voice to the right says, and I stand, flattening my tie. Michael is next to me. Eddie and Tennyson right behind me. Harrison in his office, no doubt pacing, waiting for the news.

George sits with them too. He has been here for every day of the trial, gave his evidence, and was cross-examined thoroughly. It has been tough, but he is now part of my family too, and we lean on each other, our two main priorities being Em and Rosie.

My eyes focus in on the jury as they deliver their verdict. To say the past twelve months have been turbulent is an understatement. Em has had to relive a lot of her past, which was hard to hear and harder to watch. I spent many nights cuddling her to sleep before I dreamed all night about the things I wanted to do to Jeremy. My mother had to take the stand, and for the first time in her life, she was truthful. It seems that when she found out about what her antics had actually caused, she was a little remorseful. But she hasn't seen Emily or Rosie since that day. I forbid it. Her toxicity is not allowed anywhere near my family.

"We find the defendant guilty on all twelve charges," the juror says, and the courthouse erupts.

I feel slaps on my back from my brothers and Michael, and I hang my head, relief sweeping through me. It has been a hard year for me and the firm. As soon as I learned the full extent of the situation, I packaged up all of Beasley's files and sent him a final letter of service, cutting all ties. This was soon followed by legal letters outlining his blackmailing Em and forcing George's hand to sign. Beasley settled out of court and gave the school back to George immediately in return for the case being kept private—and even better, the ten million was kept as donations to the two charities George specified. But still, his reputation started to fall into tatters, his business matters becoming affected. Last I heard, Beasley was finding it hard to secure long-term legal support and had burned many bridges within the business community. He is not the high roller he once was.

Jeremy has lived a relatively free life these past twelve months. He has appeared in court when needed, but other than surrendering his passport, life hasn't changed for him. Until today.

I watch as Jeremy is handcuffed and taken by the

guards into holding until a bail hearing, at which point it is just formalities. I know the judge, and I know he will throw the book at Jeremy.

Now as the guard walks him out, he doesn't look at me. His life is now over. His business deals will all freeze or be sold, and he is looking at many years behind bars. I can't say that he has learned his lesson, though. Men like him rarely do.

"Well done, Benny Boy," Tennyson says as I step through the aisle, and he pulls me close. Tennyson is many things, but he is always there for me.

"Good work, brother," Eddie says, gripping my shoulder. I can't speak, so I just nod, the emotions in me overwhelming.

"Let's go tell Em," George says, coming up and shaking my hand, and all us boys walk out, past the media scrum, and straight to Ralph waiting outside.

Straight home to my girls.

"So, Ben, do you think we can read *Cinderella* again tomorrow?" Rosie asks as I pack away the fairy tale into the book box in her room. The pages have been read so many times, they are starting to become worn. Her room is full of pink, very girly, and not at all how I designed this space initially. Toys, books, cushions, rugs, you name it, Rosie has it—in pink.

"Don't you get sick of the same story every night, Rosie?" I ask as I take a seat in the chair next to her bed.

My reading chair, where I sit every night, reading her a chapter at a time.

Rosie is thriving. It took her a little while to get used to my place. But she now walks around with her cane independently, and loves to run freely in the large gardens. Every night, I read her a fairy tale before bed, tucking her in tight, ensuring she knows she is always loved and safe with me.

"No way. *Cinderella* is my favorite story ever," she says through a yawn as I pull the blanket up around her chin and kiss her forehead.

"Alright, *Cinderella* again tomorrow. Sleep well, Rosie," I say, turning on her nighttime sounds, and she is asleep almost instantly. I watch her settle for a second before I walk out of her room, closing the door quietly.

The house is quiet, but not empty. There is so much life in here now; I can't believe how bare it was before. Every light in the place is on. The kitchen, although clean, has potted herbs, colorful towels, and Rosie's artwork on the fridge. It all brings a smile to my face as I walk down the hall to find Em, knowing exactly where she will be.

I pass the living room, where another box of Rosie's is stashed, along with her toys and other bits and pieces, and as my dress shoes click on the marble floor, I catch myself humming for the first time in... forever.

"Thought I would find you here," I say, stepping into the library, a room that once was like a museum. But now it's filled with so many books, candles, and cozy blankets, this room being Em's domain, and where both my girls spend most of their time.

"This book is sooo good. The couple finally got together, and it was *hot!*" Em says, not even looking at me, her head buried in her latest romance novel. I watch her as her eyes run quickly across the page. She reads almost a book a day.

"How hot?" I ask with a chuckle, taking another slow step toward her.

"Like superhot. He picked her up and threw her over his shoulder and marched her to bed," she says, still not looking at me.

"What a Neanderthal."

"Total Neanderthal, but I love it." She giggles, winking up at me, before she goes back to reading and turning the page.

I don't wait a second longer as I lean over and grab her, hauling her up off the comfy armchair.

"Ben!" she shrieks in laughter, her hands gripping on to me, her book hitting the floor as I hoist her over my shoulder and start walking us out of the room.

"Where are you taking me?" She laughs louder, and I can't help but slap her ass, which is positioned right at my shoulder.

"To bed, Doubtfire," I say as my pace quickens. My appetite for her has only grown since we have been together. I am ravenous for her daily. As soon as I get to our room, I'm tossing her onto the bed and shutting the door behind us, stalking toward her like she's my prey.

"You are crazy!" she says, laughing, her smile warming me even more.

"Oh, before I forget, I booked it," I say trying to act casual, but watching her carefully.

"Booked what?" she asks as she starts to unbutton my dress shirt.

"The celebrant." She stops then, eyes widening as she stares up at me. My favorite sight, her looking up at only me.

"Celebrant?" she whispers, her eyes starting to get glassy.

"You have worn my ring all year. Now that the past is finally dealt with, I want you to be my wife," I state, because I want her and Rosie to commit to me, to have my last name, for us to be a real family. We couldn't do it before with such a dark shadow over us. But Jeremy is now gone, and our life can finally begin.

"We're getting married," she says, her lips quirking in the corners.

"Saturday at two in the afternoon. Here at the estate. If you will still have me?" I ask, feeling vulnerable suddenly. I gave her a ring, but I never asked her to marry me. Now the nerves that most men probably feel when they are down on one knee start to creep into my body, and I swallow as I watch her, waiting for her response.

"Well, I need to check my calendar..." she says in jest, a smile spreading across her face.

"Just block out the next two weeks. I also booked our honeymoon... George will stay here with Rosie," I add at the last minute, knowing that she would ask.

"Honeymoon?"

"Is that a yes, baby?" I ask, still needing to hear the words. My hands stay firmly on her waist, keeping her close.

"Yes. Yes. A million yeses!" she squeals as she jumps up on the bed and throws herself at me. And I catch her.

Just like I promised I always would.

GRAB a special bonus scene and see where Ben and Emily are now!

Download here

ALSO BY SAMANTHA SKYE

The Damaged Billionaire

We had one hot night, and only one rule. No names.

My business is growing, my client list is long and my services are in high demand. But when I am introduced to my new client, even though his name is not familiar, his face and body I know all too well.

Tennyson is every inch the typical billionaire bachelor, extremely good looking, suave and swoony, and altogether downright dangerous.

I am hired to get his womanizing reputation under control but every time he looks at me I burn, and his touch is scorching.

But I can't fraternize with my clients, because I am in the business of cleaning up their damaged reputations, not causing them.

But there is something about Tennyson that has me breaking all my rules.

I have no problem going after what I want. But sometimes that can lead to trouble. The kind of trouble that leaves you damaged.

www.books2read.com/damaged-samantha-skye

ALSO BY SAMANTHA SKYE

The Billionaires of Whispers

Tanner

Hudson

Connor

Sawyer

Sutton

Griffin

SCROOGE: A Billionaire Christmas Story

Under The Mistletoe: A Billionaire Christmas Story

The Baltimore Boys

The Charming Billionaire

The Arrogant Billionaire

The Damaged Billionaire

The Secret Billionaire

The Bossy Billionaire

The Billionaire Babe

Men Of New York

My Legacy

My Destiny

My Fight

My Chance

Boston Billionaires

Coming Home

Finding Home

Leaving Home

Building Home

ABOUT THE AUTHOR

Samantha Skye is an international bestselling author. A country kid turned city slicker, she writes spicy and suspenseful contemporary romance novels that leave you hot under the collar and on the edge of your seat.

Samantha lives in Melbourne, Australia and when she's not plotting her next novel, she can be found travelling, drinking margaritas and enjoying a sunset or a stargaze somewhere.

To join in the conversation join Skye's The Limit Facebook group here;

https://www.facebook.com/groups/skyesthelimit books

To learn more about Samantha and what comes next in her author journey you can find her on;

Website: samanthaskyeauthor.com